CHAPTER 1
Savannah

I can't decide.

Chris-bean-a Aguilera, or Queen Latte-fah?

I've been staring at the menu for longer than is considered socially acceptable, and I still can't decide. I'm going to order what I always do. I know it. The Barbie-pink haired barista giving me sympathetic eyes knows it. And my best friend, Athena, sitting at our usual table shooting daggers into my back while she waits for me to order her first caffeine hit of the day, knows it, too. Hell, even the hero and heroine in the romance novel I'm hugging against my chest know it.

Huh. Perhaps not. Bitches Brew—the best coffee shop in town—has added new things to their menu. The Cocoa Chanel looks drool-worthy. Buttery hot chocolate with hot pink whipped cream, mini marshmallows, and edible glitter.

Ooooh. Come to mama.

But what if it's not as good as it looks on the menu board?

Nothing is ever as good as it looks on the menu board. And it's quite the beautiful-looking menu board. Everything in the coffee shop is pretty: striking, hot pink, and sparkly. First appearances come with a pink punch at Bitches Brew.

There's so much interesting *stuff*, like a pink guitar hanging from the ceiling and a pink bike mounted on the wall over a fireplace, that I almost get distracted by it all and forget I'm supposed to be ordering.

Almost. I need to focus. Turning my attention back to the menu board, I shift my weight. I need to pick something to order. It shouldn't be this hard.

But I *know* my Ruth Bader-Brewsburg, their dark chocolate mocha, is delicious. I love the depth of the coffee flavor, the richness of the chocolate, and how Taryn—my favorite barista and owner of Bitches Brew—takes the time to draw a music staff and notes with cocoa powder on top of my drink.

I do this every time. Every fucking time.

I convince myself that I'm going to stray from my boring, same old, same old and try something new. It's on the tip of my tongue, venturing out from my safe space into the unknown. But the comforting familiarity of my old favorite sinks its claws into me, just a little deeper, and I can't stop myself from blurting out the same thing I always get.

I know one thing, though. If I don't hurry up and bring Athena her Ariana Grande with an extra shot of Espresso Patronum, they're never going to find my body.

"You ready to order?" Taryn flashes me her superstar grin. I've been coming to Bitches Brew for as long as I've been a student at the University of Cedar Rapids, Iowa, AKA: UCR. Three years. And for three years I've ordered the same thing, every single time.

Maybe today, first day of my third and senior year, is The Day.

I nod and suck in a breath. "I'll have an Ariana Grande with an extra shot." A quick glance over my shoulder tells me that Athena has hit DEFCON 2.

She's starting her junior year. We met right here at the coffee shop, on our first day of college three years ago when she tried to hit on me. I was flattered, but I'm straight. She took it in stride, we got to talking, and the rest is BFF history.

She's the Geena Davis to my Susan Sarandon, the Buffy to my Willow, the Christina Yang to my Meredith Grey.

A grunt, and a string of Spanish profanities indicates she's escalated to DEFCON 1. "Better make it two extra shots, please, Taryn."

Her perfectly curled pink hair bobs up and down as she nods. "And for you?" She arches a manicured brow like she's expecting me to say something different, something new. I can't blame her, I've spent more time than usual examining her new board.

I meet her eyes, warmth blooming in my cheeks. How in the name of all that's holy does she get her eyeliner flicks so even?

The gaggle of geese hanging out around the small lake outside are honkin' up a storm. Even they know what I'm gonna order.

I heave out a sigh. Today isn't the day. "Ruth, please."

Her smile softens as she nods again. "You got it. Anything else?"

She's right. DEFCON 1 requires sugar as well as caffeine. "Hen will take the lady lips, and I'll have a dick waffle dipped in white chocolate. Please and thank you."

There's no judgment in Taryn's eyes. It's one of the reasons Bitches Brew is so popular, it's a safe space for all. A hot pink, glitz-and-glam safe space. I should be in charge of their marketing with such original taglines.

You wanna eat a dozen twat waffles and wash it down with a gallon of coffee? No judgment.

You do you, boo.

We can also work for six hours straight and use the free Wi-Fi when we are behind on projects and are butting up against deadlines. That one might be oddly specific to me, though somehow I doubt it.

Here, people can be their most authentic selves, without apologies. A twinge catches in my chest making my breath stutter. I don't really know who my most authentic self is anymore.

I thought I knew my most authentic self. I thought—I don't know what I thought—but finding the piece of paper in my dad's study telling me that I wasn't born a Bowen, that I'd been adopted as an infant and my parents hadn't told me? That shook me to my core.

It still shakes my core. I've spent the months since trying to figure out who I really am. I'd love to say that piece of paper didn't define me, or that it didn't change a single thing, but it did.

It changed everything.

I no longer know who I am. I tap my card against the machine and smile through the pain shredding my insides. My parents—my *adoptive* parents—kept it from me for almost twenty years. I've only known for a couple of months. But... How can I not be changed now that I know the truth?

The almost unhappy beep of the machine suggests a problem, and I scowl, wrinkles creasing my forehead. "Can you run it again please?"

Taryn nods and hits a couple buttons before I flap my card against the end of the machine one more time. Heat creeps up my spine and into my extremities. I place my book on the counter—cover up, because there's no shame in my smut of choice game. I know Taryn loves my hot as hell man-chest-candy covers as much as I do—then my purse.

Shit. If the card is declined again I don't think I have another way to pay.

I purged my bag last night so it was ready to collect receipts, tubes of Chapstick, and crumbs from food I don't eat avoid going back home to Minnesota as much as possible, to my parents—my adoptive parents. Something that gives me a legitimate reason to ignore my phone when their name flashes on the screen. Something to distract me from the hurricane of feelings tearing up my mind.

I shift in my seat and swear I can feel the pressure of his stare against my back. Something must show on my face because Hen raises an eyebrow.

"It's okay. We've all had crushes on hockey players before." She pats my hand, condescension and knowing hanging in the air between us. I wonder who she's talking about having had a crush on. She hates hockey. Having brothers living and breathing the sport turned her off it long ago—or so she says. Maybe there's another reason she won't step into the rink to watch a game. That's a thread that'll need to be pulled on in the future.

She picks up her lady lips pastry and drags her tongue across the seam before making moaning sexy sex noises at its deliciousness. She's tongue fucking the slit right there in front of me, in front of everyone.

"People are staring." I'm convinced the dude at Athena's three o'clock is going to come in his pants if she doesn't stop putting on a show.

She teases where the clit would be—if it were *real* lady lips —with the tip of her tongue, and the dude groans. Her smirk only grows.

"I don't have a crush on anyone." I take another bite of my dick before my high school self claws out of the box in my chest and spills the ancient history tea to my best friend.

Some things need to remain in the past, and Justin-fucking-Ass is one of them.

CHAPTER 3
Justin
(CURRENT DAY)

Yup. I'm *that* asshole. The one driving everyone in the coffee shop to the verge of losing their collective shit as I tap my pen frantically against my notebook.

Tap. Tap. Tap-tap-tap. Tap. Tap.

I'm starting to annoy even myself. But I also can't find the off switch. The tapping is helping my thought process. Or so I'm telling myself anyway.

I'm trying to make a list. Not just any list, but a list of steamy romance novels to *wow* my teammates with.

My announcement to the team that I'm starting a steamy romance book club—*Get Lit,* brilliantly named if I do say so myself—was met with less than steamy reactions. In truth, it was quite a tepid response. But they're my brothers, and they support me and my aspirations to be a *New York Times, USA Today,* or *Wall Street Journal* bestselling author someday, so they swallowed down their reticence and got on board the smut train.

Okay, so I had to bribe them with better-than-porn sex scenes and good eats while they read—which is why I'm at Bitches Brew sampling their extensive offerings while I compile my list. I can't believe I've never been here before. It's a gem, and I dig their explosion of hot pink and down to earth quirky vibe.

Research. That's why I have two plates of sugar topped with sugar, with a side of sugar sitting in front of me. At least that's what I'm telling myself. I promised the team delicious treats, and I promised them literary greatness. I groan.

GTFO—Cedar Rapids's best kept secret pie shop—and Bitches Brew have us covered for gastronomic delights—those vagina waffles might be the closest some of those idiots come to a pussy this year—but picking the books they're going to read...that's entirely on me. They've got to be good, great even.

I need to find one book a month for the next ten months, and other than adding my upcoming release—which is yet to be written or edited, but that's another problem entirely—I find myself stuck. I have too many talented indie author friends that I could showcase. And while I love all of their work, I need to impress.

As a collective, the team isn't convinced on the idea. Not on the book club, not on indie published books, not on romance novels, so I've really got to sell it. My goal is to change their minds on books, on indie published books, and on love. Some of those fuckers are cynical AF and need a little romance in their lives. Okay, a lot, but I can't perform miracles.

I tried asking them what kinds of things they want to read, but since romance isn't their jam, I was met with blank stares, shrugs, and skepticism. They have no ideas about tropes or subgenres, so it's just me—me, my notebook, my now-cold Barbara Chai-sand tea, and some scrawled notes about my boys and what I think they'd vibe with.

Since I write sports romance, that box has been filled. I need to pick a suitable rockstar romance for our budding musician, Raffi. A billionaire romance for the de la Peña twins Artemis and Apollo. Their younger brother, our rookie netminder, Ares, requested a good LGBTQ+ story to read, and I'm eager to deliver.

Tate is from Texas which *obviously* means I need a cowboy romance, and two of the guys on the team plan to enlist after graduation so I want to include a military romance as well. Scott loves sci-fi; I'm sure I can find him a sexy space-based, alien romance to enjoy.

Maybe I'll throw in a romantic suspense for good measure, a bodyguard trope. And for the last two months I could do a romantic fantasy and a paranormal romance—by that time they'll have learned to trust my judgment and won't argue when I hand them a magic-touched book that requires suspended disbelief.

I've got this.

Tap. Tap. Tap-tap-tap. Tap. Tap.

My eyes drift back to the girl from the counter whose card didn't work. She's sitting with her side-on to me, curving her shoulder to offer me her back more than her side, and it somehow feels deliberate.

Her long, honey-blond hair is braided and hanging over her shoulder, stray tendrils falling around her face and her bangs straying dangerously close to her eyeballs. She's wearing a hunter green UCR sweatshirt that drapes her to mid-thigh, leggings, and calf-length boots with a fur lining.

More interesting than her clothes, however, is the fact she had a copy of my last book hugged against her chest and seemed shameless about being seen reading it in public. I'm here for it. It was on the tip of my tongue to offer to sign it for her but she was very clearly mad at what feels like my existence.

At first I couldn't tell if she was pissed at only me or the entire universe—if my card declined unexpectedly, I'd be pretty unhappy too. But it didn't take long to figure out that she's not only *mad* at me, she's *big freakin' mad*.

Why would someone be mad at someone else for helping them out of a bind at the checkout?

Her spine is taut as she sits chatting with Athena de la Peña, sister of two—I guess three now that Ares is on the roster, also—of my teammates. Is that where I've seen her before? Athena is renowned for hating hockey, so it's unlikely I've seen them together at a game, but maybe at *The Den* post-game?

She looks familiar to me, but I can't place her.

Tap. Tap. Tap-tap-tap. Tap. Tap.

Does she always sit so stiffly?

Tap. Tap. Tap-tap-tap. Tap. Tap.

Is she always so mad when strangers offer to pay for her coffee?

Tap. Tap. Tap-tap-tap. Tap. Tap.

She shifts in her seat, as though she can feel my gaze on her back. Her attitude at the coffee bar suggests I should know who the hell she is, but no amount of racking my brain is coming up with an answer...which makes me mad that she's mad.

Tap. Tap. Tap-tap-tap. Tap. Tap.

It's the principle of the thing. Being mad at a stranger's kindness is dumb. And I'm sure my own ire is misdirected frustration at my current overwhelm, but she feels like a good enough target for it.

I write "enemies to lovers" under "brother's best friend" on my list of tropes as my phone vibrates on the table, making my cup clink against the saucer.

It's work. The on-campus bookshop, The Book Bin. I'm tempted to watch the call go to voicemail, but I just can't. When my phone rings, I have to answer it. Telemarketers love me.

"Hey, Frieda."

"Justin, how goes the word count?"

She knows I'm behind, and she knows I'm on a deadline. That Amazon countdown clock waits for no one. She also knows I need the occasional kick in the balls to get my shit together.

I sigh and rub the back of my neck.

"That good, huh?"

"I get stuck on the same part of my outline every damn time."

She laughs. "And every damn time it all comes good in the end. Quit yer moaning and gimme my next happily ever after already."

It's my turn to laugh. "What's up?" There's no way this is a social call—she's not that kind of boss—and she's not calling to check up on my progress on my current WIP, either.

There's a long pause before she speaks again. I scrawl "forced proximity" under "enemies to lovers" while I wait for her to talk.

"I know you're super busy..."

Understatement of the century. Between school deadlines, author deadlines, hockey, and my part-time job in The Book Bin, I'm running on fumes. I've even been contemplating pushing my pre-order out a bit to give me some breathing room, but God knows I need those royalties sooner rather than later.

"...but we need a couple of shifts covered if you can manage the extra hours."

"No luck filling the open position?"

Her sigh probably carries with it an impressive eye roll. One I've been on the receiving end of many times over the past couple months. "I thought I had it covered, but the guy who aced the interview never showed up for his shift. He totally ghosted me."

My head lolls back as I take in the bright lights on the ceiling. We both know I'm not going to say no. "When do you need me?"

As I scribble down the three shifts Frieda needs me to cover, movement draws my attention back to the blond-haired stranger who looks like Elsa—right down to her ice queen temperament. If she wasn't so standoffish, I'd have offered to buy her dinner just so I could stare across the table into those sea-blue eyes and at her perfectly pink, pouty, Cupid's bow lips.

When I hang up with Frieda, I add "fake dating" to my list of tropes to consider for *Get Lit*. I'm starting to feel a little better about the idea so I take a shamefully large bite of my donut.

"He cheated on my best friend in high school okay? Drop it." Her voice cuts through me like an ice pick. Then her words register like a bucket of cold water to the face.

Cheated.

High school.

The donut in my mouth turns to dust as I chew. She's talking about me. I know it. Her words are a lightning bolt into the depths of my memory, and I also know who she is now. Though she changed her hair, I'm kicking myself for not recognizing those bottomless green-blue eyes of Savannah Bowen.

Her best friend, Molly Morrison, was my girlfriend in high school, and of *course* Savannah believes the narrative that Mol told her, told everyone. Justin Ashe is a cheating asshole. Justin Ashe kissed another girl at Applebee's. Justin Ashe broke Molly Morrison's heart.

I absently rub at my jaw. Molly's personal brick wall, Finn O'Brien, left me with some bone-deep bruises that night when she fled Applebee's like her ass was on fire. I never wondered why it was him and not her brother Will who beat the shit out of me for "cheating" on her. It was written all over his face, clear as day.

I heard through the hockey grapevine that Finn finally found his balls and made a move on her after all these years. Good for him. It's about damn time. He's loved her forever.

No one beats the shit out of someone over a woman if they don't love her. Everyone knows that. Everyone it seems, except Molly and Finn. It took them a while to put the pieces together.

I shake my head, irritation prickling my skin like needles. The whole damn school heard only half the story. No one cared to hear my side. And the girl I kissed hadn't said a goddamn word in my defense either. Of course she wouldn't. She wasn't the home-wrecker—I was the asshole cheater.

I thought I'd left all that behind in Minnesota, but here we are. Savannah is telling Athena, who was undoubtedly going to tell one or all of her fucking brothers about my misdeeds and my past will be dredged up all over again.

If anyone would give me a hot fucking minute to explain myself, they'd maybe realize I wasn't a soulless, heart-breaking monster, just a naive boy, trying to do a good thing, for a damsel in distress.

Justin
(4 YEARS AGO/16 YEARS OLD)

Applebee's is quieter than usual, almost empty in fact, but the rush is coming. I'm early for dinner. And yet, my usual booth is occupied by a redhead, bent forward, hands over her face, and her shoulders shaking with the force of her heavy sobs.

I turn a full circle but don't see anyone who might have either been responsible for her tears, or there to help comfort her. It's a sign that she's in my booth, right? That means I need to go help her... Right? Dad says my "intuition" is—and I'm quoting here—"bullshit," but my gut hasn't led me wrong so far. And I hate to see someone in so much pain.

Decision made, my feet carry me toward the crying girl. I'm pretty sure she's in my grade at school, though I don't know her name. I might not know who she is, but no one should cry alone.

I clear my throat and toe the heel of one of my hand-me-down Chucks from my cousin Gabe. They're starting to get tight around my big toe, leaving red marks from the friction, but I know my parents can't afford to buy me new ones, and my grandparents just helped them replace our broken washing machine and bought me new-to-me skates, so they're tapped out too. Maybe for Christmas.

When she doesn't look up, I clear my throat again. "Uh... You okay?"

She jerks upright and blinks at me like it's a surprise to find someone standing next to her in this very public place she's chosen to have her breakdown. "What?"

"I asked if you're okay."

She gives me that look. The Girl Look. The one that says "are you fucking serious?" and simultaneously calls you a goddamn idiot. It strikes deep in my chest.

"I'm fine."

The sarcasm from her two words clings to my clothes and hair as she wipes her cheeks with the heel of her hand.

"Wanna talk about it?"

Her eyes flare wider like she wasn't expecting me to persist, and she shrugs. I slip onto the bench next to her. The sadness radiating from her feels personal, intimate, as though she needs to speak quietly and have someone beside her for comfort.

If I sit across from her, staring at her, waiting, she might not share what she needs to unload. It's easier to talk when you're not being looked directly at. You can't feel people's judgment quite so much.

She sucks in a stuttering breath before taking a sip of her pop. "My parents are getting a divorce." Her shoulders sag like a 100lb weight was placed on her muscles. "It's messy, angry..." She sniffs and her glassy eyes meet mine. "And just really, really sad."

I nod and pat her back, her misery sinking deeper under my skin. Empathy is what my mom calls it when I experience other people's emotions all the way to the center of my being. I thought it was the same for everyone, but Mom says some people feel nothing at all. I have no clue how that's even possible. She also says some people do feel things, but they aren't accompanied by physical reactions. How weird?

I've always had big feelings. Each emotion also has a physical response in my body. Anger feels like hot iron striking metal, a deep vibrating fire burning in every one of my cells. Jealousy tastes bitter, fizzing like acid in my stomach. Happiness is like stepping into the sunshine on a warm day... It's hard to believe that not everyone literally feels their emotions like I do.

My girlfriend, Molly, says she doesn't have visceral responses to her feelings. Anxiety doesn't make her feel sick in her stomach, and sorrow doesn't make her every muscle hurt like she has the flu. I guess I've always been a bit of a weirdo that way. I wonder what it would be like to not carry the weight of emotions with me everywhere I go.

I'd love to not feel things so deeply, so...entirely. I'd love to not be exhausted from sitting in a room full of people feeling their feels and living their lives like they're not painting their emotions on me. My empathy often feels like a double-edged sword—I can relate to people, connect to them but it can also be terribly draining.

Case in point: sitting in a restaurant comforting a girl I don't know over things that aren't any of my business.

The girl blows her nose and wipes her tears. "Do you know that half of all marriages end in divorce?"

I nod but stay quiet. It doesn't feel like she's finished saying what she needs to say.

"We have a one-in-two chance of finding The One and keeping them. It's so depressing." Her lip quivers like she's fighting a battle inside to stop her tears. "I feel like my whole life is a lie." Another sob rolls through her body as she launches herself at me, linking her arms behind my neck and burying her head into my shoulder.

I have no idea how I find myself in these situations, but I

really need to extricate myself from this one before someone from school sees and tells my girlfriend.

Gripping the redhead by her shoulders, I try to ease myself out of her hold. Her head snaps back a little, then her lips are on mine. I freeze. What the fuck is happening right now?

A gasp to my left wakes me out of my WTF stupor, and as I shove the stranger away from me with more force, I hear Molly say my name.

Fuck. It looks like I'm making out with a girl in my booth, our booth in Applebee's. I push back out of my seat and jump to my feet. Turning toward Molly's voice, I find no trace of her other than her family. Her brother is glaring at me so hard my own jaw clenches to mirror the twitching in his, and her folks are staring at me with that mix of parental anger and disappointment that I think they hand out to moms and dads when kids are born.

It's like a sucker punch to my gut, and my empty stomach roils.

The server behind the counter hands a bag of food to Mr. Morrison, and before I can collect my thoughts, find my voice to defend myself, or even get my breath back, they're all gone.

Double fuck. This doesn't look good. I know that. But Molly is a good person. She'll listen to me when I tell her it's not what it looked like. She'll listen and if she doesn't, I'll keep talking at her until she listens, and everything will be fine.

It has to be.

She's not my first girlfriend, but she's definitely my favorite. And while I'm not quite sure what love feels like yet, I think I might have those four-letter-feelings for Molly Morrison. And I can only live in hope that the red-haired stranger in Applebee's hasn't fucked it all up for me.

CHAPTER 4
Justin
(CURRENT DAY)

My shoulders feel like I'm carrying boulders in my muscles, and my lower back hurts like a mother-fucker. Downside to feeling all my feels so intensely is that my stress manifests itself in physical pain. Usually right across my shoulders.

Today, I get bonus back pain.

As I walk into the Trashcan—our team's home rink—for practice, I make a mental note to go see my chiropractor and to get a massage from one of our team trainers. I need it.

Seeing Savannah yesterday sent me down a memory lane I'd hoped to bury and never think about again.

The girl in Applebee's kissing me.

Getting my ass handed to me by Finn O'Brien.

The stares in the hallways at school.

The days that followed the incident were insufferable. Any street cred I'd built from being best friends with the most notorious kid in school evaporated in a puff of smoke. But those few days paled in comparison to what had happened the following week when Steve Dobbs and his parents showed up at my door accusing me of cheating on a test.

Rubbing the bridge of my nose, I force out a breath, but it doesn't carry any of my tension away with it.

I'd thought that it wouldn't matter when that douche goblin Steve accused me of plagiarizing his work because my own parents would know I'd never do such a thing, and they'd have my back.

Boy, was I ever wrong.

The truth of the matter was that Steve copied me, and when my boy Johnny caught him looking at my paper, well, I guess Steve thought he'd cut me off at the pass and tell his parents that the reverse was true. Control the narrative.

I thought my parents knew me better. While I wasn't a straight-A student by any means, I excelled in some subjects, like English, and I worked damn hard for my grades.

I snort and pull the door to the Trashcan toward me. As I step into the rink, my kit bag catches on the door and jerks me back, yanking the air from my body with a grunt. If I can't even get my ass through the door of the building... Huh. This doesn't bode well for practice.

Coach is going to have my balls in a fucking vise. And he won't be afraid to squeeze.

A shudder trickles through me at the thought of getting blasted by our leader. With so many de la Peñas on the team and their family giving so much money to the school, it can't help but feel like Coach took a risk giving me the C over one of them.

I hope it's because he sees something in me, qualities becoming of a captain, a leader, someone my teammates trust and respect—and not because he wants to stick it to the twins' asshole billionaire dad, Alonso de la Peña.

While I go through the motions of getting ready to train, my brain cycles back to a time when I wasn't so fit, so strong, to a time when my father's baseless disbelief in my character almost destroyed me.

Pads and shorts on, I tuck my foot into my skate. While things are very different now, in some ways they're still every bit the same. If it wasn't for the team, the university covering the cost of my gear, I'd still be wearing Gabe's hand-me-down skates, and my socks would have holes in the heels and toes.

When my skates are tied, I tug my socks up over my shin guards one more time on both sides. The rest of the team are getting changed around me, but I haven't spoken to a single person since I arrived, and they're all giving me a wide berth— maybe my *fuck off* vibes are strong enough to keep my brothers at bay. Or maybe no one's noticed my moodiness and they're all wrapped up in their own shit.

My dad used to always take great joy in reminding me that the world didn't revolve around me. I mean, he was right, obviously, but some days I think it should. He's mellowed out as we've both grown older, and we're pretty close these days, but man, those younger years left scars on my heart.

It's time to shake this off.

I need to concentrate on the game and keeping my spot on the team, deserving Coach's trust in me. Without the scholarship that comes with my place on the roster, I can't afford to attend UCR to get my degree. My royalties from book sales are growing by the month, sure. But that doesn't mean much when you're just starting out and have a never ending list of things to pay for to make sure every book you put out into the world is the best it can be.

Who knew how expensive it could be to pay someone to make sure you spelled your own name right in your book?

Not me, that's for sure.

And while I have an excellent grasp of the English language, I'm not too arrogant to think I don't need someone to check my work. My readers deserve my very best—even if it's expensive, even if they occasionally have to wait longer than they'd like. I have faith in my process, I do. Even if sometimes it feels like the method might bankrupt me.

With a sigh, I smooth out my shorts. Some days my dream of being a bestselling author seems pretty far away. Like today. I know I need to be patient and ride the waves, but it's hard. Some days it's really fucking hard to believe in myself, especially when a piece of my past shows up and reminds me just how much of a loser everyone back home still thinks I am.

Stepping out onto the ice, I'm resolved to leave my issues in the locker room. I'm going to kick this practice in the nuts, have a protein shake, and get back to playing catch-up on my school work and my outline. There's so much to do, and I usually thrive under pressure, but right now I feel like a stick on the ice being flexed, waiting for the puck to arrive.

One more hard hit, and I'm pretty sure I might snap. Or shatter.

Practice starts with some low intensity skating, a warm up to get the blood flowing to all parts of the body after a night of attempted sleeping and stillness. It feels good to move my joints. My knees and ankles have cracked since I was a kid and the familiar snap, crackle, and pop give me comfort as I roll out my shoulders and glide across the ice.

"You good, Cap?" Raffi Shaw must have been nominated to come check up on me. He's frowning, poised like he's ready to dart out of my personal space if he needs to. It's almost funny. Maybe my resting bitch face is as strong as my fuck-all-the-way-off attitude today.

I nod. "I'm fine. Didn't get much sleep." Tiredness is a great scapegoat for damn near everything. Because damn near everyone on the planet can relate.

Quiet? Tired.

Moody? Tired.

Forgetful? Tired.

He doesn't need to know that I stayed awake staring at the

ceiling as I replayed the conversation I overheard between Savannah and Athena. Or that I can recall, in meticulous detail, the lecture my dad gave me on the day Steve-fucking-Dobbs came by the house—tone, inflections, subtext and disappointed eyes included. All Raffi—all any of them—needs to know is that I'm tired.

He elbows me with a knowing grin splitting his face. "Hot date? You finally water that dry spell of yours?"

If only. "Nah, man. Just busy as fuck, y'know?"

He pats my chest. "Too tired to sleep. I get it."

Coach blows the whistle and calls *Chase the Rabbit*—my favorite puck handling and skating warm-up for honing my on-ice awareness—as our first drill.

We line up and get assigned our roles and partners. Reds and blues, rabbits and chasers—or, as I like to call them, hunters. But unlike Elmer Fudd chasing Bugs Bunny, we're on skates at high speed, holding sticks and controlling pucks, not hunting our wabbits with a double-barreled shotgun, tiptoeing through the forest.

It's a messy drill, and if we don't keep our wits about us, we could end up crashing into any one of the other moving targets on the ice.

The players tagged red are rabbits, and all the blue players —including me—are hunters. The aim of the drill is for the hunters to chase the rabbits, following as close to them as possible, without losing control of the puck, or falling on your face. After about thirty second bursts, we switch roles and the hunters become the hunted.

I'm paired with Apollo de la Peña. He's faster than his twin brother, Artemis, and not as broad so he'll be tricky to stay close to. It's good though. I fucking love rising to a challenge.

When the first whistle blows, Apollo darts off at speed with me close to his heels. Thirty seconds later, we switch and start over. By the time the drill is over—with only one minor collision between Scott and Tate—and we move onto a five-on-two keep-away drill, sweat stings my eyes, and my muscles burn.

It's knock out time.

The first batch of ten skaters—including me—slides onto the huge Raccoons logo at center ice. For this drill, every player starts with a puck, and the goal of the game is to keep control of your puck while you knock other players' pucks out of the designated boundary—namely the logo painted under the ice.

Last player standing with a puck wins.

The whistle blows, and I push off into movement, cradling my puck with the blade of my stick like the basket of eggs those kids protected from their sensei in season five of *Cobra Kai*. None of these fuckers are crushing my egg.

Does Savannah like hockey? Or does she hate it like Athena? Does she like *Cobra Kai*? Will she be at the game tomorr—?

I hit the deck hard, and my head smacks back, helmet bouncing off the ice. My chest constricts, burns at the sudden loss of air from impact with the hard surface underneath me. I don't want to open my eyes to see the bemused gazes of my teammates, but if I keep them closed, they might think I'm really hurt and not just lying here with wounded pride.

Salty sweat streams into my eyes the second I crack them open. I nod that I'm okay, and my teammates burst into collective laughter. Great. They didn't even wait for me to get up on my skates first.

Artemis leans over me, hand outstretched. "The fuck was that, Cap?"

I wave off his hand and roll onto my knees, sucking hard and deep at the thin, cool air in the rink, trying to convince my struggling lungs that I'm not actually dead, it just kinda feels like it.

Did a semi-truck burst through the walls of the Trashcan and take me out of the drill? I rub at my chest. My hands are bare. I must have dropped my gloves and stick in the fall.

"I'm good."

Standing on shaky legs, I avoid making eye contact with any of the guys gathered around me, and you better believe I'm not looking in the direction of Coach's undoubtedly fire-fueled glare right now either. Embarrassment claws at my throat as I force out a laugh.

"Which of you assholes crashed into me?"

My head bounced around inside my bucket, but I'm fine. If I told them I was distracted by a girl they'd never let me live it down. Hell, *I'm* never letting me live it down. One errant thought about Savannah, and I ended up on my ass staring at the rafters. Talk about a sign.

Artemis jerks his chin. "You should know better than to keep your head down, Cap. That shit's for the rookies."

"Sure you're okay?" Tate narrows his eyes like he's not convinced.

"Just rattled my chiclets." I wiggle my jaw back and forth as if to emphasize the fact.

He nods and steps out of my way. The whistle blows and we all freeze in place like we forgot Coach was there too. "Hit the showers. And Ashe?"

"Yeah, Coach?"

"Try to stay upright at the game tonight."

"Yes, Coach." My heart rate and breathing return to normal as I hit the locker room, determined to put Savannah Bowen completely out of my head before I take to the ice tonight.

She's here.

Savannah Bowen is in the stands watching me play hockey. And by play hockey I mean get my ass handed to me by everyone on the ice—including my own fucking team.

I tried. All afternoon I fucking tried to clear some space in my mind. Meditating, affirmations, yoga, even an ice bath to soothe my still aching muscles from getting crashed into by our resident moving wall de la Peña.

It was starting to work, too, and no sooner had that thought crossed my mind when I spotted the flowing honey-blonde locks of one Miss "He's nothing but a cheating asshole" Bowen. I know where I went wrong—I tempted fate.

But are you fucking kidding me? Is Mercury in retrograde? That little fucker ruins damn near everything.

There are thirty seconds left in the first period, and we're down by two goals. I'd love to say neither of them were my fault, but I was on the ice for both, and from the scowl Coach is shooting my way, that fact didn't escape him, either. And the fuck-off-and-die vibes Ares de la Peña is throwing me from the crease suggests I'm not his favorite person right now either.

Peachy.

Just fucking wonderful.

This girl has been back in my orbit for less than thirty-six hours, and she's already fucking up my goddamn life just by existing. What else did she tell Athena? Did the de la Peña sister tell her brothers?

My gaze skims along my teammates sitting next to me on the bench. Do they all think I'm the untrustworthy asshole Savannah says I am? Do they still have my back out on the ice?

Rationally, I know it's an overreaction.

Or is it, though?

I mean, I thought my dad wouldn't take Steve Dobbs' side, and look where that got me.

It's different now though, right? These guys, my friends, my teammates, they know the real me. We've won together and lost together. The ride-or-die energy from my brothers is one of the reasons UCR hockey is so damn popular and renowned across not just the state of Iowa, but the whole country. We're more than a team. We're a family.

As I trudge to the locker room at the end of the period, a not-so-tiny voice at the back of my head reminds me that Dad is family too, and he still took someone else's side over mine. He didn't believe me when tears spilled down my face, when I swore until I was hoarse that I didn't—would *never*—cheat on a test.

Molly didn't believe me when I told her that I didn't—would *never*—cheat on her, either.

My shoulders curl forward with the weight of, well, everything. My heart is heavy, my mind is busy, and my muscles ache. It's been a long time since I've suffered from depression but I remember the darkness. And if things keep going the way they are...

I huff out a sigh. The faintly familiar tug of gloom pulls at my being.

I need to dust it off. Stop being dramatic. Stop anticipating things that haven't happened yet. But mostly? I need to get my head the fuck back in the game before Coach benches my ass and I lose my spot on the team.

CHAPTER 5

Savannah

Skimming my fingers along the spines, I suck in a deep breath through my nose. There is no greater scent than the smell of a bookshop. Fact. Freshly cut grass is a close second but the scent of bound together paper doesn't trigger my allergies or require a big enough dose of antihistamine to sedate a bear. Therefore, books win. Books always win.

I don't *need* new books, but since when has that ever stopped me from dropping into a bookstore when I'm passing?

My phone buzzes in the butt pocket of my jeans, pulling my hand away from the perfectly printed spines lining the shelves.

Athena: Got another fucking ticket.

In the quiet of the store, I swallow a snort. I think this is her third traffic violation in three months. It's partly because she drives like she's Max Verstappen behind the wheel of his

Formula One car and also because she drives a car that attracts attention. A *lot* of attention.

She says it's because she's a woman and the cops have little dick energy, but I've been in a car with her and barely lived to tell the tale. Agro—her midnight blue Nissan GT-R—is every guy's wet dream. He's her baby, and she whispers sweet nothings to him as she floors the gas.

She's a woman with a deep need for speed who thinks speed limits are a suggestion and who doesn't mind dropping cash on paying tickets. Just as well, since she's a frequent flyer.

Vannah: I-380?

Athena: You know it.

Athena: I don't think there's a single person alive in Cedar Rapids who hasn't gotten a ticket there.

Vannah: I've never gotten a ticket. Anywhere.

Athena: That's 'cause you drive like Miss Daisy.

Vannah: I don't know who that is.

Athena: My eyeballs hurt from the major roll they just did.

Her eyeballs must always hurt from eye rolling. It's her raison d'être.

Someone shuffles into the aisle behind me as I shake my head at my bestie. She's a fierce, strong, and independent woman, but she has a chip on her shoulder the size of Colorado, and a cursory relationship with the law—especially when it comes to breaking the speed barrier on I-380.

I turn to find a tall, gangly guy with a bright red face scanning the shelves. He opens and closes his mouth before rolling his lips between his teeth. Turns to the bookcase behind him and repeats the process.

"You okay?" I tilt my head. We're in the steamy romance aisle, and from the tiny beads of sweat forming along his hairline, this is the last place on earth this guy wants to be.

He flicks a glance my direction before looking back at the books, then back to me, back to the books. His whole body is taut as though he's ready to bolt at any given moment, and my insides hurt at his discomfort.

"I can't see what I'm looking for."

I'd figured that much, but I don't want to spook the guy with my glib sarcasm, so I nod. "Maybe I can help you find it."

He's got to be a freshman, eighteen, nineteen years old at most. He checks over both shoulders, for what I'm not sure. I've never felt safer than when I'm inside the walls of a bookstore. There's something oddly comforting about being surrounded by generations of stories.

"I'm...uh..." He scrubs at the back of his neck so hard I'm scared he's going to scrape his skin off.

Is he a criminal? What is this guy's deal?

I shift my weight from one foot to the other, suddenly regretting the fact I didn't just walk on by. Why can't I ever just walk the fuck by? I don't know how many times Hen has grabbed me by the cheeks and chanted, "Not your circus, not your monkeys, Vannah-Banana," right in my face.

Not my circus, not my nervous AF and sweating profusely book-searching, potential criminal monkey. And yet here we are.

"I'm looking for a book by Saxon James."

Luckily for perspiring dude, I'm a whale—someone who reads at least a book a week—an ARC team member for many indie authors, and an avid reader of steamy sports romance of all flavors, which means I know exactly who he's talking about.

"They have a special section for—" Ah. That's when it hits me like a smack upside the head. Saxon writes gay romance. The pleading in this kid's eyes silently begging me to stop talking out loud causes my heart to constrict so much I'm afraid it might stop working.

I give him a warm smile. "How about you tell me which book you're looking for, and I'll go get it for you, okay?"

The relief in the guy's face is real as his body sags and he nods. "It's called *Presidential Chaos.*"

I pat his biceps as I pass him, desperate to give him some kind of comfort in the moment. I want to tell him there's no need to be afraid, there's no reason for him to be ashamed. I want to say that I believe love is love, and there is no judgment when you're in the safe space of a bookshop but the words feel empty, hollow in my mouth.

So I stay quiet, make my way to the LGBTQ+ section of the store, and scan their selection. They have it on the table display. In fact, they have both the smokin' hot man-bod cover and Saxon's adorable illustrated cover as well.

I'm guessing this guy's an illustrated cover kinda reader. I pick up a copy, and am ready to make my way back to the stranger standing in the steamy romance aisle when the hottie on the cover of *Shameless Puckboy*—by Saxon and her co-writer bestie Eden Finley—makes eyes at me.

Not today, Satan.

I close my eyes and shake my head. Chant to myself in a resolute whisper. "I don't need any more books. I don't need any more books. I don't need any more books. I don't...need... Fuck it."

I snatch the delicious puck boy from the top of the stack on the table and lift the book so it's at eye level. "You really are shameless."

I hurry back to where I left the guy standing, hoping he hasn't fled the scene in the meantime. He's moved to the end of the aisle and inched himself toward the crime section, but he stayed where I could see him when I returned.

My heart squeezes as I hand him the book and again at the gratitude painted all over his face. He hugs the book against his chest before making eye contact for a beat. "I'm just...not ready yet."

The flexing organ in my ribcage threatens to burst at this poor man's vulnerability. I want to hug him, to squeeze him until he feels better. I want to give him my number and tell him I can be there for him. But I don't want to make him feel any more uncomfortable than he already does. So I press down my urge to help him somehow.

Instead, I blink back the tears forming in my eyes and give him what I hope is a reassuring smile. "I know you didn't really choose to share this with me, but thank you anyway."

He nods, pausing like he wants to say something else, an awkwardness hanging heavy between us in the aisle of the store, and then he's gone.

I lean against the end of the bookshelf for a long moment, gathering my thoughts and emotions. Gravity pulls at my ass, and the temptation to slide down the wood and plonk myself right there on the floor of *The Book Bin* is strong. But I don't. I don't have time to dwell on the agony in the stranger's eyes.

I need to haul ass out of there before other books make eyes at me and silently plead for me to take them home.

My resolve was strong when I walked in, but now... Now I have one book cuddled against my body and two more are calling me from the end of the steamy aisle. I saw them on TikTok, and I'm tempted... I just...can't...

"Want a job?" A woman's voice pulls my attention to the next aisle next over. She grunts as she pulls herself to her feet with a groan and presses her flat palm against her lower back, stretching out.

I look around but no one else is there. Is she talking to me?

"Yes, you." She smiles at me, and I feel sunshine in my bones. "Any chance you'd be interested in a part-time job?"

I've been in The Bin, as it's affectionately termed, more than my share of times over the years, so I know for a fact this isn't common practice. I've never been offered a job free with purchase before.

She wants me to work here? Surrounded by all this temptation? Is she insane?

I almost laugh. I've been searching for a job all summer. I want to save money, build security, and here the book dealer is standing in front of me and offering me a job where I would undoubtedly spend more than I made.

"You handled that situation very well. Better than I probably would have. You'd be surprised at the amount of shame people bring with them to the bookstore." She shrugs. "Compassion is a pretty big deal inside these walls."

Her name tag tells me her name is Frieda, and she nails me with another one of those body-hugging smiles. "We hired a new guy a few months ago. I tried to hire another two but"— she shrugs—"they never showed up."

I glance around the store. It's my first time here so far this semester, but it's always been one of my favorite places to spend time. And God knows I need a job now that I'm actively avoiding my parents. The reliable flutter of rage ignites in my stomach, and I'm grounded in my righteous indignation. How could they keep such a *huge* piece of my identity a secret from me for all those years? Who does that?

The idea of asking them for money or, well, *anything* is as enticing as the idea of the pap smear I'm scheduled to have next week. And I still owe them a little for the repairs on their car.

It wasn't my finest moment. I flipped all the way out when I discovered I was adopted. It still makes me cringe just to think about it.

Slamming the door of the house. "Borrowing" my parents' car. Ignoring their pleas to stay and talk about it, to not go driving in the rain at night. My vision blurred by tears as I sped away from the house. The thud as I hit the deer and careened out of control. I vowed to repay them every damn penny for repairs.

I need this job. I need to clear my conscience, repay my debt.

Would there ever be a better job for me? Spending time surrounded by tales of tragedy and love? It feels like it's meant to be. Kismet. Yuanfen. Fate.

"I'm flying home for Thanksgiving." I'd rather scrape my skin off with a potato peeler than see my parents, but I promised my sister, Sophia, that I'd go back to Minnesota for the holiday.

"Not a problem. We've got the schedule covered for Thanksgiving since our other recent hire is traveling then, too. You could start the week after Thanksgiving."

"In that case, I'd love to." I'll have to be disciplined to the extreme and not allow myself to buy all the books. As much as I'd love to take them all home with me and spend my days stroking and sniffing them, I don't have the funds or the space. I nod, determined in my decision. "You might have to keep me from buying *all* of the books with my salary though."

Frieda laughs, the sound joyous and uplifting. She's one of the warmest people I've ever met; it's hard not to love her already. "I feel that. I'll run interference on all your book purchases." She pauses and nibbles on her lip. "Is it a bad time to mention that we have a staff discount?"

I pay for my book at the counter, chatting with her about the layout of the store and the duties involved with the position she's offering. I feel good about it. Book addiction aside, I'm taking back control of at least a little piece of the chaos that has been my life lately.

I started the week with two goals: find a job and Google my birth mom. One out of two ain't bad, right? Now that I have a job under my belt, I'm coming up short for any more excuses to keep me from hitting the search engine.

As I leave the store, the tinkle of the bell above the door seems to taunt me like it knows all my secrets. *Deer Killer* it chimes. The dumb bell knows I'm a coward, that I've typed my birth mom's name into the search bar countless times over the summer, but I haven't been able to push the enter key.

Killer. Coward.

For a bell, it certainly is opinionated.

Fine. It's not the bell. It's my own critical inner voice giving me shit. Some days I'd love to reach into my mind, pull her from the depths of my gray matter by her roots and beat the ever loving snot out of her.

Bitch is loud.

The only way to shut her up in this moment is to head home and look up my birth mom. Sounds easy enough, but man, even the thought makes my stomach churn. I've had so many questions over the past months, and I'm too fucking scared to find the answers. But maybe it's time.

I crack my knuckles one by one as I stare down the Google homepage on my laptop screen. I need to know. I need to know where she is and anything else I can find out about her. Does she have a family? Is she local?

Questions I'll never have the answer to if I don't suck it up and look, ricochet around in my brain. I throw back a shot of tequila and shudder as it burns through me, its warmth rippling out to my limbs. It's time. I need this.

I type her name into the bar, *Amara Declercq*, and wait as

though the act of typing it alone will bring me the answers I seek. It's the same every damn time.

Throwing back another shot, I scrunch my eyes closed. When the shot glass hits the table I smack the enter key on my laptop before I can change my mind. It's done now. No take-backs.

I open my left eye a crack, squinting at the screen. My hands are clammy and shaking, and when I try to pop my knuckles again I get nothing but disappointment.

Heaving in deep breaths, I face my past. There's no need to scroll. My own eyes meet my gaze, staring right back at me from the screen. The knowledge is deep in my chest. That's her.

Part of me is glad she has an unusual name so I don't need to scroll through pages and pages of Jane Smiths to find the right one. But the other part of me is freaking out that Google found her in under three seconds. Her. My birth mother.

When I click the photo, my stomach sinks. Tears prick my eyes as I gulp once, twice, a third time but the wave of emotions hitting me from all sides can't be swallowed down.

Deceased.

A tightness bands around my chest as I scan the obituary. She was an only child, her parents both died a number of years ago, and according to the article, she never married or had a family of her own. She was an elementary school teacher in Wisconsin.

Grief consumes me like a black hole, and I'm powerless to escape its gravity. I hover the arrow over the X at the top of the page, hoping that clicking it closed will ease the agony stirring inside me, but I pause when something catches my eye.

She died a week before I found my birth certificate in my dad's study. If they'd just told me about my life, my past, my birth mom... I could have tried to connect with her, had a chance of finding out who I really am.

But now—I sniff and swipe at my tears—that's never going to happen.

Deceased.

I slam my laptop closed with a sharp click. I'm never going to forgive them for lying to me. Never.

CHAPTER 6
Savannah

I made a mistake.

My stomach is curdling. I can't breathe. I don't know where October disappeared to, but I want it back. I hate flying at the best of times, then add in the all-consuming dread at seeing my parents for the first time in a couple months, and I'm a walking ball of anxiety.

I need sedation, but I was all out of anxiety meds. My PCP wouldn't renew my prescription over the phone, and I didn't have time to go see her. I should have made time. I should have found a way.

Right now, standing in the surprisingly short line for security at Cedar Rapids airport, I have regrets. Many of them, in fact. I don't want to see my parents. I don't want to look at their guilty faces and listen to their guilty voices while the fire of rage still burns bright in my chest.

I don't want to. But here I am.

My palms are slick with sweat, and a bowling ball is sitting in my gut.

I should have driven.

Flying is never the right choice for me, but it's so much

quicker, not to mention, I got a great deal on the ticket. And I thought I'd have my trusty happy pills. I know, I know, it's poor planning, but I'm freaking out too much to be angry at myself.

If it wasn't Thanksgiving tomorrow, I wouldn't even be here. But no matter how hard I tried, I couldn't find it in me to punish my little sister for our parents lying to me for years. While I'm still pissed at them, I miss her. I miss them all, even if I am still seething at my folks.

We always love making Mom's life miserable when she's in the kitchen trying to prep Thanksgiving dinner, and we're determined to sample things ahead of time.

I sigh and push my carry-on suitcase forward on the belt toward the scanner. It's butt-crack-of-dawn o'clock but the airport is pretty quiet despite the holiday. Maybe no one else really wanted to go home, either.

I walk through the security arch and pick up my bag, thanking the TSA agent and flashing him a smile. I've always wondered what the most interesting or hilarious thing they've ever pulled out of someone's bag is, but I've never had the guts to ask them.

They thought my bath salts were drugs once. Another time I had a sniffer-trained Beagle bark at my backpack, which scared the shit out of me. Obviously. I mean, I *knew* I didn't have anything illegal in the bag, but for a really long fucking moment I wondered if a Mexican cartel boss had somehow planted cocaine on my person.

What had the Beagle taken offense at?

A fucking apple, abandoned and long forgotten about, languishing at the bottom of my bag. My heart had threatened to explode as I waited to see what they'd found.

A motherfucking apple.

I've never carried fruit on a flight again.

And after they pulled out a giant pink vibrator from the

girl next to me in the security line when I flew home for Christmas last year, I stopped carrying my Buzz-tastic battery operated boyfriend with me too.

No fruit, no vibrators.

I would literally die if that happened to me. I can walk into Bitches Brew and order myself a dick waffle, but the idea of someone reaching into my case and pulling out my portable, personal peen in a crowded airport? The bowling ball in my stomach shifts, and I swallow against the wave of nausea. Fuck no.

It's a small airport, so it doesn't take long to walk to my gate. My feet stutter to a stop when a familiar head of blond hair appears in my line of sight.

I groan. Out loud, because of course Justin Ass is going home to Minnesota too. There are two direct flights from Cedar Rapids to Minneapolis every day—he couldn't have taken the one at 6:30pm instead of the 7:00am?

Of course he couldn't, that would have just made my life too simple. And I guess he'd have missed out on an entire day with his family too. Sighing, I admit that would be a lot to ask of someone who doesn't seem to know or care that I'm so mad at him for being at the same college as me.

I've managed to avoid him since that fateful day in the coffee shop, but this, ha! You couldn't write this.

I check behind me, half expecting to find a disheveled-looking author scribbling notes about my life into a spiral bound notebook. If it was happening to anyone but me it'd be hilarious.

But it is me, and it isn't fucking funny. I wipe my free hand on the thigh of my jeans and shiver. It's colder than usual for November and according to the weather report there's a storm brewing but it can't make up its mind whether it's going to hit Iowa, Illinois, or Minnesota. Maybe it'll coat all three states with a thick layer of snow.

You'd think with the advances in technology we've made as a species over the decades that the weather people could predict accurate weather.

I feel like I'd be better informed if I'd consulted my Magic 8 ball.

That thing has helped me make some of the most challenging decisions of my life.

Anyway, when I bolted out of bed at four this morning to pack at the last minute, it seemed like a good idea to leave my winter coat in Iowa to save from having to drag it around the airport. Travel light. It was such a great idea at the time.

Like I said, I have regrets. And they seem to be multiplying.

I find a chair as far away from *him* as possible but keep my eyes on him like a cat chasing a laser. Not that he seems like he's going to move, but just in case. I can't risk him seeing me and having to make small talk with him.

There are fifty seats on our tiny plane, but I can still work with that. With any luck we'll be at opposite ends of the plane, and he won't even know I'm there. I'm glad I usually wait until the end to board rather than being one of those eager beaver travelers who jumps up as soon as boarding starts.

Hell no. I don't want to be on that damn bird for a single minute longer than I have to, so I wait. I stay out of sight until the last possible minute before handing the desk agent my phone.

Part of me hopes it's rejected, that there's some issue with my ticket and I won't have to walk down that jet bridge. I'm drenched in sweat and probably look somewhat deranged. It ain't pretty.

At least I have an aisle seat so I won't feel trapped against the window, and I won't be able to fixate on whatever is below the clouds.

At the bottom of the bridge I hand my small case to the

guy loading baggage and smile my thanks at him despite my nerves. I hesitate at the last step before boarding, staring at the edge of the plane like it might move if I pick up my foot.

The flight attendant grins at me. She's way too fucking cheery for 6:30am. She bids me good morning and steps back like I don't have enough space to board. I try to press down my terror, paralyzing every muscle in my body, and smile back at her, but all my energy is currently being used to not run, or puke, or pass out.

The fight or flight response is in high gear, and I really need to get my ass onto the plane before I make a scene. She checks my boarding pass and points to row four. I'm on the left-hand side of the plane, and the poor son of a bitch who has to witness my nervous breakdown over air travel is—fuck, shit, fuck, fuck, motherfucking fuck, of course it fucking is.

Justin lifts his head as I approach the empty seat next to him, and his eyes darken. Not in a sexy kind of way, but in an almost murderous kind of way. He doesn't seem to even try to hide his dismay as I move closer. Huh. So I guess he remembers me after all.

Maybe it doesn't have to be this way. I clear my throat and turn to the flight attendant. "Excuse me?" I can't sit next to him. There doesn't seem to be another free seat, but it's worth a shot. I need to move. "Can I sit somewhere else?"

Justin's grunt pulls my attention back to him as his nostrils flare, but he says nothing.

"I'm sorry, but there are no other seats." She gives me a look through her smile. A look that says I must be out of my ever loving mind to want to move away from the hockey boy who smells like sunshine and looks like he belongs on a different kind of runway.

It's fine. It's totally fine. I have my book, it's just a seventy-minute flight, I can absolutely, positively ignore Justin Ass for an hour. It's not the end of the world.

Okay, fine. It's not like Molly and I have stayed besties over the years. I came to Cedar Rapids and we drifted a bit. But we're still friends, we still catch up from time to time, and I follow her Twitter account daily. I don't care how hot he is. I'm still loyal to her, and loyalty means something to me, even if it doesn't mean jack shit to the guy to my right.

The plane door slams shut, and I swallow down the yelp at the back of my throat. He shifts in his seat beside me but I don't look at him. I can't. He's about to witness one of my biggest embarrassments and greatest fears, and I'd rather have a colonoscopy than be here.

It might be the end of the world.

I should have driven. Sure, it's just over a four-hour drive home, but right now I'd drive to the fucking moon and back if it meant I could be away from this situation. My leg is bouncing so hard it feels like the whole plane is vibrating because of me. Beads of sweat prickle across my hairline, my shirt is damp under my arms and in the small of my back, and my chest is pulsating with quick breaths.

I squeeze my eyes shut.

It's just an hour. It's just an hour. It's just an hour.

The chances of us having an accident are slim. There is plenty of space for all of us, it's not really the tiny tin can it seems to be. There is enough air for everyone. We aren't going to suffocate or crash. It's all going to be okay.

It's just an hour.

The hard plastic of the arm rests is comforting, and I hold on for dear life. My fingertips hurt as my grip tightens with each passing second.

The funniest part about all this is that the plane hasn't even started moving yet. That's when the real fun begins. It's not funny at all. By funny I mean sheer terror. Why did I do this to myself? I say every time that I'm never flying again, and

I mean it every single time. But this time I *really* mean it. I do. I'm never flying again.

"Are you okay?" Justin's voice is soft and somehow right next to my ear, sending a shiver snaking up my spine.

Like he'd care if I was okay or not.

"I asked, didn't I?" His breath tickles the side of my heating cheek as he huffs out air.

I guess I answered him out loud.

"Is there anything I can do?"

The captain's voice crackles over the speakers as he tells us there is a delay, and we need to stay seated on the plane with our seatbelts fastened for an indeterminate period of time before we can get a takeoff slot. A hysterical laugh bubbles up in my chest.

Once again: you couldn't write this shit.

Tears sting my eyes as I flutter my eyelids in a vain attempt to keep them at bay.

"Hey, hey." Justin pries my hand from the arm rest and slides his warm hand into my super sticky palm. "It's okay. You're going to be okay."

His tone doesn't carry any sarcasm or condescension. I expect amusement on his face when I turn to look at him, not the deep furrow in his brow and concern swimming in those blues of his.

Danger. Danger.

I grope around in the basket of emotions behind my ribcage, frantically searching for the anger, resentment, and vehement dislike I have for this guy. He's a cheater. I hate cheaters. I hate him. He hurt my friend and made her cry. He doesn't deserve my time.

Cheater, cheater, pumpkin eater.

And yet, here he is, my teenage crush sitting next to me on a plane, face grave with concern, holding my hand to soothe my terror, and I don't even think I hate it.

This is bad.

His face softens at whatever he sees as he stares at me. If I wasn't already sweating from the terror of being stuck on this God-forsaken plane, I'd be perspiring under his gaze.

Stars above, he has pretty eyes.

This is really bad.

"Would a distraction help?"

It's cute that he thinks he can distract me from the fact I'm on a plane, so I nod. Things couldn't get worse than this, right?

"You want to talk to me about that book you're reading?"

CHAPTER 7
Justin

S avannah's eyebrows shoot up, and my chest tightens even more. Book porn chat is not the distraction she was hoping for, it seems.

"I wasn't judging your choice of genre at the coffee shop. I know you think I was, but I wasn't. In fact, I've started a spicy romance book club for the hockey team."

She stares at me like she's waiting for the punchline. *It has to be coming*, her eyes say. She thinks I'm pulling her leg. "We read the book you had in your hand at the coffee shop by J.R. Blake for our September read. And last month we read *False Start* by Melissa Ivers."

I've read her hockey romance series, but hadn't yet read her football novella. Savannah looks kind of amazed I even know who Melissa Ivers is.

"I—" She clears her throat. "I haven't read it."

"It's hilarious. I never knew there were so many euphemisms for dick."

That draws a laugh from her. If there is one thing I've learned about reading romance novels it's that just about everything can be made dirty. But man, Ivers takes it to another level.

"What's this month's book?" she asks cautiously.

Her voice sounds not convinced, like she thinks I'm bullshitting her. And who could really blame her? A group of burly, toothless, smelly hockey players sitting around in a circle reading and discussing romance novels? It's unlikely.

"This month we're reading *On the Ropes* by Kathryn Nolan."

"I'm noticing a sports theme here." Her death grip on my hand eases just a smidge. If she lets me go I might retain function in it after all.

I snort. "I have a carefully crafted plan, thank you very much. I'm diversifying in the coming months." I lean back into my seat a little, but don't take my hand from hers. In fact, I give it a squeeze to reassure her that I'm not letting go and that she really is going to be okay.

She might hate me on principle, and a tiny part of me might wish I could hate her back, but I've never seen someone so utterly terrified to be on a plane in my entire life. Or anywhere at all for that matter. Her earlier fear seemed paralyzing. And no matter what she thinks about me, I can't just sit here and watch her hyperventilate and cry her way through the next ninety minutes.

I wish I could. All that judgment and distaste for me has been clear in her blue-green eyes. She's only talking to me right now because the air travel powers that be thought it would be fun to sit us together. I bet she'd rather walk to Minnesota right now than accept any help I could offer.

And yet, the twitching muscle in her face, her scrunched up shoulders, and the tears still welling in her eyes have brought me to my knees and punched the air from my lungs. She needs someone, and I'm here. After she survives the flight without hyperventilating until she passes out, she can go back to hating me.

It's not like my love of romance novels and support for indie authors will wear her down any. It's definitely not enough to make up for all the pain she thinks I caused. But it's a start, common ground, something to keep her attention from her terror.

"I have a list of tropes, subgenres of romance, and each month I show them the three books I've selected that they get to choose from. Most votes wins."

"Sounds like a very logical system."

Maybe now she'll believe me. There's no way someone could come up with such a creative and complex lie at the drop of a hat. Okay, maybe there's someone out there who could, but that's not me. I'm a plotter, not a pantser.

"Are your teammates enjoying the smutty reads?"

I idly stroke the back of her hand. It could be to comfort her, but truth be told I really need to check that I still have mobility in my digits. She's got me in such a tight grip, I'm losing feeling.

"Y'know, they're enjoying it more than I expected them to." I relax further into my seat, and her death-grip tightens around my fingers. She'd lost all color in her face, but now she's starting to look a little green.

Dear God, I hope they have barf bags in the seat back pocket.

"It took a while to get some of them on board. Most of them signed up because I asked them to, not because they're big readers or into romance—novels or otherwise."

That makes her lips twitch. "Real life hockey players aren't quite the same as book boyfriend hockey players."

"Facts." I crack a smile. She's not wrong. Romance authors rarely write about the toothless grins, and some of the pathetic attempts to grow mustaches for Movember. If it wasn't to raise awareness for testicular cancer, prostate cancer, and men's suicide, I'd want some of the guys on our team to stop trying before they end up mistaken for suspects on *Dateline*.

"There were four of us that first month, last month there were six, and I'm hopeful that another one or two of them will join this month."

"The month is almost over."

I heave out a sigh. "I know. Between school, hockey, and my job, I've been slammed. We all have. We're meeting next week to talk about it. Those that have read the past two books have enjoyed the process, if not the books themselves. They're enjoying the discussions about the characters and plot." It's on the tip of my tongue to tell her I'll have one of my author friends hanging out with us at *Get Lit* but I'm not going there.

Her pallid face pinks up a little. "Are you planning to read any more of J.R. Blake's books at your book club?"

"You like 'em, huh?"

She gives me a jerky nod and shaky smile. "He's my favorite romance author. So full of emotion. He really digs deep, you know?"

Boy, do I ever. Grinning, I want to tell her it's me. I'm him. I'm J.R. That those emotions are my own, and that sometimes it feels like if I don't get them down on paper they'll tear me apart at the seams.

But I bite my tongue. "I've got *Hot Motherpucker* on the list for next month." I shrug. "I'm trying not to have the same author over and over again, or the same subgenres and tropes, but... I know what I like. It's hard not to stick to sports romances every month when they're just so damn good."

Her eyes light up. Her smile is real this time, and I feel it everywhere. Damn, she's pretty.

"That's one of my top picks. Harry is one of my favorite book boyfriends. He's so swoony." She nods. "Great choice."

"Thanks," I mumble, watching my thumb move back and forth on her pale skin.

Praise kinks aren't my jam, and hearing her validate my book selection is one thing, but hearing her gush over my words, my characters? Wow. That's...something else. Her muscles loosen around my fingers. She doesn't let go, but my extremities are less at risk of popping off the end of my arm at least.

We fall silent for a beat, just sitting, staring. The heaviness of my past crushes my chest, weighing down my limbs and making me feel like an awkward teenager for the first time since high school. The only reason anyone knew who I was back then was 'cause of Johnny. He wasn't an all-bad guy, just broken and misguided. But everyone sure as hell knew who he was. And since I was his best friend, or rather his only friend, they all knew me, too.

The captain's voice comes over the speakers and announces we've got a takeoff slot. He reiterates the need for our seatbelts, but his voice turns to background noise as the sharp intakes of breath by my side drown out everything else around me.

What is this woman's damage?

Her hand seizes around mine. I clamp my lip between my teeth in a bid not to yelp out loud. I'm a strong guy, but it turns out that when Savannah Bowen is propelled by crushing fear, she's pretty savage herself.

As the plane judders and starts moving, my stomach sinks. I admit, when I'd seen her sit down next to me and heard the captain announce a delay, I was convinced this was my very own forced proximity romance novel come to life.

If I was writing the story myself, our plane would have been canceled, she'd have beaten me to the last car at the rental place, and I'd have somehow convinced her to let me tag along for the ride. Maybe bribed her with snacks and candy to let me go with her.

We'd have snarked and bantered our way through as much of the 272 mile drive as we could before we got to a hotel for the night. A hotel—which of course would be in a place that was booked out for the holiday—save for one room, with one bed, that we'd have to share.

The story writes itself in the back of my mind as her trembling hand clutches mine. I wish I had use of all of my appendages so I could grab my laptop from under the seat in front of me and start pounding the keys. I can't help it—the muse wants what the muse wants. And right now, since there's no chance of my very own love story with the beautiful woman next to me who happens to hate my guts, I want to write it.

In my fictional, forced proximity story I'd of course be a gentleman at the hotel and offer to sleep on the couch, or the floor, hell, even in the bathtub if it made her feel comfortable.

But it's the Midwest, right? So it would be cold, really fucking cold. Like freak blizzard cold. The heating could be broken in the hotel, and the icicles around her heart would eventually thaw and she'd let me lie on the double or queen bed with her.

Crap. I need to stop this thought process as my dick likes this story more and more.

The plane trundles toward the runway, and the closer we get, the louder and shallower Savannah's breaths become. Her ashen face had tiny beads of sweat on it before, but now there are large droplets running down her face and trickling down the side of her nose.

Why would anyone do this to themselves? Why would anyone put themselves in a position to be so utterly terrified? Why didn't she just drive?

My questions pop up like moles in Whack-a-Mole. I try to

smack them down while I frantically search for something, anything I can do to distract her from her fear. I'd love to say it's because she looks like she's going to puke all over both of us, but I can't take the waves of suffocating emotions rolling off her. And it's all I want to do, absorb it all so she doesn't feel any of it.

She's muttering to herself now, something about changing doctors and never flying again. I don't think she realizes that she's rocking back and forth and looks like she might be summoning a demon from the depths of the underworld.

If I was writing this, right now my hero would kiss the heroine to snap her out of her traumatized state. He'd just grab her by her gorgeous sweaty face and lay one on her, right there during takeoff.

But this isn't a romance novel, and I'm not sure I could grab her face even if I wanted to. My fingers are turning blue as pins and needles stab through them. She may be cutting off the circulation to my brain, too, and that's why I can't think of something else to talk to her about.

"Savannah?"

She shakes her head, still muttering under her breath, the roar of the engine and the rattles and shudders of the body of the plane drowning out whatever she's saying to herself.

She scrunches her eyes as the wheels lift off the tarmac beneath us, and her cheek flexes so much I'd be amazed if she didn't crack a tooth.

I could never do what she's doing. I'd have said "fuck this shit" and walked the 272 miles rather than go through what she's going through. She's so fucking brave.

Fuck it.

I slide my arm around her shoulders and pull her close. Her whole body trembles as I hug her to me. It's awkward over the armrest, but I can't flip it up right now, and even if we'd leveled off in the air and I was allowed to, Savannah is now clinging to me like a freakin' spider monkey.

Her nails dig into my thigh, pinching through my pants, her face is burrowed into my shoulder, and her hair tickles my nose. She smells of pineapple. I don't know if it's her lotion, her shampoo, or something she uses on her lips but all I can smell is pineapple. I kinda want to lick her to see if she tastes like it, too.

The plane shakes from side to side and her nails sink deeper into my skin. That's going to leave marks. I shush her, sliding my hand up and down her spine, over the bumps of her bra strap and back down, rocking her back and forth.

I'm sure she has a return flight, and I know she won't tell me when it is, but maybe I can convince her to coordinate somehow, or maybe she'd let me drive her back. Oh! Maybe I could ask Mom to ask Aunt Jennie if she could pick up a horse tranquilizer from the vet office she works at, and I could shoot her up with sedatives before she gets on the plane.

Her fear has exhausted me, so when she falls asleep on my shoulder and her body goes limp against mine, I'm not surprised. In fact, relief courses through my veins but I'm afraid to rest my head against hers in case she wakes up with a start and hits me with a head-butt.

I want to bury my nose in her hair, though. I want to brush my head from side to side in her soft locks and take a deep inhale so the hairs tickle my nose again. I want to drown in the scent of pineapples.

Do I have a sudden and consuming crush on the woman in my arms who hates me? Absolutely.

It seems to be my calling card, falling for unavailable women. Getting myself into awkward situations with people I barely know. Feeling more for people than they feel for me.

It's my MO.

Sure, I'm lonely. But that's not why I'm drawn to Savannah. She's striking—high cheekbones, full, pouty lips, beautiful locks of golden hair, bottomless sea-blue eyes.

Maybe I'm a masochist, drawn to her vehement dislike for me.

Maybe that's my kink.

At some point I must doze off, because the next thing I know I'm jolted awake by the head-butt I predicted. Savannah's ponytail connects with my eye socket as she jerks her slumped head back. We're descending, so my guess is that the change in air pressure woke her up.

Our eyes meet as the wheels touch down on the ground, hers wide and afraid. It's taking every ounce of strength I have not to tuck that stray wave of hair behind her ear and caress her face. My heart's racing, and I'm intoxicated by the scent of pineapples and Savannah's close proximity to my...everything.

She's still holding my hand. Her chest brushes my body with each heaving breath, and if I move myself an inch closer, our lips would be touching. Fuck. I want our lips to touch.

The tiniest frown appears, wrinkling her forehead as though she can read my mind, as though she knows I want to kiss her fear away, drawing it from her body and into mine so it can't wreck her anymore. Her gaze flickers to my lips and back to my eyes. Like she might be thinking about kissing me too.

She wets her lips.

I shift in my seat.

She closes her eyes.

I lift my hand to cup her jaw.

The crackle of the speakers sparks us out of our stupor, and I jump back so far from her that I hit the back of my head off the window. She looks at my outstretched hand like I'm offering her a palm full of dog shit. Her expression morphs from the delicate, vulnerable, kiss-me face of just a split second ago, and is instead replaced by a scowl and venomous eyes.

Is she upset I didn't kiss her? Is she upset I almost kissed her? Is she embarrassed about her fear of flying? Of piercing my thigh with her nails? Who knows? I certainly fucking don't.

All I know is she's looking at me like she's contemplating my death, and if she stares at me much harder, she might actually succeed.

The "fasten seatbelt" sign turns off with a chime. The cabin door opens. And before I can blink, Savannah is on her feet, grabbing her purse from the overhead locker, and out the door without a backward glance.

I rub the back of my neck, staring at the hole in the side of the plane where she disappeared out onto the jet-way.

What the fuck just happened?

CHAPTER 8

Savannah

Waiting for my bag to appear in front of me on the jet-bridge might be the longest four minutes—and counting—of my entire life. My anxious stare flicks back and forth between the passengers deplaning and the magic door my case will come through any second. The door that needs to hurry the fuck up and open so I can flee the scene before Justin steps off the goddamn plane.

He's either waiting for everyone else to disembark to give me time to leave, or he's trapped and no one will let him out into the aisle to leave. Either way, I'm happy. The longer they keep him there, the more chance I have of getting away without having to see him again.

I bounce my weight from leg to leg, while simultaneously trying to press my knees and thighs together, desperate for the restroom. Moms are always right—I should have gone before I left. Ugh. There was zero chance I was going to amble down the aisle of that death-trap in flight to try to pee. Hell no. I had no choice but to hold it through my entire ordeal. I'm paying for it now, though.

Goddammit, they need to hurry up with my bag.

And I better not fucking sneeze because I'm 100% sure I'll piss myself.

Every time I board a flight I think it'll be different, easier, not as terrifying, but it never fucking is. It's always the same, every single time. I try not to let my fears dictate my life but this, this isn't cool.

I know one thing's for sure, unless I have a purse full of happy pills, I'm never boarding another plane again in my life.

Blowing out a hiss of air, I pray to the bladder gods they won't embarrass me in this moment. Peeing yourself in front of your enemy isn't sexy or funny.

My enemy.

Justin Ass is still my enemy, right?

Right.

The fact that he was concerned and attentive and even let me drool on his shoulder means nothing. It doesn't change a goddamn thing. It *can't* change anything.

Uteruses before duderuses.

He's still an ass. He broke my bestie's heart. My loyalty remains with Molly, no matter how nice he was to me on the plane. No matter how much I wanted him to lean just a little bit closer until our lips met.

I don't need to kiss Justin Ass, no matter what my tingling girl parts said. Or continue to say.

I need to have sex, that's all it is. The fact I was so drawn to Justin just confirms that it's been too long since I've enjoyed the company of a member of the opposite sex. I am so starved of human touch that I contemplated kissing Molly's cheating-ass ex.

Damn. That's bad. I definitely need to get myself laid. It's going on the to-do list for when I get back to UCR, right next to cleaning my sheets and booking a waxing appointment.

The door opens, a gust of cold air blows up the jet bridge, and I shiver involuntarily. Jesus. I can't risk another shiver. No unplanned movement or my bladder might just give up on me. The baggage handler lines up the bags. Of course mine isn't one of the first out.

I'm whispering prayers to any God who will get me to the bathroom without leaking when my case finally appears. Popping the handle up, I drag it behind me as I walk as fast as I dare without risking spreading my legs too much with each stride.

Oh God. I'm not sure I'm going to make it.

I shuffle-run through the airport cursing the fact not every airport in the country is small and quaint like Cedar Rapids, and burst through the door of the restrooms with mere seconds to spare.

I don't even take an extra beat to lock the door to the stall. I slide my case in front of it, and hold it in place with my foot while I take a moment to enjoy my blissful relief.

Is there anything more satisfying in life than making it to the bathroom in the nick of time? I flush and leave the stall, only to come face-to-ass with Justin. He's standing to my left at a urinal I didn't notice in my haste to empty my bladder. His trouser snake is on full display. His not-at-all-tiny trouser snake.

I swallow and fight the urge to lick my lips. I'm not sure I have any moisture left in my mouth, it seems to have dried up at the sight of him with his hand on his dick.

His eyes widen, and his cheeks turn pink. I consider fleeing to the ladies room to wash my hands but then he might think I don't wash them at all. And that's almost worse than standing in the men's bathroom trying not to make eye contact with his still-on-display cock.

I clear my throat and look at anything that isn't...*that* as I tug my case toward the sinks. Embarrassment sears every inch of my body. Going back to the jet bridge where I was praying not to pee in front of him and just pissing my pants right there would be better than this.

He tucks away his junk and pulls up his zipper before joining me at the sinks.

"Don't say anything." My voice is almost a growl as I lather up my hands and rinse them under the water.

From the corner of my eye I can see him roll his lips between his teeth as though trying not to smile which only fuels my embarrassment and anger even more.

I don't dry my hands. Instead, I spin on my heel and grab my case, making a beeline for the exit, passing three very confused-looking guys on my way. They'll figure out that they're in the right bathroom when they see the urinals I power-walked right by.

Maybe I can get through baggage claim and to the exit before he's done in the bathroom, especially now that I don't have a full bladder weighing me down.

Shit. I stumble to a halt. Mom's going to be waiting for me in baggage claim. In all the flight panic and the pee-fiasco, I'd almost forgotten that I'm not really ready to see my parents.

I rub my hands on my pants, back and front to soak up some of the beads of water before making a decision.

I'll take Mom discomfort over having to face the guy whose peen I just saw. So I take off like an Olympian at the starting line. The end is in sight, I can *see* the glowing exit signs above the doors. All I have to do is find Mo—nooooooooooooooooo. No, no, no, no.

Mom isn't alone. She's chatting animatedly to a woman a few inches taller than her. The stranger has blonde wavy hair, and the closer I get to them, the more familiar she looks. She's a female version of Justin.

My stomach sinks. They're smiling and laughing as they talk, comfortable, like they've known each other for years.

There's no way I can grab-and-go Mom, and Justin can't be too far behind me.

This is a disaster.

Another disaster.

"Mom?"

"Savannah!" Mom abandons her conversation and launches herself at me like she half expected me not to show up at all. Her hug is bone-crunching, all consuming, and warm despite the chill to the air. Tears well in my eyes as I scold myself. I won't cry, not here, not now. I'm still mad at my parents for lying to me, for not giving me the chance to meet my birth mom, even if Mom's hug feels pretty damn good.

"Ready to go?" I flash a hopeful smile.

She knows how traumatic flying is for me, and right now I just want a nap. It's still way too early in the morning to be dealing with people. Especially very specific people whose cock I just saw. In front of my very eyes.

One very, very specific delicious person who I've had a crush on since I was a teenager. A very delicious person who, until today, I thought was nothing but douchiness thanks to being BFFs with Johnny White. I think I might have been a little wrong about him, and I don't know what the fuck to do with that any more than I know what to do with the mental images of that mondo cock I just saw in the bathroom.

Mom returns my smile, but half-turns back to Mrs. Ass. Ashe. Fuck.

"Savvy, this is Mandy Ashe. She and I go way back. We went to high school together but fell out of touch over the years. We were just catching up. Did you know her son goes to school with you?"

Do. I. ever. Yeah, Mom. I do know he's in school with me. I give a tight-lipped smile and nod as Mandy's face brightens.

Oh no. She's looking over my shoulder like the light of her life just appeared. Dammit. Dammit, dammit, dammit.

"Hey, Mom." Justin brushes my shoulder as he passes, then grabs his mom in a bear hug.

Okay, that's kinda sweet.

Nope. No. No. No. No sweet. No hot. No wanting to climb that tree-trunk dick like a freakin' Bengal tiger.

Cheating cheater who cheats on all the things. Tests and women. I don't want his dick. He *is* a dick. A cheating dick. We don't hold space for cheating dicks.

Ovaries before brovaries.

Ovaries before brovaries.

Ovaries before brovaries.

The warmth at seeing the smile on his face as he hugs his mom drowns out the chant in my head.

"Hey, honey." She squeezes him before stepping back. "This is Abby Bowen, and her daughter Savannah. She goes to UCR. Do you know her?"

The corner of his mouth twitches as he meets my gaze before those perfectly kissable lips tilt into a smile. "We sat together on the plane. Hi, I'm Justin." He reaches a hand to Mom who takes it and gives a shake.

"Abby. It's lovely to meet you, Justin."

It's not lovely, Mom. He's the enemy.

She gives him a warm smile before flexing her eyes at me in an "isn't he so dreamy" kind of subliminal message. Yeah, Mom. But all that glitters is not gold. And this guy may be enchanting on the outside, but inside he's a cheater.

Cheater, cheater, pumpkin eater.

"We should…" I hook a thumb over my shoulder toward the exit beckoning me to safety. Okay, so not safety, but away from *him*.

Mom flaps her hand at me. "Excuse her rudeness. She doesn't like to fly."

I half expect him to snort an "I'll say," but Justin's face turns more serious as he nods, holding me hostage with those eyes.

Sigh. Those eyes.

Wait. Does he have a full-size suitcase? He has hockey games to get back to, so I know for a fact he's not staying long, at most a couple days.

What the hell kind of diva is he that he takes an entire case back home for Thanksgiving? I guess he couldn't fit all his douchiness into a carry-on bag.

Even as I think the words I know they're not true. He's been nothing but sweet since we left Cedar Rapids. But it's a front. It has to be. No one cheats with someone out in the open like he did and isn't a dick.

Mom claps her hands together, her "great idea" signal, and I groan, out loud, drawing a strange look from Justin. "I know. We should all get together tomorrow for Thanksgiving dinner."

My stomach drops. This is not a good plan. Sometimes Mom acts without thinking. This is clearly one of those times.

I expect Mandy to wave it off. It's Thanksgiving—everyone has plans already, and everyone hangs with their family. There's no way. They definitely have plans and can't just abandon their own celebration to come and join ours.

There's no way. Dammit, Mandy, tell me there's no way.

Except Mandy looks at Justin, asking a silent question with her eyes, and I'm waiting for Justin to shake his head, or tell her they can't because they have plans when he smiles and nods.

What. The. Fuck?

"We'd love to." Mandy grins at Mom and they turn toward the exit. Justin grabs my case and follows behind the moms leaving me standing wondering what the hell just happened.

I wouldn't fucking love to. I can think of eleventy billion

other things I'd rather do than have Thanksgiving dinner with the Ashes.

Jumping out of a plane at 30,000 feet for example.

Or using a cheese grater on my fucking lady garden.

How did this happen?

Mom doesn't even pause or stop to check I'm following her. She's so engaged in her conversation with Mandy that it's kind of cute.

Justin, on the other hand, stops and casts a glance back over his shoulder. His mouth tips up again in that infuriatingly smug smile and he shrugs.

I know Mom's plan. She's playing matchmaker, thinking it's cute. She thinks I need a boyfriend, that I need to settle down with a nice boy and give her thirteen grandbabies after I graduate college. I hope that's what happens, too, but not with him.

He throws me one more smile before turning back and following the moms out the door. I'm left with nothing else to do but follow behind.

My feet carry me toward the exit, but what I really want is to do a 180 turn and get my ass back on a plane to flee the impending clusterfuck of a Thanksgiving I'm facing.

CHAPTER 9

Justin

Maybe I'm living my very own forced proximity romance novel after all. This is all working out perfectly. Sitting next to Savannah on the plane I realized that I do care what she thinks about me. I don't just want to change her mind about me, I want her.

All of her.

I want to take her on dates, figure out what makes her smile, and help her chase her every dream. Yup. It's a lot, way too fast, way too soon. I want to kiss those tantalizing lips, I want to tangle my fingers in her honey gold hair, and I want to drag my tongue over every single inch of skin on her body.

I'm crushing. Hard.

And the conflict was written across her features. Like she was trying to process the Justin she heard about in high school against the one she saw sitting with her on the plane.

The look on her face when her mom invited us for Thanksgiving dinner was priceless. It took everything I had not to laugh out loud at the stunned disgust painted on her delicate eyebrows. We don't usually do much for the holiday.

We eat turkey, we watch football, and Dad and I pass out in a meat coma on the sofa the way God intended.

Mom does the Black Friday thing with her sister and comes home with a bunch of shit she doesn't need, just 'cause it was on deep discount. Then she spends the weekend trying to figure out who's getting what for Christmas. She's gifted so many waffle irons that I've lost count. By this point I think a few people have been given two.

The idea of spending the holiday across the table from a girl who's trying so hard to hate me has my muse in overdrive.

I pull out my phone on the ride home and start a new note, frantically typing as Mom drives and tries to make small talk. It's not the book I should be working on, but sometimes the ideas that come to you in a moment of inspiration? Sometimes those are even better than the ones you'd planned out to the letter.

Fingers crossed this is one of them.

I guess Mom sees I'm writing and goes quiet, knowing that when I'm creating I need to concentrate. Instead she sings along under her breath to the Christmas music radio channel she switches on at the start of November every year without fail.

By the time we get home, I'm ready to take a break. We have dinner, I unpack—giving Dad most of the 6-packs of Spotted Cow I picked up from Glarus Brewing Co. in Wisconsin while I was in town for a game.

"I'm going to bring a couple to the Bowen's house tomorrow."

Dad's jaw drops open and he clutches a 6-pack to his chest. "You...what? My precious Spotted Cow? You wouldn't!"

Mom rubs my arm, laughing. "I think that's a great idea, sweetie. You brought more than enough for your dad. I told

Abby I'd make my chocolate mud pie for dessert and bring a couple of sides, too. You want to help me in the kitchen?"

Our turkey is already thawing, so Mom decided she'd cook it tomorrow anyway and give me a meat-coma-care-package to take back with me since my case is now empty of all the beer I hauled across state lines.

Once the boys get a whiff of my luggage, it won't last long. I'll make her team-famous Thanksgiving leftover hotdish. Mom always makes sure she sends enough food to feed an army—or a college hockey team—plus a second mud pie for me to bring with me, too.

She makes the best mud pie in the freakin' state. For real. It won first place at the state fair two years in a row, beating out her baking nemesis Matilda-Mae Bolt. Who—Mom thinks —uses a box mix for her brownies, which is unforgivable in the Ashe household.

I tug off my sweatshirt and leave it over the back of a dining room chair as I get to work. I'm shredding a block of cheese for the mac and cheese—Mom says it tastes better than the pre-shredded stuff—when she bumps me with her hip.

"So."

Here it comes.

"Savannah Bowen, huh?" She waggles her brows at me like she knows things. "I'm guessing she's the reason you agreed to break tradition from leaving your ass-print on my couch for Thanksgiving."

Moms always know. There's no point in denying it, so I keep grating and nod. Maybe if I stay silent it'll pass quickly. Like a kidney stone.

An indecipherable squeal bursts from her and she gives me a squeeze. "I knew it. She grew up nice, didn't she? I see pictures on her mom's social media sometimes, but she's turned into a stunning young woman"

Yes, she did. She really fucking did.

Mom frowns as I pop the grater off the plastic tub below and clip on the lid.

"I couldn't help but notice that she didn't seem to return your affection."

When my brows twitch, she taps the side of her nose. "It looked like Abby had asked her to go get a colonic instead of sharing her Thanksgiving meal with us. But I know you can win her over." She pinches my face like I'm still her plump-cheeked toddler. Some days I wonder if that's how she sees me when she looks at me. "There's no way she doesn't fall head over heels for my boy."

Despite her conviction, I'm not so sure she's right that I can win Savannah over. But I'm going to give it my best shot. One thing's for certain, though. If my face happens to end up in the vicinity of those luscious lips of hers, I won't stop myself this time.

I didn't sleep. Every time I closed my eyes I saw Savannah, and my dick twitched to life. I spent all night with a raging boner for a girl who tried to kill me with her eyes.

I jerked off in the shower this morning—twice—but it didn't help. My dick knows it's not her hands, or her mouth, or her pussy wrapped around it. No matter how much I imagine, or want it to be.

Since Abby suggested we go to her house for Thanksgiving lunch, I guess they have evening plans. That, or she and Mom want to spend all day getting reacquainted. It wouldn't surprise me. Mom was so excited to have bumped into her at the airport.

They can catch up while the rest of us watch football on TV. And Savannah... I dunno what she'll do.

Either way, I'm now looking at the crappy selection of

clothes I brought home with me, wholly unprepared for a winning-the-girl type of situation.

Mom comes into my room and laughs, probably at my surly face at the outfit choices I've lain out on my bed. She offers me the bag she's carrying. "Here. Wear this."

Savannah isn't going to care what I'm wearing, so for a moment I consider choosing the tatty, old UCR Raccoons tee that's crumpled under my pillow to wear to bed.

Inside the bag Mom handed to me is a Raccoons-green polo shirt and a soft navy sweater with new dark-wash jeans.

"It was supposed to be part of your Christmas gift, but I feel like you could do with wearing something...eh...nice today." She winks.

I want to groan but I'm grateful and pull the tags off the new clothes. "Thanks, Mom. You're a lifesaver." Grabbing the back of the shirt I'm wearing, I haul it over my head before I realize she's still standing in the doorway, nibbling on the inside of her cheek, a frown pinching between her eyes.

I've seen that look before. "What's wrong?"

"I don't want to meddle. Or gossip."

I slide my new polo on and fasten two of the buttons, leaving the top one open. "But?"

"Abby said something at the airport while we were waiting for you guys to arrive."

"Okay?"

Her forehead is wrinkled, and the crow's feet at the corners of her eyes are more defined when her frown deepens.

"Mom?"

"She's having a rough time right now. Savannah, I mean. She could probably do with having a friend around, that's all."

If she thinks I'm letting her get away with that vague, click-bait-y sentence, she has another think coming. I fold my arms. "Spill."

"Over the summer...Savannah learned that she's adopted.

Abby and Kev hadn't told her yet—she found out on her own." She hugs herself, chafing her arms. "Abby says she's barely talked to them since."

I rub the back of my neck. "Abby just told you all this while you were waiting in baggage claim? After not talking to you for what...decades?"

Her face softens. "Moms talk, kiddo. We understand each other. Abby's really worried about Savannah. I guess she just needed an outsider to confide in. Sometimes unburdening yourself, even to a stranger, helps get things straight in your mind."

"And why are you telling me?"

"Forewarned is forearmed, Justin. She's fragile right now, hurting, angry and if you want to pursue something with her, I figured it might help if you knew what she's dealing with going in."

If Savannah hasn't spoken to her family for months, she probably hasn't been looking forward to seeing them for the holiday. Add in her fear of flying and it's no wonder I almost choked on her anxiety.

Damn, she really is brave as fuck.

I finish getting dressed, and by the time I get downstairs, Mom has the cooler ready to go. Dad's wearing a plaid shirt and khakis. I don't remember the last time I saw him so dressed up. I guess since we'll be peopleing for Thanksgiving, we needed to ditch our customary wardrobe of pjs and fluffy slipper socks for something a little more outside-world-appropriate. I have to admit, it's kind of nice.

We load up the car and hit the road to the Bowens' house. My shoulders are tight, and while I'm looking forward to seeing Savannah again, part of me can't help feeling like we're about to intrude on a private family moment that we have no business being anywhere near.

Dad reverses into their driveway—backing into parking

spaces is a habit I picked up from him and it drives Mom irrationally mad—and I suck in a breath. Savannah will either welcome the distraction of having us around, or try to kill me with her laser eyes again.

It's time to find out which it's gonna be.

CHAPTER 10
Savannah

I've fluctuated between panicking over lunch this afternoon and being angry at Mom for inviting the Ashes over at all today. While part of me—a teenie weenie part, like way down deep—is glad to have a buffer around for at least part of the day, the other is tangled up in nerves, embarrassment, and a healthy dose of resentment.

She couldn't have invited someone else? Someone I wasn't trying to get space from? Someone whose dick I haven't seen waving in the wind?

Ugh. Talk about a hockey stick.

I need to stop thinking about his dick.

But really, he could cleave a woman in half with that thing.

I fan my face with both hands like I'm drying my mascara or lipstick. But neither need it. My face is just hot because my memory is making my cheeks singe.

By the time I figure out what to wear and get my ass downstairs, the Ashes are already in the house. I didn't hear them arrive—maybe I was in the shower or drying my hair. When I see Justin in his perfect-fitting jeans and navy sweater looking like the All-American boy next door at the sink helping Mom rinse potatoes, I stop dead.

His dad sits next to mine at the dining table and they're both wearing shirts—like Sunday shirts, not graphic tees.

While my yoga pants and Care Bears shirt are comfy as hell, I'm *wildly* underdressed for this. I pivot on my heel and make a break for the stairs only to come face-to-face with Justin's mom. Mandy pins me with a knowing smile and the back of my neck prickles with beads of sweat.

Busted. "I...uh..." I point finger guns at the stairs behind her. "I didn't realize you were here already. I was just going to get changed."

She pats my shoulder as I dart past. "It's good to see you again, Savannah. I love your hair."

"Thanks," I squeak and take the stairs two at a time. She's in her Sunday best, too. I'm the only one letting the side down. I guess I hadn't considered that we'd level up our outfits just because Mom's old friend was coming over. My bad.

And I certainly didn't want to put too much time into picking my outfit just because Justin would be here.

I throw on one of my church dresses, a blue one—Mom says it matches my eyes, and I love it even more because it has pockets—smooth my wavy hair one last time, and hurry back to the kitchen where I find Mom and Mandy.

"There you are. I thought you'd dropped off the face of the planet or something." Mom puts a pot on the stove and jerks a chin toward the living room. "Everyone else is in there."

"I thought maybe I could help you guys out in here."

They share a look before Mandy gives a small shake of her head. "Savannah, honey. We've got this covered. Why don't you go hang out with Justin in the living room?"

As subtle as a low-flying blimp, Mrs. A. Thanks.

"But—"

"Mandy's right, Savvy. Everything's under control in here.

Too many cooks spoil the broth and all that. Why don't you go and make sure your sister isn't driving poor Justin mad."

Poor Justin, my ass. If anyone deserves to be driven crazy by Sophia, an excitable nine-year-old girl who is going through her "boys suck" phase, it's him.

I lean on the doorframe to the living room taking in the situation. Dad's sitting on the couch with Justin's dad. They're sipping on what looks to be craft beer of some kind chatting about hockey.

Justin and Soph sit cross-legged next to the coffee table playing Game of Life. Justin occasionally chirps up adding to the hockey discussion going on behind him, while somehow keeping up a conversation with my sister too. She appears to be over her "Ew. Ew. Ew. Boys suck" phase because tiny love hearts are popping out of the side of her head as she stares at him.

Something warm stirs in my stomach as he patiently waits for her to take her turn. She asks his opinion about something on the card she's drawn and grins at him when she moves her piece. He's engaged in the game and in her. He doesn't seem at all bored or grumpy at the fact he's hanging out and playing board games with a kid less than half his age.

"There you are, sweetheart."

Dad's voice makes me yelp in surprise.

He tips his beer at me with a grin. "Justin brought a couple six-packs of Spotted Cow. You know how I love craft beer."

That I most certainly do.

Justin shrugs like it's no big deal. "I usually bring home a few packs from my travels. I don't always have time to visit the breweries and microbreweries themselves, but I've worked out where I can get mine and Dad's favorites in most of the states we play in by now. I figured you can't go wrong with bringing good beer when you're crashing someone's Thanksgiving plans."

Dad chuckles and takes a sip before smacking his lips together. "Feel free to crash our Thanksgiving any time." He raises his bottle to Justin, and I suppress another groan.

Mom and I have made it our life's mission to find new and exciting craft beers for Dad to try over the years. Birthday, Father's Day, Christmas—any excuse for a new beer for him to try. He's had Spotted Cow before and loved it. Justin has unknowingly become one of Dad's favorite people.

Dammit. With Mom and Mandy's obvious desire to match-make Justin and me, I was kind of hoping Dad would be on my side.

Justin 2.

Savannah 0.

This can be fixed. I walk to the wall where my phone is charging in the far corner of the room and disconnect it.

> Savvyanna: Hey Molster, long time no see. I'm in town for the holiday and was wondering if you'd like to hang out.

I almost fist-pump at my little victory and drop my phone in my pocket. A moment of grounding, a reminder of where my loyalties lie. That ought to do it. Talking to Molly will center me and renew the strength of my allegiance tether to my old friend.

It doesn't matter that he's gorgeous. It doesn't matter that my little sister is looking at him like he's the best thing since sliced bread. It doesn't matter that he brought Dad one of his favorite craft beers, or that he helped Mom in the kitchen with the food prep.

Justin and Soph have turned their attention back to their game, and I'm itching to join them. I *love* board games, and my parents have an extensive collection spanning back to their own time at college. We never miss a chance to pull out a box and let our competitive natures take over for a while. Especially when we have company visiting.

My feet carry me toward the coffee table, and I fold my legs under me as I drop to the floor next to Sophia.

"He's pretty good," she tells me with a sharp elbow to the ribs. Of course he is.

Justin puffs out his chest. "Thanks. You're not so bad yourself."

Soph grins and takes her turn. His mouth opens, closes, and opens again. And I can't tell if he's pretending to be a fish or if he's got something on his mind he wants to talk about.

My phone buzzes, distracting me from staring at those lips, that jawline, that face.

> Molly: Sure thing. Waffles?

I grin at her predictability and nod like she can see me.

> Savvyanna: Just say when.

There's another message on my phone that I must have missed.

> Athena: I'm so sorry for your loss, girl. I know she wasn't in your life, but it's still a loss.

> Athena: I can't imagine what that feels like. Finding out you're adopted, then finding out your birth mom is dead—and so recently too. Ugh.

> Athena: I wish I had something profound to say, but all I got is: it's shit.

Savannah: I'm still pissed. I didn't get to tell my parents I looked her up, either. They invited some people over for TG dinner. Probably to avoid having to talk to me. It's like this giant elephant is in the room, taking up all my oxygen.

I rub my chest, suddenly aware of how true that is. Despite not being ready to see my parents, I know we need to talk. They should know what I found out about my birth mom, and I have to find a way to process this anger fizzing and hissing under my skin.

Mom's excited to see her old friend, but she hasn't talked to me yet and I expected that we would. We've kept it light so far, talking about school, my new job, and what I plan to do while I'm in town visiting.

And yeah, some of that is my fault, but jeez. Maybe they're as scared to talk to me as I am them, and having the Ashes over is a way to help...somehow? Or at least distract.

Who knows? All I know is I have this aching pit in my stomach, and I feel icky in my own skin.

I cast a glance at Dad whose sad eyes are on me while he chats with Clint. He offers me a small smile that I try to return. He knows I'm hurting just as much as he is, too. I've always been his little girl.

I just don't feel like it anymore.

Justin

Savannah has been quiet all afternoon. She chatted with her little sister during our Game of Life. She helped me set the table ahead of the mouthwatering dinner our moms are serving up onto platters right now. But her eyes are melancholic, and she's emitting such overwhelming distress from her every freakin' pore that I can almost taste it in the air.

Is it me? Is she this upset because we're here? Or is it seeing her parents again after learning about her history?

Part of me wishes Mom hadn't told me about what Savannah's going through right now. But the rest of me is kind of grateful, even if I do feel like I have some sort of unfair advantage over her somehow.

The drone of pleasant conversation buzzes around the table as we eat, but Savannah only speaks when someone asks her a direct question. I want to reach out to her, to hold her hand, or pat her thigh.

I'd try to stroke her foot with mine, but she's sitting next to her dad, and I really don't want Kev to think I'm coming onto him, so instead, I sit through dinner aching to help.

We dive straight into dessert, none of us wanting to wait

even ten minutes to let our food settle before Mom's pie is brought to the table. I resist licking the dish—only just. If I was in my own home, I wouldn't give it a second thought. But here, well, I'm making an effort. Though the idea that it might make Savannah laugh, even for a second, has me wondering if I should do it anyway.

Mom wags her finger at me. "Don't. You. Dare. Justin Phillip Ashe. Don't you dare."

Savannah's eyes cut to me, fork paused en route to her mouth with her last bite of pie. In fact, everyone's staring at me.

I hold my hands up in surrender. "I don't know what you're talking about." My lips twitch as Mom's face breaks into a smile.

"I'm sure." She swipes the near-empty pie dish from in front of me and places it on the counter behind her. "Where are your manners?"

I shrug. "I didn't do anything, Mom. You can't scold me for thinking about doing something."

She turns to Abby. "Justin sometimes forgets his manners when it comes to my mud pie. He has a penchant for licking the dish."

Sophia gasps a "no." Savannah's dad snorts.

"I don't blame him." Savannah speaks around her mouthful of pie. "I probably would too if I lived in close proximity to this pie. It's amazing, Mrs. Ashe."

Mom preens. She's a feeder. There's rarely a day when she doesn't make something delicious from scratch. The kitchen is her domain, and she's a culinary artist. I guess I got my creative gene from her. Dad, on the other hand, burns toast.

When we're all done with our food, Abby makes coffee for her and Mom.

"You want help cleaning up the kitchen?" Savannah offers. I can't tell if she's really offering, or if she's just being polite.

"I'll help, too." Anything to spend a few more minutes in her company.

She looks like she bit into a lemon but doesn't fight me. It's a little victory, but little still counts.

At the sink, Savanna's shoulders curl forward, and I wonder how she's still standing. I want to hug her, to carry some of that emotional weight for her, but I'm half-scared that if I step into her space right now she'll butcher me with the carving knife she's moving from the cutting board.

She empties the dishwasher while I fill the sink with warm, soapy water. When she stands up straight, our elbows brush, and she apologizes. I'm dying to talk to her, but I can sense she needs some space and quiet.

As the sink fills, I cover some of the leftovers with plastic wrap, and I get a whiff of her citrus shampoo as she passes. They won't last long, they never do. If we stay for any length of time I bet Dad and Kev will go for round two. Mom brought a wheel of brie, a Granny Smith apple, and some fig preserve just in case there's an opportunity to make turkey sandwiches. They're the *best*.

We both reach for the same dish in the sink and our hands tangle together. Jerking back our hands like we've been electrocuted, we both smile, still quiet.

Dad and Kev have already moved on to the second pack of Spotted Cow.

Savannah stacks the dishwasher in silence, and I get to work on scrubbing the pots. She casts occasional furtive glances at me, like she's expecting me to fill the quiet with idle chatter. And while it's tempting—so fucking tempting—the quiet seems to be working for her. So I stay silent, trying my best to give her what she needs.

Her shoulders have softened, her jaw isn't flexing, and she *feels* calmer to me. When she's done loading the plates and filling the dishwasher with detergent, she starts the wash cycle and picks up a towel.

She's standing so close to me that our elbows are almost touching. I should be a gentleman and give her more space but every time our skin connects, a little flutter of electricity skates up my arm, and honestly, I don't want it to stop.

We still haven't said a single word. The air around us is heavy with unspoken words. It's getting to the point that I might need to clamp down on my tongue to keep from saying something. It's almost turned into a silent challenge, and I'm not going to lose by speaking first.

I'm rinsing out the last pot in the sink when a shriek bursts from her, followed by a string of curse words. When I turn to her, she's clutching her hand and droplets of blood ooze from between her fingers.

"Shit. First aid kit?"

"Under there." She jerks her chin to the cabinet under the sink.

"I've got you. How bad is it?" I'm already crouched low to the floor, holding the cabinet door open and groping inside for the first aid bag.

"I think a Band-Aid would do." She hisses as she examines the cut on the side of her finger. "It's not too deep, it's just bleeding a lot."

Rising to my feet, I already have the kit open and am digging for something to cover her wound, but she's moving away from me.

"Where are you—?"

She plonks down on a dining room chair and leans forward, putting her head toward her knees. "Not great with blood." She looks up, giving me an embarrassed smile. The color has drained from her face like she's lost half of the blood in her body.

She holds her hand out for me to give her the Band-Aid, but instead I hold mine out. "I've got it."

She looks at me, then her finger, then back to me before she reaches her injured hand toward me and puts her head back down near her thighs with a groan.

I clean up the blood, put the Band-Aid on—making sure she was right about the severity of the cut—before sliding my knuckle under her chin and tipping her head back so she can see me.

"All good."

She glances at her hand like she doesn't believe me, then breathes out a sigh. "Thank you."

Just like that, we're back to within kissing distance, staring at each other, holding each other in our orbits. I search her eyes, waiting for some kind of demand to stop what I'm doing and get the fuck out of her space, but none comes.

She smells like chocolate. I risk sliding my palm along her jaw to cup her face, and she sucks in a sharp breath which she holds onto. Our noses touch so I tilt my head, ready for her lips to cushion mine.

"Justin!" Sophia's voice permeates the quiet. There's a shake of a board game inside a box, the pieces rattling against the cardboard.

Savannah jolts, our foreheads smack, and pain jabs into my forehead as I shoot to my feet. What is it about this girl? Why is she so intent on damaging my pretty face?

"Yeah, Sophia?"

"You can call me Soph. My friends do." She flashes me a shy smile, and I nod returning her smile.

"Can we play Monopoly next?"

"Sure thing, kiddo."

I chance a look at Savannah, whose head hangs in her hands. When she doesn't move, I squeeze her shoulder. "You okay?"

She nods. "Just queasy." After a beat it's as though she realizes she just told me being a nanosecond away from kissing me makes her feel ill. She pulls her face from her hand and waves her bandaged finger in my direction. "Blood."

I grin, a warm feeling coming over me. That's not a "fuck no." "You wanna play Monopoly with Soph and me?"

She pushes to her feet. "I'm not sure you're ready for that, Justin Phillip Ashe." She grins and plants her hands on her hips. "You might be king of your ice castle. But in this house" —she jabs a thumb at her chest—"I'm the queen of board games. And unlike my little sister, I won't let you win."

She's right. She totally kicked my ass at Monopoly, and from the beaming smile that lit up the whole room, she enjoyed doing it, too. She's not a humble winner, either. Nope. She's a gloater.

Our dads moved into Kev's man cave an hour ago, while the moms sat drinking coffee and chatting in another room to hang out without disrupting our game.

Abby sticks her head around the doorway. "We're supposed to be going out soon, Savvy. We told Uncle Jim we'd stop by to see him and the family."

Savannah's face falls as she holds her little silver top hat pinched between her finger and thumb. "I forgot." Her voice is flat, and the light dims from her eyes.

Family.

I imagine that the meaning of that word has changed a lot for her over the past few months, and she's struggling. Hell, anyone would.

If I woke up one day and discovered the foundations of my life to be different to what I thought, it'd be like...betrayal? I dunno. But it can't be easy for Savannah. She sets the piece back down on the board and slips her thumbnail between her teeth like Mom does when she's got a lot on her mind.

"Oh. I didn't realize she had plans." I urge my cheeks to heat with faux-embarrassment as I push to my feet. "I...uh..." Savannah's eyes are locked on me. I rub the back of my neck. "I asked Savannah to come out with me...later..."

Abby's brows shoot up her forehead, and her eyes widen. I swallow hard, half expecting Savannah to snort, object, or throw something at me.

"I've been meaning to ask her out for a while, but with school, work, hockey... I just haven't found the time." I'm laying it on thick, knowing what moms are like. I heard her and Mom whispering in the kitchen about trying to get Savannah and me together. "It's totally okay, though. We can reschedule."

I can't risk looking at Savannah in case she's horrified, but even if all I do is get her out of the house and away from her parents for a while to catch her breath, that'll be enough. At least for now.

This isn't a knee-jerk reaction for me, just opportunism. I've wanted to ask her out from the minute I met those sea-blue eyes at the coffee shop. In the split second before she registered who I was and her gratitude was replaced by low-key loathing.

"You..." Abby points at me, then at Savannah. "You asked Savannah out?"

"Like...on a date?" Mom's voice comes from the doorway behind Abby.

I nod, my face heating for real now. This probably wasn't my smartest plan, and Savannah still hasn't said a goddamn word so I'm out on this branch all by myself.

Sophia makes an *ooooooh* kind of noise before bursting into giggles, and Savannah jumps to her feet. She'd probably rather barbecue her soul and feed it to a hellhound than go out with me. But she tosses me a grateful, genuine smile, and it seems that at least for now, she'd sooner spend time with me, than with her family, because she's nodding.

Relief uncurls the tight knot in my chest as I let go of a slow breath. "Yes, Mom. Like a date. I didn't realize they already had family plans."

Savannah flinches at my word choice. Shit.

Abby's brow furrows. "Let me call Uncle Jim and see if he can do tomorrow instead. We still have a few days of you in town." She smiles. "There's no reason for you two to change your plans." Whether she's excited that I'm taking Savannah out, or simply humoring Savannah so she doesn't lose her shit, I'm not sure. Either way, we're now committed to a fake date and I'm not, for one second, going to waste it.

Maybe if I can convince her I'm not demon spawn, she'll agree to give me one for real.

CHAPTER 11
Savannah

I can't believe he just said that. And as much as I want to fight it, to tell everyone that he's lying and making dates up, another part of me just needs air. We've played the happy family all afternoon, and I'm drowning in the lie. What's a little fake date to go with the fake perfect family?

I'm not happy. Our family isn't happy. Not right now at least. I'm pissed at my parents, and despite a few cursory sad glances over dinner, we've just ignored the whole thing in lieu of keeping up appearances.

Faux feelings are exhausting. Smiling when I just want to cry is exhausting. And having an *actual* perfectly happy family in my space all day has been pretty fucking exhausting too.

I guess you can never tell. Maybe the Ashes have a thousand issues also. But from the outside they look every bit as happy as we look right now.

I need to get out. Even if that means going out with Justin. He's been kind and considerate all day, and I'd be lying if I say it hasn't worn down my resolve to hate him on principle, but I've been looking forward to putting some distance between us.

Spending the day with someone you've almost kissed twice isn't easy. Especially when you actually *want* to kiss him.

Ugh. My loyalty lies with Molly and chicks before dicks is a gender-wide rule for us. But maybe...just maybe...he's not actually an ass. And maybe Molly would understand if she'd seen just how tempting and delicious he is. Maybe if she smelled him she'd get it and give me her blessing to kiss the enemy.

I swallow as our moms share a not-so-secret look at Justin's announcement that he's taking me out. They're clearly trying —and failing—to be chill. Mom even squeaks. Good Lord. We need to leave before they start picking out a wedding dress and hiring a carpenter to build us a white picket fence.

Dad comes in to say goodbye to Justin before we leave. And instead of giving him the "*You better take care of my daughter*" speech, he thanks him for the beer.

"Don't mention it. I've got your list now." Justin pats his butt pocket. "I'll see what else I can find for you on my travels."

Dad beams like all his Christmases have come at once, and his smile only grows when Justin tells him there'll be tickets at Will Call for him and me for tomorrow night's game against the Minnesota Snow Pirates.

It seems that no matter how much I try to get away from Justin Not-an-Ass, the more I end up in his sphere. Maybe it's like getting caught up in a riptide current—you just have to stop flailing and struggling against the pull before you're too tired and dragged out to sea.

Justin places his hand in the small of my back, sending a shiver up my spine. He turns me toward the door. "We need to leave before they start picking out baby names and Mom crochets tiny baby hockey skates." His low voice at my ear sends sheets of gooseflesh over my skin, and I snort.

Mom rolls her eyes and mutely scolds me for being so gross and snorting. Sophia saves me from the mom-glare and launches herself at Justin, looping her arms around his waist and smashing her face against his body in a bone-crunching hug. All twelve foot of him crouches down to her level, and he ruffles her hair. My insides melt, dissolving into a pool of goo at the sight of him being so sweet.

He's inching more and more into perfect book boyfriend territory by the minute: massive dick, impossibly good looking, charming, kind, sensitive, helps the heroine, wins over her family... The list is growing.

And let's not forget we're on near-miss-kiss #2.

My body heats. He's taking me out, but I have no idea where. I don't think I'm upset about it. Didn't I want time away from him? Why are my feelings such a contradiction?

"They're watching through the blinds so I'm going to open your door for you, okay?" he says as we walk toward my parents' car in the driveway. "My mom would kick my ass if I'm not the perfect gentleman. She raised me better than letting you open your own door." He winks at me then moves a step ahead.

"You're driving?"

"I'm driving."

I'm kind of glad he's taking charge. I'm falling apart inside, and I know from past experiences that it's not a good idea to drive while upset. A ripple of guilt hits for the animal I killed a couple months ago when I fled the house after finding my adoption papers.

His hand only leaves the curve of my spine when he gets to the passenger door of the SUV. I hand him the keys while he reaches out and pulls the handle. Door open, he sweeps an arm at the seat inside. "Your chariot awaits, milady."

I giggle, taking my seat, and since he's closing the door, I buckle up. As he circles the car, the blinds move again, and his mom gives us a thumbs up out the window.

Justin heads out of the neighborhood without telling me where we're going or why we're on this "date" in the first place. I should probably ask, or care, but the more miles we put between me and my childhood home, the more into myself I've curled. Shapes pass outside the window in a blur of movement and lights.

After about fifteen minutes, maybe, the car slowing down jolts me back to awareness. I don't know where we are, but it's dark, quiet, and there are no streetlights or people to be seen. We're in an empty parking lot, though I can't tell where the parking lot might be.

Either he's brought me here to kill me, or he wants to try the kissing thing again. The. Fucking. Audacity. Of this man. He totally had me fooled that he was some adorable, sweet, kind, and sensitive guy, but really he just wants to find somewhere dark and quiet to have his way with me.

Would that be so bad? Probably not as long as he knows what to do with that lightsaber he has tucked in his pants. But it's the principle, damn it. The presumption.

I spin in my seat to confront him. He puts the car in park then turns on the interior light over the center console and shakes his head. "I figured you'd want somewhere quiet to sit for a little while. I can go take a walk if you need space, or we can just sit here. I have the Kindle app on my phone." He waves his phone at me. "I'm good."

Wow. Way to punch my righteous indignation in the vagina, Justin. Am I impressed at his consideration or disappointed that he doesn't want to scratch the itch brewing in my panties?

Ew. That kinda makes it sounds like I have crabs. But I definitely think it's both. I'm impressed and disappointed, which serves only to confuse me even more.

Searching his face, it hits me. He knows. I can tell by the sympathetic look he's giving me that he knows why I'm upset. "Your mom tell you?"

He hesitates for a moment, like he's afraid to answer but nods. "If you need to get things off your chest I'm here."

"What book are you reading?"

"Just starting the last book in the Bastards at Boulder Cove series, Twisted Secrets."

Rachel Leigh. I love that series. I haven't started the last one yet. I'm a sucker for a good bully romance, add in the "*why choose?*" three hot as fuck men, a strong female, and just enough mystery to keep me reading... Well, let's just say I binge read the shit out of those books. And if Jagger came alive from the pages and walked up to me in the street? I'd bend right over where I stood and take that monster cock like a champ.

My face heats. I know someone else who has a monster cock, just like Jagger.

Jesus. I'm still staring at Justin silently like an idiot.

"Savannah?"

I blink. "Yeah?"

"Do you need me to give you space?"

"I think I'm okay."

With a nod he turns the light off and pulls out his phone. I watch him read for a beat or two. Is he really just going to sit there and read in silence?

Either he doesn't feel my gaze on him, or he chooses to ignore it, but he seems to be happy enough to read his book. Not that I blame him. It's a really good fucking series.

I unclip my seatbelt and pull my knees up to my chest, planting my feet on the seat, and stare out the window.

I don't know how long I look out into the darkness but after a while Justin starts the engine and after a few minutes warm air curls around my cold skin. "You sure you're okay just sitting there?"

He wiggles his phone at me again like it's all the explanation I need and turns his attention back to the screen.

I don't think I've ever met someone this okay with holding space for someone else. I mean, Athena knows by now that sometimes I'll need a little time, but she'll still pepper me with questions. Or she'll check—repeatedly—to make sure I'm okay, or that I don't want to go do something other than just stew in my emotions. But Justin just sits, reading like he has nothing but time, and like he knows I don't have a solid enough grip on my emotions to engage yet.

Hot tears course down my cheeks, and I turn my head away from him so he can't see. After a few minutes he shuffles in his seat before his body brushes my arm. He leans over the arm rest separating us and into the back seat. A box of tissues drops on my lap before he picks up my hand and curls his fingers around mine, locking our hands together.

Then he goes back to his book.

"I'm not normally this emotional." I sniff and dab at my tears with a Kleenex.

He strokes the fleshy part of my thumb with his. "It wouldn't matter even if you were."

My tears continue to fall, my whole body shaking with the need to purge my feelings, and all the while, Justin definitely-not-an-ass strokes my hand and doesn't let go.

When I'm finally done, I turn to him. "You know what'd be nice?"

"Ice cream?"

I smile in the darkness. How'd he know? "Ice cream."

He locks his phone and tucks it into his pants pocket. "You want McFlurry ice cream, milkshake ice cream, or somewhere like Marble Slab ice cream?"

So many choices. And it occurs to me that I appreciate him giving them to me. Huh. We'll unpack *that* later.

"McFlurry. Then I can get some fries, too."

He starts the car and grins as though I picked the best possible option. "You read my mind."

"You're not judging me for wanting food so soon after that huge dinner we had earlier?"

"This is a judgment free space. Besides." He taps his stomach. "Hockey player, remember? We can put away a lot of food. Any time is a good time for eats."

He keeps hold of my hand the whole way to McDonalds, and I let him. His warmth is comforting, and when he starts humming grossly out of tune along to the radio, I think I've finally found his imperfection.

The man is tone deaf. Actually, that's not even fair to tone deaf people. Justin Ashe singing should be a crime against humanity. I try to hide my wince but his voice is literally stabbing at my ear drums with a rusty blade. It hurts.

We pull into McDonalds' parking lot just in the nick of time. I was seconds away from snatching my hand from his and clamping it over his mouth.

"Dine in or drive thru?"

I'm not quite ready to go back and face my folks yet, so I opt for inside.

"Take a seat, I'll grab the food. McFlurry and fries?"

I nod. What he actually gets doesn't really matter, I just need to feed my feelings so I don't cry again.

Shit. I don't have a purse with me. I didn't think to grab it in my hurry to escape the meddling moms and my "Justin Ashe saved me from my family" stupor.

"I..." My cheeks burn. "I don't have any cash with me. Let me run outside to see if Dad left any in the car."

He arches a brow at me. "Sit."

I cross my arms, the temptation to tell him to go to hell pretty strong.

"I've got this, Savannah."

Generations of independent women in my family turn in their graves while I submit to letting him pay. It's just a few bucks, I assure them quietly. I'll pay him back.

After a few minutes, a tray with an ungodly amount of food on it is placed in front of me and a bashful Justin slides onto the chair across the table.

"I might have gotten carried away at the counter."

"You think?" I laugh and swipe a fry. Crisp, salty, and fresh from the fryer.

"I panicked. Everything sounded good so I just..."

"Ordered all of it?"

He hands me my McFlurry and more fries than I can eat while he unwraps a double cheeseburger and takes a bite. He looks so happy right now I almost want to take a picture. My stomach flips. We had such a huge Thanksgiving dinner... surely he's about to make himself sick on cheeseburgers?

"Justin?"

His face jerks up at my voice, and he tips his head but doesn't speak. Another check in the pro column. I hate when people talk with their mouth full.

"Thank you."

He swallows, shaking his head. "You don't have anything to thank me for."

I guffaw. I beg to differ. "You helped me on the plane." I stick out my index finger, counting on my digits. "You brought my dad his favorite beer." My middle finger is next. "Played with my sister." Ring finger. "Manufactured an escape plan without being asked."

His free hand wraps over mine, bending my extended fingers back toward my palm and puts his burger onto the wrapper on the tray.

With a squeeze of my hand he leans forward. He must be a full moon, and I'm the tide because I'm leaning toward him whether I want to or not. He's got ketchup at the corner of his mouth and before I can control myself, my thumb is brushing it away. It'd be weird to lick it off my thumb, right?

He smiles at me, and my insides warm. "Thanks."

"Don't mention it." I'm free-falling into those crystal blue eyes, and I don't want it to end. Time stops and the only people in the world, the entire universe, are him and me.

My heart thrashes against my ribs. My pulse races. My hand is probably sweaty under his. Maybe third time is the charm? Maybe this is where I get to kiss Justin at long last. Maybe a kiss is all I need to get him out of my system.

The corners of his lips twitch, and in the moment, my inner monologue is screaming "the penis shall never get between us."

Besties before testes is a great idea in theory, but I don't think whoever created the Girl Code had ever come face to face with Justin Ashe before. I lick my lips, salty-sweet from my ice cream and fries. I wish it was him licking the salt from my lips. Desire laps low in my stomach.

Movement in my periphery breaks his spell as I hear my name.

"Hey, Savvyanna." Molly Morrison is walking past our table with a couple of guys and another girl. She's only looking at the back of Justin's head, she can't possibly know it's him, can she? I flinch back and jerk my hand from his all the same, just in case. Sisters before misters. I'm itching to bolt out of my seat and throw my arms around her, but the girl she's with is literally dragging her toward the door. Hugs will have to wait.

"See ya in the morning." She winks at me. I could swear she's muttering something about getting sausage under her breath.

They're heading toward the exit, and she doesn't stop to chat. I force out a breath as the door closes behind her group. When I turn back to Justin, he's picked up his burger and has taken another huge bite.

His eyes swim with hurt and unspoken accusations. This guy has been nothing but amazing to me since we boarded the plane in Iowa. We've actually spent quite a nice day together. He chews his food in heavy silence and that's when I realize: it's me.

I'm the ass.

CHAPTER 12
Justin

I have three emails from my editor. Usually, getting one email from her isn't good. So the three unread emails staring at me from my inbox make me shiver. She's probably pissed. I really don't blame her. I've been late on my last two deadlines and haven't confirmed whether or not I'll be sending her my shit on time this time either.

I'm a terrible client. I mean, I pay her on time, and I thank her in all my books, but praise the stars the woman is as flexible as she is or I'd be screwed. I'm a small fish in a big literary pond right now, but when I make it big, I'm gonna give her a raise. Or buy her a koala. She loves koalas. And chocolate. I'll buy her an entire bathtub filled with chocolate. Hell, maybe the tub will be made of chocolate too.

When I got home from my not-a-date with Savannah I locked myself in Dad's office and wrote for hours. It didn't matter that I have a game tomorrow, or that I was exhausted from hours of empathizing all day with the Bowens, or that I was pretty butt hurt that Savannah bolted away from me like I was on fire when she saw Molly Morrison at McDonalds. It also didn't matter that it wasn't what I was supposed to write. I was compelled to sit at my desk and let the words flow.

I don't remember the last time I managed a 10,000-word day, never mind 12k, but last night felt pretty damn good. I got some sleep and am now back at my desk to go over the words I got down—just to make sure they weren't turkey-influenced babble-crap, which is a distinct possibility. Sometimes it's best not to let my stream of consciousness make it onto the page.

It's not the book I'd planned to write, but I haven't opened that manuscript since I left Iowa. Instead, I'm working on this fresh new document that came to me on the plane. Is the heroine a honey-blonde, crystal blue eyed beauty who's afraid of flying? Maybe.

Whether or not Savannah can make up her mind about me is irrelevant. My muse made me her bitch, and I'll write until my fingers fall off. I'm simply a vessel for the story.

A soft tap on the door draws my attention from cycling the words in my manuscript. I change the word "anal" to "a nap" and grin at how different the story would be if I just left it the way it was before I noticed the typo.

The door opens, Mom steps in with a plate of cinnamon roll French toast and bacon, and my stomach growls its thanks.

"Thanks, Mom."

She pats my shoulder and rests her butt against the edge of my desk. "You were up late pounding those keys last night. Have you flipped your schedule? You usually write better in the morning."

I can't say my parents have always been supportive of my bid to be a self-employed creative. Coming from essentially poverty and a scarcity mindset has left its impact on all of us, but once they realized it was something I needed to do, something that lived and breathed in my veins, they were 100% on board. And for some reason, Mom really likes hearing about my process.

I chew on a piece of bacon before I answer. "Inspiration struck. I'm still a morning writer." I smile. "I have to be. Between work, school, and hockey...I'm dead on my feet in the evenings these days."

She nods like she gets it. She probably does. She and Dad have worked so hard to save us from the brink of bankruptcy more times than I can count. One time when I was in middle school she worked three jobs, kept the house, and somehow managed to still be the best mom in the world. I have a sneaking suspicion that all parents are Fae—it's the only explanation for how they keep their heads above water.

"Savannah is certainly very pretty inspiration for your work." She nudges me. Here it comes. "Speaking of Savannah."

Nice, subtle segue, Mom.

"How was your date?"

Instead of answering, I cut a piece of French toast that can't possibly fit in my mouth but I try anyway.

"That good, huh?"

I groan, both at her observation and the explosion of cinnamon sugar on my tongue. I take my time chewing, trying to decide what I'm going to tell her.

"A problem shared..." She's said that phrase forever, though she rarely needs to finish her sentence.

I sigh. "She's holding on to ideas from high school, about who I am, or rather who she thinks I am. I'm not sure I can get her past it."

It's Mom's turn to sigh. "Cheating?"

"She was Molly's best friend in high school. I know Girl Code dictates she needs to make a voodoo doll of me and stick pins in my eyes out of loyalty to her friend. But people change. I was kind of hoping she'd give me a chance to at least show her I'm not the guy she thinks I am." I swallow. "And I don't care what you and dad believe, I never cheated on that test paper."

"I know you didn't." Mom's eyes soften. "And if she doesn't see the real you, then she isn't the one for you." She rubs my back with a splayed hand. "What's for you won't pass you, Justin. And if she passes you, maybe at least you'll get a fictional happy ever after from your attempts at wooing her."

I laugh and pick up a piece of bacon. "No one says woo anymore, Mom."

"This mom does. And she has also believed you from the day you told her you didn't cheat on your test."

We both know Dad never believed me. Not then, and not now. No matter how much I proclaim my innocence, he's just not interested. As though the accusation alone was proof enough of my guilt, and enough to condemn me.

Mom leaves me to finish off my breakfast and my edits. The words in my document from last night aren't bad. In fact, I kind of like them. One good thing about being so painfully aware of my feelings on a cellular level is that when I need to bleed them onto my pages, I can, though it can be just as draining as feeling someone else's emotions.

Rereading my work, I experience Savannah's terror on the plane, and I laugh at her bursting out of the bathroom stall, seeing my cock on display. Even if I never publish the words I'm writing, I'm enjoying the process and the story is alive on my screen.

When breakfast is finished and my work is done, I spend a few minutes centering myself and getting ready for the game. I don't have the bandwidth to let Savannah cloud my thoughts all day. I need to focus, bring myself into game-day-space and get ready to kick ass on the ice—not so I can impress her and her dad in the stands. Nope. I just don't want to let my boys down. That in itself is motivation enough not to think of the fact she's going to be there watching.

She's not here.

I left tickets at will call for her and her dad, but it's not her sitting next to Kev in the stands. He seems to have brought along one of his buddies, which wouldn't usually bother me, but while I've spent the day trying to put her out of my head, I'd been looking forward to seeing her again.

We're up by two—make that three—by the end of the first, and the guys are faring well on the ice despite my being distracted by the notable absence of my blond inspiration.

The UCR Raccoons are a force to be reckoned with this season and what's more, everyone knows it.

Why didn't she come?

I push the question aside and refocus on my team.

Ares skates out to meet Lincoln Scott as he maneuvers into position to take his shot. A gasp ripples around the crowd as everyone holds their breath, waiting for the lamp to light. When Ares does the splits and makes an impressive glove save that should have been close to impossible, the spectators groan, some boo, and Lincoln looks like our netminder just killed his puppy.

I don't blame him, they're now three-nil-down and Ares is in danger of doing that thing goalies do that we're not allowed to talk or think about until the final buzzer. We still have a lot of play left, so I'm not counting my chickens. Or goals for that matter.

Despite his asshole attitude and playboy nature, Ares de la Peña is one of the best goaltenders I've ever seen play. Maybe the fact he moonlights as a stripper accounts for his flexibility between the pipes, but he's also wicked talented. And he knows it. He shoots water in his mouth and over his face from the bottle resting on top of his net before taking up his position again.

I have to admit, I wasn't sure what we were getting ourselves into when Coach signed him. But so far, other than having the reputation for fucking anything that moves, his on-ice performance has been beyond reproach. I've gone from apprehension at his joining our team, to hope for our success.

Maybe this is our year.

I glance down at the C on my chest. I worked damn hard to become captain of this team, and my pride warms me against the chill of the rink.

After the period break, the teams face off again, and there's a shift in the mood. The Snow Pirates are frustrated, missing passes, and fumbling plays. Russell Stewart has been offside twice since the first whistle of the period blew.

As much as I love winning, playing against a team coming apart at the seams can be dangerous. The air changes, anticipation crackles against the surface of the ice.

Apollo de la Peña turns over the puck at center ice after picking Luca Hook's pocket. Apollo is now on a one-on-two breakaway and dekes around their last defender standing before chipping the puck over Séb's shoulder.

It's a beaut of a blink-and-you'd-miss-it kind of goal, but instead of letting their heads drop, the Snow Pirates sink into their bad moods and get aggressive.

In the marrow of my bones I feel a fight brewing, so it's no surprise when Russell Stewart and our de la enforcer, Artemis, drop their gloves. It's not a short fight either—the guys are well matched and strangely alike. Both are stoic, calm, and patient, the anchors of their teams. The irony that our cool headed, calming influences are also our enforcers is not lost on me. Though it does mean that when they drop the gloves it's for a good reason, and not just because they're quick tempered.

By the time the linesmen intervene, there's still no winner, but Artemis has blood trickling down the side of his face from a cut over his eye and Russell's nose is bleeding. Their fans boo Artemis as he skates off the ice for medical treatment. I'd guess a couple of stitches, or some glue, and he'll be back out and ready to hand the Snow Pirates their asses in the third.

We're playing them again tomorrow before heading back to Iowa, and no one likes to lose in their own barn. The Snow Pirates are going to be out for blood.

I'm not too worried though. My guys can take it. We'll give as good as we get, and then some. We're going all the way this season. I feel that in my bones, too. It's our time to shine, and I won't let some hot-headed douchebags come between us and the Final Four.

CHAPTER 13
Savannah

"You wanna tell me why you were looking so cozy with my cheating butt-face ex last night, Savvyanna?"

My stomach sinks as Molly drops onto the chair facing mine at the Sugar Bean. Their coffee's not quite as good as Bitches Brew and the vibe's not as cool either, but it's Molly's favorite place to mainline caffeine on campus, so here we are.

"I...uh...I..."

She came in, fists swinging. While I'd hoped she hadn't figured out it was Justin I was with last night, I'd also hoped that if she had figured out who he was, she'd at least let us stuff our faces with caffeine and sugar before she gave me shit about it. Wrong on both counts.

I heave out a sigh. While I haven't seen her in a long time and our check-ins are reduced to once every few months when one of us remembers to text or call, she's still my oldest friend.

"He was saving me from my family."

Molly's brows shoot up, and she holds up her hand like a stop sign. "Coffee first, then confessions."

Cappuccino and an almond croissant for me, and her own

oversized tumbler from home filled with cold brew and a donut for Molly. I take a bite of my pastry to buy some time before I have to spill my guts to my astute friend.

She takes a long slurp, closing her eyes and inhaling like the coffee is breathing life into her lungs before waving her hand at me. "Proceed."

I can't help but smile. You always know what you're going to get with Molly Morrison. There's no subterfuge, no miscommunication, she's as straight as a freakin' rod. It's kind of comforting.

"I found out a couple months ago that I'm adopted." I wait for a reaction, but her facial expression doesn't change.

"Is that why you blew off my last call?"

I nod and take another bite, washing it down with a sip of my coffee. "I'd just found out. I was kind of reeling." I wince. "Stole Dad's car and ran away in the rain."

She arches a brow. "How'd that work out for you?"

"Killed a deer."

She winces. Animal murderer. It's like the worst crime in the world. I could have told her I knocked down twelve old grandmas who spent their lives dedicated to curing cancer and that would have been more socially acceptable than killing a deer.

"Busted up the car pretty good, too."

She scrunches up her whole face.

"It's been a rough few months."

She sips her iced coffee. How she can drink something with ice cubes in it when it's so cold outside is beyond me.

"So it would seem." She tips her tumbler at me. "But I still don't get how you ended up sharing fries and getting all up close and personal with Justin Ass."

A flush heats my cheeks. I wish I'd gotten closer and even more personal with him. And while I don't say that out loud, she can probably tell from my face.

"I sat next to him on the flight Wednesday. When we landed, our moms were talking in baggage claim and suggested Thanksgiving. After dinner, Mom said we were supposed to go visit family..." Emotion clogs my throat.

"And you're struggling with the concept of family right now."

I nod. "My birth mom died, Mol. She's gone, and I can't ask her why she gave me up for adoption. I can't get to know her, or much of anything about her."

Molly pats my hand, her cold fingers sending a chill up my arm.

"And I'm pissed at my parents for keeping it from me." The familiar flutter in my stomach confirms I'm still mad at them. "Anyway, I guess he realized I needed to be rescued, because he swooped in and took me for a McFlurry."

"Falling for each other over McFlurries. How adorbs." She slurps at her drink, pinning me with a probing stare.

"It's not like that." I take a gulp of my coffee to wash the lie from my tongue. "And adorbs? Who are you and what have you done with Molly Morrison?"

"Quit deflecting. We've known each other for a long time Savvyanna Bowen. I know when you're lying, to me, or to yourself. You like that boy."

It's on the tip of my tongue to deny it, but part of me doesn't want to because she's right. I do like him.

She steeples her hands together and leans forward over her drink. "Did you go to pound town?"

Not for lack of wanting to. "No. I saw you and..." I draw my finger around the edge of my saucer. "We came close to kissing. But when we were like...right there...I was reminded of my loyalty to you, his cheating past, and I heard you in my head saying 'once a cheater, always a cheater.' I jumped away."

"I saw." Her mouth forms a grin but her eyes say something else. "If you need permission to go for it with him"—she shrugs—"feel free." She takes a huge bite of her donut, licking jelly from the corner of her mouth. "I don't mind if you want to date him."

"But...?"

There was definitely a "but" in her tone, and there's reluctance in her expression.

"I just want you to be happy, Savvyanna. But I'm not sure Justin's your guy." She pauses and takes a drink. "Maybe he's changed. Maybe he had a reason for cheating on me, I don't know. Maybe he's telling the truth that he didn't cheat on me, or that term paper. Who knows? But it's a pattern of behavior that isn't ideal. A pattern I don't want my friend getting tangled up in."

She takes another bite of her donut. "That said." She swallows. "I know how compelling those baby blues of his can be." She falls quiet for a long beat, like she's thinking things through in her head. "Ultimately, it's your funeral. He cheated on me. He might cheat on you, he might not. As long as you go into it with your eyes open and your heart protected, that's all I can really ask for. I don't want him to hurt you."

Her eyes darken, and she curls her bottom lip between her teeth. She'd walked into Applebee's with her family and seen him kiss another girl. She said it was an image she wouldn't ever be able to unsee, and I'm pretty sure her heart splintered into a million pieces at the sight.

That moment changed her. She became brasher, more confident, and *I don't give a flying fuck*. She shut her emotions down hard and fast and went from the "relationship" type to the "never being tied down for as long as I live" type.

Justin Ashe shifted something in Molly's world, and she'd never be the same because of it. She probably wants to grab me by the shoulders and demand to know what I'm thinking even entertaining the thought of kissing the enemy, but she doesn't. She's a good friend who doesn't try to sway me from making my own decision, even when she very clearly thinks it's a mistake.

She just tells it like she sees it, or, in this case, has lived it.

I didn't expect to get her blessing to pursue something with Justin, but now that I have it, I want it to feel...different, lighter somehow. It's not the overwhelming relief I expected it to be.

My life is a constant juxtaposition of opposites: strong and weak, on the defensive and on the offensive, sweet and sour. My moods can change like the weather. I find that if I just wait long enough my frame of mind will shift like the pendulum in a grandfather clock.

Maybe if I wait long enough the pendulum will swing away from Justin Ashe, and it won't be an issue anymore.

A girl can dream, right?

I have no idea why I'm standing outside Justin's childhood home right now, but I am.

Okay, I do know why. My official excuse is that I'm returning his mom's dishes from Thursday, but the truth is that I really want to see him again.

I skipped the game last night in lieu of spending the night getting mani-pedis with Mom and talking through some stuff over a bottle of wine. I tried to avoid the conversation about my birth mom but avoidance didn't go so well. We'd both ended up in tears, and I still don't feel better about any of it, even after we'd talked a little. I'm not convinced Mom feels any better either.

Anyway, Justin may not have even noticed that I wasn't there with Dad last night, but I feel guilty for not showing up. I want to apologize and tell him I'll be there tonight instead. Dad gave me a game report, and it sounded like quite the barn burner. De la Peña got a shutout between the pipes, gloves were dropped, and I kinda want to go just to see if the bad vibes from last night are carried over—Dad says it's near certain.

I love watching grown men beat the snot out of each other on the ice. I know they're trying to move away from violence in the sport but damn, there's something so hot about watching them throw down.

It would be so much easier to leave the empty dishes on the step and haul ass like I'm on fire, but as I stare at the red painted door, I'm drawn to stay.

I shift my weight from foot to foot, but I still can't bring myself to ring the doorbell. I'd like to think I'm a strong, brave, and independent person. But standing in front of this door has my insides churning, and while I don't need to pee, I might wet myself.

I've never been this nervous about talking to a boy before. Possibly it's because Molly said she's okay with me pursuing something with Justin, and I'm resigned to admitting that I do like him. Everyone does stupid shit in their lives. Stupidity doesn't have an expiration date either, so there's every chance he'll end up doing something stupid in the future too.

Though if he ever cheated on me I'd cut off his ginormous cock and feed it to whatever animal I could find to eat the damn thing.

I'm trying not to care as much about his past, his mistakes, and I'm trying to focus on anything but the fact that I want to climb that boy like a tree.

I'm not succeeding. I really do want to climb him. And considering he's a million feet tall, I probably could, too. Scaling Mt. Ashe. If that's not the title of an erotic romance novel, I'll eat my hat.

I'm still standing on the front step like an idiot when the door opens, taking my breath as it swings away from me.

Justin is shirtless—which, considering it's Minnesota in November, is kinda badass—and hot. It's so very, very hot. *And* he's barefoot. His blond hair is damp and strands of it hang down his forehead. He smiles at me as he leans his forearm against the edge of the door.

Every drop of blood in my body rushes south, and I remind myself with a little in-my-head chant that I'm standing in the street and can't just tug down those shorts and lick him like a sucker.

Oh God. Oh God. Oh G-O-D. I looked at his V. He's got a *very* nice V, and I already know it leads down to a *very* nice cock.

I want to trail my tongue down his very nice V to his very nice cock and do all kinds of things that would make both our moms blush.

"Hey." He catches my chin and tips my head back so I meet his stare. "My face is up here."

Who cares where his face is? Okay, another lie. I want his face crammed between my thighs while I ride the shit out of his tongue though I'm not telling him that.

But maybe my face is telling him that without my permission because he's grinning at me like he's the big bad wolf and I'm Little Red Riding Hood, and he wants to eat me for supper. I volunteer as tribute.

Why did I come here again?

Words. I need to find and use words. Despite the running commentary in my head, I haven't said anything out loud to him yet. I think I'm being hypnotized by his nakedness. That's a thing, right?

"Savannah?" His eyes sweep across my face, and I think it's his smile bringing me under his spell. Should I cover his mouth with my hand and stop him?

I clear my throat. "Y-yes?" Get it together, girl. It's like I've had all of the most embarrassing moments of my entire existence this week, and he's been there to witness each and every one.

"You wanna come in?"

I nod and step through the open door. He brushes the side of my arm as he closes it behind me, sending a shiver through my body.

"Mom asked me to return your mom's dishes." I turn to face him and he's *right there*, like, the tip of his nose is touching mine.

I'm a goner.

He's right. Fucking. There.

No one can be this close to someone so good-looking and not turn into a puddle of need. Especially when they're lacking clothing. It's just not humanly possible.

"She's not here." He takes the dishes from my trembling hands and sets them...somewhere. I don't know where, nor do I care.

"Savannah?"

"Yeah?" My breath is a whisper on the air, fluttering with anticipation.

"Can I kiss you?"

I love that he's asked for my permission, I do, but my body aches for his hands on me, and if I don't taste him soon I may die.

Exaggeration? Maybe.

But I don't want to find out.

I nod, and my tongue snakes out between my lips, dampening them. His hand cups my face, and I tremble—this time not from the chill in the air, but from the skin to skin contact at last. He lowers his lips to mine and plants a kiss so soft I'm not even sure it counts as a kiss.

A voice inside screams that it's not enough. I lean into it, hungry, desperate for more, but torn, because I want to savor the soft and delicate way he's touching me.

Pressing my mouth a little harder against his, I sigh in relief as he responds in kind. His tongue moves along the seam of my lips, firm yet tender, and my jaw slackens, granting him access.

I've never been kissed like this before. Slowly, deeply, and so fucking tenderly that I might cry from just the way his tongue brushes against mine. I feel it everywhere—where our tongues meet, where he's holding my face, where my nipples press against the fabric of my bra. And I want more. I'd grab his shirt and pull him to me so he can't stop, or put any kind of distance between us, but he doesn't have one on.

My fingers find their way onto his chest, skimming over his heart, and his pec muscles as they move up the column of his neck and into his hair. Crossing my wrists at the nape of his neck, I try to draw him into me more. Our heads switch from one side to the other as our kiss deepens again.

It's slow, lazy, as though he has all the time in the world to kiss me, and he wants to savor every damn second and commit it all to memory.

This is the kiss wet dreams are made of.

I curl my nails into his hair and groan into his mouth. The kiss grows more urgent, quicker as pure need drives me forward. I demand more with my tongue. His hands glide down the sides of my ribcage and hook around my thighs.

He picks me up, wraps my legs around his waist and backs me up until my spine hits the wall. A picture frame—or something—crashes to the floor, but we don't stop. I can't stop. I need to keep kissing him. He is the secret to immortality—all I need to do is kiss Justin Ashe forever. And I'm never letting him go.

His rock-hard dick is pressed against my aching pussy. I know it's huge, I know he'll destroy me with it, and I know it'll probably hurt in all the best possible ways, but I need it. I need him.

It's as though our kiss ignited a magical tether between us. It's burning bright and luminescent, anchoring us to each other, and if I stop kissing him, it might burn out. I tilt my hips against his hard on, and he groans.

He steps toward me, pinning me with his hips against the wall, and I cling to him as though we're forty stories high and if I let go, I'll fall to my death.

He drags his lips across my cheek, smearing kisses along my jaw, but I'm not ready to be done with his lips on mine. I pull him back. He smiles against my mouth as he kisses me again with renewed energy. He tastes of spearmint. The dampness of his hair does little to cool the fire burning from my fingers to my toes.

His bare chest presses me into the wall, the ridges and planes of his chest firm and toned. His arms flex as I trace my fingertips along the top of his shoulders and down his biceps. He's not straining to hold me. I've never had a guy pick me up and hold me against a wall before and now I want it every day.

His hips grind, sliding his cock along the length of my core. If I wasn't quite so afraid of falling on my ass and making an idiot of myself, I'd dry hump him through those shorts. His hands curl into my ass cheeks as he pins me in place.

His kiss is consuming, equal parts give and take. I scrape at his chest with my nails, forgetting I'm the one still wearing a shirt. I need to take it off. I need to feel his skin on mine. I need... everything, and I need it all right now. Right this second.

Another thud makes me vaguely aware that a second frame has fallen from the wall. But when a gasp that isn't his or mine reaches my ears, my eyes pop open, meeting his mom's gaze over his shoulder.

My galloping libido comes to a screeching halt—for real, I can hear the deafening record scratch over Justin's almost animalistic grunts and heavy breathing. Mandy rolls her lips, clearly fighting a smile as I try to extract myself from her son's delicious mouth.

I'm supposed to be embarrassed. But I'm more pissed off at the fact I have to stop. She interrupted the best kiss of my life. *She* should be embarrassed, dammit.

"Justin?"

"Yeah?"

"Your mom."

His lips are on my neck, sucking. Ten bucks says he leaves a mark. "You really wanna talk about my mom right now?"

I guess she can't contain herself anymore because she bursts into a fit of giggles. His head jerks back, his cheeks flush red, and his eyes widen as though someone sprayed cold water onto his back.

His forehead drops to my shoulder with a pained groan. I fight a smile. It's nice to know he's as distraught about the situation as I am. His mom is still there, still laughing. She's bent at the waist, and I'm pretty sure tears of laughter are falling onto the tiled floor.

Justin lowers me to the floor but doesn't move. Probably because his dick hasn't yet gotten the message that we're in time out.

Mandy excuses herself, breathless and still laughing. She offers me lunch, but I don't think I can sit across the table from her any time soon. Especially since all I want to do is tear off my clothes and mount her son until we're both exhausted, breathless, and sated.

He needs to start his pre-game prep and head to the rink, and I don't get to kiss him goodbye. As he walks me to my car, my lips are still swollen and tingly, and my pussy is on fire in my soaked panties. If I wasn't 100% convinced his Mom was watching out the window I'd beg him to finger me against the side of my car just to take the edge off. Though I'm really not sure it would take the edge off. It wouldn't be enough.

I give him a shy smile as I unlock the car door. "I wanted to tell you that I'll be at the game tonight. I'm sorry for missing last night."

He brushes my hair off my face and half-shrugs. "It's all good."

I grab the hem of my shirt, twisting it between my fingers so I don't reach out and tear off the shirt he threw on to walk me to the car.

"So, I talked to Molly. She says we can date if we want to." I search his face, hopeful he'll agree and we can skip ahead to having a shameless amount of sex.

His face falls. The desire and lust that was just swimming in his eyes is instantly replaced by disappointment and pain.

I don't understand. Isn't this good news?

He takes a step back, and the space he's created between us chills me to the bone. I don't like it. I'm craving his warmth, his touch, his skin against mine. I fight the urge to shuffle toward him.

"Justin?"

He swings his arms, slapping his hands against his thighs. "Oh. Well, thank fuck for that. God knows we couldn't date —hell, I can barely sleep without permission from Molly fucking Morrison."

He doesn't seem angry exactly, but bitterness drips from every word. I open my mouth to answer, to tell him that my loyalty to her had been keeping me from being open to something blooming between us but he's already gone.

I'm once again left staring at the red door in the cold, wondering what the fuck I'm doing here.

CHAPTER 14

Justin

It's possible I might have overreacted earlier.

I mean, kinda sorta. Once or twice in my life I've been accused of being overly emotional, and the mere mention of Molly Morrison giving Savannah some kind of *permission* to date me boiled my blood on the spot.

I knew she was tethered to our past by her loyalty to her friend, by everything she'd heard about me, by her preconceptions and misconceptions. But I'd hoped that it was the fact she was spending some time with me and seeing for herself that I'm not a douche canoe that brought her around. Not because Molly Morrison said so.

I'm grinding my teeth as I tape my stick before the game. I'm supposed to be pepping up my boys, filling them full of you-can-do-it speeches about kicking the Snow Pirates asses in their own barn for the second night in a row. But all I can think about is Savannah fucking Bowen.

Kissing her felt as easy as just being. She tasted sweet like sugar and all things nice, and when I left my mark on her neck, something primal inside me reared up and beat its chest. I hadn't meant to leave a hickey, but I also don't regret it.

Her mom's going to know where she got it, too. Even if Mom didn't call Abby the second Savannah left to spill the tea like her high school crush had just invited her to prom. She'll know, and that makes my chest heat.

But the Molly thing. Ugh.

One of the lines of tape on my stick are crooked so I have to pull off a couple rows and do it over again. Like the tape, my head's not on straight either, and I need it to be on straight, dammit. The Snow Pirates are going to be out for blood on the ice, and I really have to keep my wits about me.

The last thing I need is to get benched—or worse, lose my C because I'm unfocused and dropping the ball—or puck, I guess.

Thankfully, no one is paying too much attention to me, because it takes three more tries to tape the blade of my stick. If that's not a sign of looming catastrophe, I dunno what is. I've been taping my own stick since I was four years old. I can do it in my sleep.

Shit.

This is going to be a monumental fucking disaster.

This is bad. This is very, very bad. It's like there are six crazed bulls dressed in Snow Pirates shirts on the ice at all times. But instead of a red flag, they're charging at every UCR player that comes off the bench.

Scott Raine took a hit so bad he needed his shoulder popped back in by the trainer. Our very own Bash Brothers, Artemis and Apollo, have barely left the ice all night, and Ares's skill is being thoroughly tested. Lincoln Scott's slapshot is brutal, and he's hit at least two bottle rockets so far—one of which required Ares to get a new water bottle.

It's dog eat dog out there.

We're down by one, but I'm not too worried. The Snow Pirates are bringing the brawn, but we have speed and skill on our side. And no offense to the home team, but we have the better netminder, too.

Coach calls a time out. He wants to put me out on a line I don't usually play with to see if we can face down the Snow Pirates' wall of muscle with some of our own. My head says Raine would be the better choice, but my heart flexes that Coach thinks I can pull it off and stand up to the Destructo brothers—Hook and Stewart.

As soon as I step on the ice Hook heads my way. He digs me with his shoulder as he passes but I hold steady. Thank fuck. Falling on my ass would result in lifelong ridicule by the home fans. They'd never let it go.

Luca Hook settles next to me for the faceoff. We're both bent forward, leaning low. Artemis has my back, so I know no matter what goes down on this shift, I'm not going to be left out to dry.

The ref leans over Slater Goodwin and the rookie Snow Pirate, Theo, puck in hand. If I was a betting man I'd say Slater has it in the bag, but I've heard rumors about the hot shot rookie and how quick he can be off the draw.

"Molly Morrison says you have a lil peen," Hook tells me.

What the fuck?

I bite down on my mouth guard and focus on the puck drop. The ref switches Goodwin out of the faceoff and Tate Myers takes his place. Tate's quick, but against Theo...the odds are no longer in our favor.

"I'm gonna call you tiny dick from now on."

My dick is anything but tiny and even if it was I have the added advantage of knowing that Molly Morrison never had that pleasure. Hook is on the hunt for a fight, and with all this charged energy searing through my veins, well, I'm fine being the one to give it to him.

"If you wanna go, Hook, just say so. You don't need to make up some bullshit story about your former teammate's sister just to rattle my cage."

I'm almost on my ass before I know what hit me. He exploded like Mentos in Coke. But I plant my blades, straighten my spine, and... hesitate. If I drop my gloves and he doesn't, I'll get in shit—with the refs, with Coach, with my team...

But my pause is unwarranted. Hook flings his gloves onto the ice, and the crowd goes wild in the stands, whooping and cheering as he and I circle one another, unbuckling our helmets, preparing to strike.

He hits first, hard and fast, but I deflect it and throw back a punch of my own. Beads of sweat trickle down my temples, my neck, probably my ass crack. If I had tits I'd have under-boob sweat, too.

I can't let him win. He represents everything I'm pissed at right now: my opponent, my ex, and he's the blockade to the woman I want to do dirty things to until she's coming and panting my name.

It takes a moment after the loud crack for the pain to hit and to realize he's hit my jaw. That's gonna leave a mark. I hit back in kind, hearing a satisfying crunch as his nose gives under my fist, and a trickle of blood weaves down his lip.

He strikes back, and his knuckles leave a gash over my eye. I'm blinking blood, my vision is swimming and red. Panic sets in. I'm ready to swing blind if I have to, but the lineswoman mercifully steps in and calls time on our fight, sending us both to the box to sit on the naughty step.

One of my teammates pats me on the back on my way across the ice, and I can't tell from Coach's scowl whether he's pissed or thrilled—they both look the same on his inexpressive face.

It's one of the highest penalty minute games I've ever seen, and by the final whistle I'm pretty sure the only people who didn't get penalties were the coaching staff.

What a fucking riot.

We won, though. Barely. But we scraped the second win of the weekend. The team is loaded back on the bus, heading home to Iowa. My flight's not until tomorrow morning though, so I hit up the bar, owing it to my teammates to have a drink to celebrate wiping the floor with the Snow Pirates on home ice.

Even if that means drinking by myself in a bar surrounded by said Snow Pirates. But this was my home turf before it was theirs, so they can fuck right off if they think because I'm a Raccoon I can't drink in my hometown bar.

The bartender hands me an ice pack for my face—apparently the Snow Pirates have a full service bar. I kind of like it. We should invest in ice packs for behind the bar back home. I hiss, wincing as it connects with my stitches. Beer will help. A nice buzz will take the edge off my throbbing face.

The bartender places a beer in front of me. I haven't spoken a word, and I'm starting to think this place runs on telepathy when he jerks his head to the left. Finn O'Brien tips his bottle to me and flashes a grin.

He's such a dick. But he's a dick who bought me a beer so I'm not complaining. Plus, I broke his friend's nose, and I feel pretty good about that.

"Good game." He takes a long pull from his bottle.

"You too."

"It was fun to watch." He grins again.

I wave the ice pack at him in case he forgot I have a busted up face.

He nods and takes another drink. "You deserved it."

He can't possibly know that's the truth, but he's also not wrong, I did deserve it. Lashing out at Savannah wasn't my smartest move, and yet I haven't apologized or tried to take it back. I'm right in my indignation—she shouldn't need someone else's permission to make a decision to date me. That's completely fucked up. We're consenting adults for crying out loud.

Finn turns to me, presumably because I stopped chirping back at him. "Girl trouble?"

I take a drink, trying not to react. I'm not sure how he's managed to guess that I'm thinking about Savannah, but he's too close to the mark, and I'm not getting all emotional with Finn five stitches O'Brien.

My fingers drift up to my forehead but stop short of touching the old scar. Five stitches and a fucking scar O'Brien. He whooped me pretty damn good when Molly stormed out of that restaurant after seeing me "cheat" on her.

"You just won back to back games against the reigning champs. It has to be a girl making you do those grunty noises."

"Don't you have somewhere better to be?"

"Actually man, I don't." He comes closer and pats my back. "You wanna talk to Uncle Finny-Winny?" He takes another drink, and I'm done.

"Thanks, but I'd rather give myself a prostate exam." Truth is I'd love to talk to someone about it all, but my boys are on their way out of state, and I'm not giving a Snow Pirate any ammunition against me—especially not someone who's fucking my ex.

"Suit yourself. I'd better go find my girl, anyway. Have you seen her? She's here with a blonde from out of town."

My skin tingles under his scrutinizing stare, and it's taking all of my strength not to get whiplash snapping my neck to look for Savannah around the bar.

"I knew it." He points at me, turning to lean his back against the edge of the bar.

I finish my drink in two gulps and grab my coat. I need to put space between Savannah and me. It's time to clear my head, think things through, and try to figure out what—if anything—I want to do.

"Thanks for the beer, man."

"She's at your three o'clock."

I did not need to know that. And I'm struggling to act like I don't care.

Finn taps the side of his nose like he's been told the codes to the nuclear football. "It'll be our little secret."

When I said I needed space between Savannah and me, I didn't mean this much space. I take it back. It's been a week since Thanksgiving. We're both back in Cedar Rapids, and while I've seen her a couple times from a distance, I haven't been in her space. I don't like it.

Her bruise has likely faded, leaving no trace of our earth-shattering kiss on her flawless skin.

I just finished up a shift at the bookstore, and I'm waiting for the new girl to show up to take over. The guys are all assembled at the couches ready for this month's *Get Lit* book club. Frieda ordered pie from my favorite pie place—GTFO— and if this chick doesn't hurry up and arrive for her shift, I'm going to miss out.

"This pie's disappearing fast, Cap." How Tate enunciates around the mouthful of pastry and fruit he has in his mouth is anyone's guess. But somehow he yells that warning at me and doesn't spit out a single piece of pie in the process. That's pretty impressive.

"Sorry! Sorry! I'm so sorry, Frieda! I got held up and I couldn't find my phone to call—God." Savannah stops dead as she spies me behind the counter wearing our navy-blue polo shirts with The Book Bin logo over my heart.

I tell myself to make a joke about her calling God but I'm

too busy trying to urge my tongue up from the floor and back into my mouth.

How the hell does she make a work polo look that good? She has sex hair. It's wild and unruly from the wind outside, and I want to bury my fingers in it and kiss that subtle pink lipstick off her lips.

"Justin?"

Say something, you fucking dumbass. "Hey, Vannah." I frown. "Sorry. Savannah." I want to smack myself in the face. With a bat. Or a wall.

Her pink cheeks darken and her lips twitch into a small smile. "Vannah's fine. I didn't know you worked here."

I give her a shrug. "I didn't know you worked here either." Could have guessed, though. SB is on the schedule, I just didn't think SB was Savannah Bowen. *My* Savannah. It's like the cosmos are bringing us together at every turn. And yet I'm bumfuzzled every goddamn time. Clearly I'm destined to marry this woman. "I guess we didn't get to employment history."

"I'm new. I just started a couple days ago."

This conversation is fucking painful, and I'm acutely aware of the fact that half my team is sitting six feet away watching this train wreck with interest.

"Tate's eating your pie, Cap."

Fuck the damn pie. I hold up two fingers over my shoulder.

"Your hockey player book club?" She tips her head.

I nod, and one of the guys at the table says something about being famous. "Frieda said we could have it here since it's quiet."

I hate this. Our conversation is stilted, our bodies stiff, and I just heard Scott snort out a laugh behind me.

I had my tongue in this girl's mouth last week. My fingers

pressed into her ass cheeks, and my dick rubbed against her pussy. Granted it was clothed, but still. I was *right there.*

She turns her head to look over at the boys, making the faint yellow bruising still on her neck visible. I barely hold back a predatory smile.

I fucking did that. Though right now you'd never be able to tell that I would have fucked her against the wall if Mom hadn't burst in. So why can't I talk to her now? Why can't I tell her I'm sorry for snapping at her over Molly? Why can't I walk up to her, cup her face with both hands and move in for round two of the epic kissing?

"Would you mind holding the fort while I go drop my bag out back? I'll be just a sec."

I nod and watch her walk away from me, her hips swaying with each step. My dick remembers what it's like to be nestled between her thighs, and if she'd let me, I'd love to bury it between her ass cheeks too.

Fuck.

I shift my weight, but it does little to tame the semi sprouting in my pants.

In the reading area behind me, my teammates make crashing sound effects. They're howling with laughter at my utter bombing with Vannah. Did she say I could call her Vannah out of politeness? I'll have to check. It feels weird, she's Savannah to me.

I turn back to my team, and they're all staring at me expectantly. If they think I'm going to have some kind of therapy session with them about Savannah, they have another think coming.

One thing's for sure, though. I'm going to take a look at the work schedule as soon as these assholes are gone for the night.

CHAPTER 15
Savannah

I never knew a bookstore could be so busy. I thought physical books were a dying industry, but I'll be damned if I haven't been rushed off my feet every day this week. I know it's the week before Christmas and all, but my hands and feet all have blisters, and my blisters even have blisters.

I'm not sure if it was Frieda's doing, or if Justin tinkered with the schedule, but we've been on the same shifts a lot. And on the days we weren't working the same shift, he's either here before I arrive, or after I'm scheduled to leave.

While it was probably Frieda playing matchmaker, I'm hoping it was Justin. There's a tension brewing between us that I'm not sure I can fight for much longer. We still haven't talked, not about our kiss, about Molly, or about the fact I want his dick between my legs for real. Sans clothing.

It's been weeks.

Much to Athena's amusement I burned out the motor in my favorite vibrator. It just gave up on me. It said, "Girl, stop trying to pretend I'm Justin's Anaconda. Give it up." Then it died.

Athena's tried to set me up with a few of her single guy

friends over the past few weeks but I keep saying no which seems to only piss her off more.

I told her what went down between Justin and me over Thanksgiving. All the cautions in the world from her about dating a hockey player don't make a damn bit of difference. My pussy has locked onto Justin Ass like a monster-dick-seeking missile.

There's no take-backs, no abort button.

The pussy has been deployed.

It doesn't matter that she says hockey players suck. It doesn't matter that he cheated on my bestie a few years ago. It doesn't matter. Nothing fucking matters except this deep ache driving me toward him.

My nipples tingle every damn time I see him, and when I watch his slender fingers as he's stacking books on shelves I imagine them rolling and flicking my nipples. And my clit.

I bet I couldn't even fit half his cock in my mouth if I tried. It'd be like trying to cram a Coke can into my mouth, but I wanna try.

I need a new vibrator.

Today's the last time I'm going to see him before I head home for the holidays. I know from our frustratingly polite conversation that he's going away with his family for a while before the team's upcoming trip to Ireland for some exhibition games. They have a couple weeks off from games, and then on New Year's Day they fly over to Europe.

"I have something for you."

I scream like there's a serial killer coming at me with a knife and spin to face Justin, who somehow crept up on me in the space opera aisle. My heart is pounding, partly thanks to the adrenaline coursing through my body, and partly because he's so close.

It's like there's lightning coming off his body, and my skin is screaming for it to fry me.

My crotch wants to party right here in the bookstore.

"F-for me?"

He nods and gives me his "Savannah" smile. I've noticed over the past few weeks that he has a series of smiles. Not all Justin Ashe smiles are created equal. They're all delicious, of course, but the one he gives me, and only me? That's my favorite.

"Actually, I have something for Soph too."

It's the last time I'll see him before Christmas, and I don't have anything for him. I feel terrible.

"I didn't get you anything, Justin." There's a lump in my throat, and I'm praying I don't cry again in front of this beautiful man.

He hands me two gift bags, and my eyes fill.

"Justin..."

"It's nothing much. Open it. The blue bag is yours."

My hands are shaking, but curiosity burns bright in my body. What's in the bag? Hopefully it's something small, like a succulent, or one of the journals he saw me lusting over when we unboxed the delivery last week.

I pull the book out, peeling off the tissue paper and tucking it back into the bag, and my breath catches in my chest. Oh, holy moly. It's not a journal.

He's only gone and got me an advanced copy of J.R. Blake's upcoming release. I'm holding a copy of my favorite author's next book before it's even available to preorder.

I don't have words. I can't stop the tears. All I can do is stare.

"I have an in with the author."

I'll fucking say.

"It's signed."

Is he nervous? Why the hell is he nervous? He rocks back on his feet, and I don't dare meet his stare in case I burst into hysterics.

The hand holding my new book shakes so hard I'm convinced I'm going to drop it and ding the corners. "Justin...I can't accept this... It's too much."

I peel back the cover. My name is written in hot pink Sharpie, and there's a quote about dreams I can't fully see through my tears. My body heaves with sobs as my emotion bursts out from my eyes.

He doesn't hesitate. He pulls me against his chest, curling his arms around me and shushing me softly in my ear. This might be the most thoughtful and perfect gift I've ever been given, and I don't know what to do with that. Other than cry some more of course.

"Would it help if I told you I ordered them for book club too?"

I sniff. There's probably snot on his shirt. I know I should care, but he doesn't seem to, and I'm too busy trying to process, while simultaneously cursing my tears. I can't get a good whiff of his delicious man smell 'cause of my stupid snotty nose.

"Are they all personalized?"

"No, pretty girl. Just yours."

Just mine. Pretty girl. What the hell is happening right now?

"I was wondering."

My head hits the underside of his chin as I jerk upright. Pain radiates through my skull and I hiss out a cuss.

"Shit, are you okay?" He examines my head, his concern wrapping itself around me like a warm blanket on a cold night. I hit him—shouldn't I be the one asking if he's okay? And why the fuck do we keep smacking our heads together? Is this some kind of message from the universe?

"I'm good." I rub my crown. "Startled more than hurt. What were you going to say?"

"Your flight leaves tomorrow morning, right? To go home to Minnesota?"

I nod slowly, not sure where he's going with this.

"I'm booked to go on that one too."

Wait, what? "I thought you were going to Aspen...or Angel Fire...somewhere with the skiing and the snow." I shiver. I'd probably fall off the ski lift and get stuck under it—that's the level of confidence I have in my ability to control giant sticks strapped to my feet. They'd undoubtedly find my body dangling by the feet from the bottom of the chair lift someday.

"I am. I'm going home first. And I figured..." His face is red as he shrugs and tucks his hands into the front pockets of his jeans. It's so fucking adorable I want to pinch his cheeks.

"I figured you could do with the company on the flight. We could ask to sit together when we check in." What he's not saying resonates inside my chest. He wants to take care of me on the plane.

This boy.

This boy is growing on my heart like a rose bush up a trellis.

"Mom wants you guys over before we go on vacation," he says. "Just eggnog and charcuterie boards. She lives for the holidays. I told her I'd ask if you guys wanted to join us..."

The unasked question is left hanging in the air as I fight the now familiar urge to wrap my legs around his waist again.

I of course say yes.

"I'm sorry I snapped at you over Molly. It's a," he sighs, "Sore subject."

I don't press him, and I gratefully accept his apology. When I leave, it's in a blissful haze of excitement. When I get back to my place, I cram all my crap into a case for my trip, unable to shove all the butterflies in my stomach into their box.

"What's your deal?" Athena asks. She's been calling me a deserter and traitor for an hour now as she lies on my bed flicking through some car magazine she gets delivered every month from Europe.

"I don't have a deal."

She arches her microbladed brow, dipping the magazine from her face so she can scrutinize me. "You never take this long to pack. Are you nervous about seeing your parents again?"

My parents. In all the rush leading up to Christmas vacation I'd kinda set them aside. It's been easier to separate myself from those emotions and compartmentalize that situation while I worked on school and at The Book Bin rather than face them.

But now I'm faced with going back again, and I'm just not sure how to handle anything. I think my disassociation from the whole thing is because of overwhelm. For those few months I built myself up to finding information about my birth family, only to learn my birth mom had died, and now the goal of finding her is gone, I'm kind of stuck in limbo.

I'm scared that if I keep going down the path of pushing my family away, they might actually leave. And I just... I don't want that. But I'm hurt, and I definitely don't feel like I can trust them. As dramatic as it sounds I feel like my whole life has been a friggin' lie, and I just don't know how to come back from that. My usual joy for the holidays has been overshadowed by a sadness I can't shake.

"Yeah."

She drops her magazine onto the bed, nailing me with a stare. "That's not it. Talk to me, Goose."

"Hen, just drop it."

Not even the infamous quote from her favorite movie will get me to spill.

She rolls her eyes. It makes me want to hold up a scorecard

giving her a perfect ten. "It's the boy, isn't it? The hockey player. You're seeing J-boy again."

She must see something in my face, because she grins. "You have such a shit poker face, Banana. So you're more worked up about seeing the boy with the giant meat whistle than you are over your first Christmas as an adopted child?"

The air explodes from my lungs with an *oof*. "Don't hold back, Athena. Tell it like it really is."

She shrugs. "You know I don't pussyfoot around. It's why we work so well together as a best friend duo. Straight as a rod, no place for bullshit. Yadda, yadda..." She waves her hand. "Stop deflecting. You want him, right?"

I nod, afraid to say anything as though the walls have ears and they might hear my confession.

"He wants you?"

I abandon my fourth packing attempt and cross the room to my bookcase. It's a small dorm room, tiny in fact. I feel like I definitely got the runt of the litter when it came to personal space allotment from UCR.

Athena keeps offering for me to move into her apartment with her, and I keep saying no. I don't want to take advantage of our friendship. And while the apartment is hers—she told me that each of the de la Peña kids got gifted an apartment near UCR from *Daddy Moneybags* when they graduated high school—I just can't do it.

A tiny voice in the back of my head whispers that I'm scared. It's true. I don't have that much of a circle. My family, Athena... Uh... My family and Athena, that's pretty much it. If Hen and I move in together and get on each other's nerves... well. I might end up losing her, and that thought makes me queasy.

I slip the book Justin gave to me from the shelf and hand it to her. She looks at me like I've lost my mind. "Are you trying to distract me from my questions with fictional hotties?"

"Open it."

She does, and she's still clueless. "I don't get it."

"It's by my favorite author."

She sits upright in the bed, puts the book on her lap, and reaches behind her to fluff the pillows. "I can see that, but I still don't follow."

"Justin gave that to me earlier."

It takes a moment for understanding to clear the confusion from her face. She looks at the book, then up to me, then back to the book. "Girl. He wants you so bad." She waves the book at me, and I suddenly regret letting her touch it. If she drops it and dents a corner I'm going to beat her to death with it.

She doesn't have far to reach when she hands it back to me. "Well, you really need to move in with me now. You're not going to want to bang him in the hockey house, and he's not going to even fit into this sorry excuse for a room, never mind onto this matchbox bed."

I huff out a breath. "We'll make it work." My body has woken up at the idea of banging Justin. I've stopped fighting the flicker in my chest when I think of him, and instead, I just sink into the warm fuzzies like it's where I belong.

"I need a puke bucket." Athena wraps her arms around her stomach and makes gagging noises. "This is so sickeningly sweet. I'm gonna blow."

I toss a throw pillow from near her feet at her face, and her gagging noises increase. "Why do you hate hockey players so much anyway?"

I've asked her before, and her answer is always the same. Her face darkens, glimmers of something I can't identify passing across her features, and she goes rigid. "I just do."

"One of these days you're going to let me know your damage."

"Not today. Today we need to unpack those floral undies

you just shoved in there thinking I couldn't see, and find the sexy, sexy lace."

I like her confidence. It's contagious and intoxicating, but it's also short lived. When she heads back to her place and I hit the hay, my nerves return. So many thoughts I can't quiet swim around my mind as I try to sleep. I end up covering my face with my pillow and screaming into it like I've lost my mind.

Because it kind of feels like I have.

What if the kiss didn't affect him the way it did me? What if he doesn't really want to give this thing between us a shot? What if we do give it a shot and he cheats on me? What if Molly isn't really okay with it and she was pulling some reverse psychology shit on me in the hopes of making me come to my senses and step out from under the spell Justin's magic wand has clearly cast on me?

Another growl tears from the back of my throat as I flip onto my stomach. If overthinking was a subject at school I'd have a PhD in it. I can't silence my thoughts, so when I haul my ass out of bed at the butt crack of dawn to catch my flight, all the triple shot coffees in the world aren't enough to make this zombie-scarecrow hybrid hot mess express in any way vaguely human.

Justin meets me curbside at the airport. He opens the door to my Uber, kisses me on the cheek, and grabs my bag from the trunk. And suddenly I don't give a shit that I'm about to step onto another metal death trap.

I like this.

I like it a lot.

But can I trust it?

He checks his huge bag at the check in desk, and I can't help but smile. He tells me he's got more beer for both our dads and some cheese curds he picked up in Wisconsin for his mom. Considering the size of the case I'm convinced he's trafficking an entire dairy farm across state lines. He's even hit with an excess baggage fee, but he doesn't seem at all fazed.

When he's ditched his 63 pounds of cheese and beer, he turns to me and smiles. My insides feel like winning the jackpot on a slot machine. The lights flash like crazy all at once, there's an obnoxious ringing sound, and a huge payout. That smile could light up an entire Kingcaid casino.

Taking the handle of my carry-on, he offers me his open palm. My stomach flaps and twists as I slide my hand into his, staring at our joined hands while he leads me through security.

Huh. I guess we're doing this dating thing, then. *hell yes*

CHAPTER 16
Justin

Christmas was amazing. I kissed Vannah—it's growing on me—under the mistletoe at my parents' house every chance I got. Mom had very sneakily hung mistletoe everywhere she could think of, so there was quite a lot of kissing.

I went skiing in Aspen, played hockey in Belfast, Northern Ireland, ate entirely too much artisanal cheese, and now I'm back at UCR things are...awkward.

It's not like I've never dated girls before. But I've never dated one I've felt *this* deeply for, this quickly. It also doesn't help that we spent the first few weeks of our "dating" life long distance. We've talked on the phone once or twice but it's mostly been texts between runs on the slopes, or before or after games—the six hour time difference with Ireland is not conducive to getting a relationship off the ground.

I want this woman. Mind, body, and soul, for the rest of our lives on this planet and whatever lies beyond. Forever. And I know it as surely as I know the sun rises in the east and sets in the west. I also know if I say it out loud to *anyone*, even Mom who is already buying pastel yarn to make tiny little hats for her future grandkids, they're going to think I'm crazy. Because it is crazy. It's too soon. I don't know her all that well.

But I love fast, and I love hard. And I know down to the core of my being that I'm already falling wildly in love with Savannah Jane Bowen.

I just need to keep it to myself for a while until I can make her fall wildly in love with me right back. That means having a plan. Asking her out for a real, official date. And getting all the other knuckleheaded shit stuff off my desk so I can spend time with her.

My latest book launched over the holidays, and it's doing well. But I'm still drowning. Writing to deadline in the twelve weeks between releases is crippling me. I need to find a way to write more, and faster, so I can get a step ahead of the deadlines looming in front of me.

Writing this many words in this many days is something I do because I have to. I'd much rather have a book on the shelf all ready to go for the next publishing day. I almost laugh as I save and back up my document in three different places.

If wishing made it so.

I'm told there are people out there who do it. It's gotta be witchcraft.

Over the past week, I've had three different people messaging me to see if I want to join their list-aiming anthologies. And while it's been tempting—like, it's literally my dream to reach a bestseller list—I need to do it by myself.

I need to prove—to myself, my father, and anyone else who believed I cheated on that stupid term paper—that I don't need to copy anyone, or ride anyone's coattails, to succeed. That my own work, as sometimes off the wall and quirky as it is, speaks for itself.

I want to earn it solo. And while part of me is scolding myself at saying a polite "no, thank you" to the emails I've gotten, I know it's the right choice for me.

Hitting the list requires patience, sustainable strategy, and playing the long game. Putting out good quality books, building my brand and reader base over time, and hoping that a little growth with each book will lead to big growth overall.

My next deadline is just under nine weeks away. I wrote every day while on vacation, and almost every day in Ireland. It doesn't help that I'm working on two manuscripts. The book I *should* be releasing next, and the book I *want* to release next.

I'm still writing words in the story I started when I landed in Minnesota with Savannah that first time. I want to binge-write it and publish it ASAP, but I can't because I don't know how our story goes yet. This requires yet more patience. Ugh.

But my heart isn't in the book I'm supposed to be writing. It's flat. I'm at the murky middle where I can't see the shore-line in any direction, and I'm lost out at sea. My characters have abandoned the outline I was so sure this time they'd follow.

They've set fire to the metaphorical life raft I sent them in my back up plot idea. They snapped my olive branch of recon-ciliation between character and outline. And they've gone off on some random tangent with no directions, GPS or road signs, and I have no fucking clue what they're up to, or how they're going to get to where I need them to be.

I'm about to resort to violence.

You'd think because I'm the author of the story that I might have some semblance of control over the stubborn assholes in my books. But no, it's an illusion, a mirage, a big fucking lie. I am their bitch and completely at their mercy.

My author friends say to suck it up and dig in. Push through the awkward middle bit to get to the downward slide into *The End*. Some books are easier than others, but this book? This book is like a bunion, rubbing against the inside of my shoe.

It's on my mind constantly, which doesn't bode well for

the other areas of my life. My game on the ice is slipping because I'm distracted trying to figure out how the fuck to untangle the mess of drama my characters just jumped into like it was a bowl of vanilla freakin' pudding.

Geronimooooooooooooo! They took off from the edge before checking with me and belly flopped right into the delicious dessert and now they don't want to leave.

Of course this is all metaphorical, though the more I think on the pudding thing, the more I wonder if I should just throw in a big-ass bowl of pudding into my manuscript. Couldn't be any worse than the dumpster fire I've written so far.

My beloved car broke down two days ago, and I'm waiting for the mechanic to give me an estimate for how much that's going to cost. She's quaint and well loved, which is realtor speak for old as shit and falling down around my ears, but she gets me from A to B, and I don't have the cash to sink into a new ride for the foreseeable.

Slamming my laptop shut, I push to my feet. We've got a game tonight, which means I have to set aside the book stuff, my money stuff, and get into hockey mode. It's hard. I've worried about money since I was old enough to understand the concept of bills, or money in, money out, and since I was old enough to understand the conversations I overheard between my parents.

I check my phone now that my allotted writing time is up, and there is a weird combination of messages on my screen.

> Tate: I know you keep the team's group chat muted, so I wanted to prepare you. We got a pig, Cap.

> Savannah: Good luck tonight. I'll be in the stands during the game, and at the bar after.

Mom: How's things going with Ms. Bowen?
We haven't heard anything from you for a
little while now.

My chest tingles at the thought of seeing Vannah after the game. It's been too long. I plan to kiss her until she agrees to come on a real date with me. I even know where I'm going to take her and everything. But I'm too stuck on the pig to even contemplate a reply.

Justin: Like... to eat?

I open the group chat. There are 300 unread messages in the thread. I'm almost scared to open it but I need to know what's waiting for me when I get to the rink.

I don't need to scroll back through all 300 messages to find what I'm looking for. As soon as I click the message, a picture of a pig dressed as a raccoon pops up on my screen. Oh, Christ.

The message underneath is from Ares.

Ares: Meet the latest Raccoon. Our new
mascot: Bacon.

Of course that's what he's called him. I don't even know what to do with this. Who just ups and gets a fucking pet potbelly pig?

Someone with a shit ton of money, who gives no fucks, and who is more impulsive than anyone else I've ever met. To be fair the pig is kind of cute, and it could have been worse, he could have picked up a raccoon. That would have been much worse—those suckers are vicious as fuck and hard as hell to train.

All things considered, he's been restrained in Ares terms. So I can't be too mad. The team is typing their adoration for our newest team member and I wonder what other carnage happened in the 299 other messages in the text string leading up to the pet pig.

Ares messages that Bacon will live with him, but we all have visitation rights and can take him for sleepovers if we want. He says Bacon is a chick magnet. He's also going to find someone to take him to games to cheer us on, and I wonder if an arena of screaming fans is the best place to take a poor, defenseless pig.

I also think it's a bit presumptuous to stick him in a raccoon costume on his first day. Doesn't he need to see us play first before he decides if he's a fan or not?

I tell the guys to focus, not on the new porcine in raccoon's clothing, but on the fact we need to concentrate for the game later and cut out distractions. Distractions like a shiny new pet. And a beautiful woman cheering me on in the stands.

Cutting out distractions would be easier if they didn't come to the rink. Bacon tottered around the locker room getting ear and belly scratches from all the players, right up to the point Coach burst into the room and told Ares to get him the fuck out.

I'm not sure where he put the pig, if he brought a crate with him or what, but he moved him pretty damn quick. Bacon's kind of cute, though, and he has his own Instagram. He already has more followers than the team account which is embarrassing.

The game was... Ugh. It was fine. It wasn't great and it wasn't awful. It was just okay. Mediocre. We aren't a mediocre team, though, so even though we scraped a win by only one goal, it feels like we lost by 100. I even scored the game winning goal. And I still can't be happy about it.

I'm in my suit post-game, leaning against the bar and surveying the crowd. I know Savannah's here—not only did she tell me she would be, but it's as though her energy is charging the air around me. I feel her. I just don't see her yet.

A beer appears in my periphery on the bar to my right, and I spin to face the person who brushed against my back to put it there. It's her, my Savannah, beam of sunshine and sugar, lighting the place up with a radiant smile.

She's wearing a Raccoon's jersey that falls to her mid-thigh, and I swear to all that's holy if it's crested with a name and number on the back that isn't mine I'm going to lose my shit.

If it's blank and doesn't have a name and number on it, I'm reaching behind the bar to our emergency supply of autograph Sharpies, and I'm going to fix it right here in the bar.

"Justin?" Her forehead wrinkles with a frown. "Why do you look murderous when your shot won the game?"

"I was just thinking that if you have someone else's name across your shoulders, I'm not going to be okay about it."

She laughs and sips her beer. The long pause before she answers almost suffocates me.

"I don't have a name on my shirt. It would be a little..." She taps the rim of the bottle against her plump bottom lip and suddenly I couldn't care less about the shirt, I want my dick in her hand. "Presumptuous...wouldn't you say? Getting your name on my shirt is kind of a big commitment. We're not there yet." Her eyes hold hope. "We haven't even had a real date."

Or maybe I just think they hold hope. I slide a knuckle under her chin and drop a light brush of my lips against hers. "I'm happy to wait. But you will have my name across your shoulders someday soon."

She's not wrong. We do need to go on a real date. And then another. I'm already in with both feet, but she's still reluctant to trust me, and trying to get to know someone over the holidays between deadlines, travel, and hockey, certainly hasn't been easy.

A couple of guys are waiting to talk to me. She gives me a look that says "go ahead," but I don't want to. I want to talk to her. She doesn't give me a choice though, because before I can say Gordie Howe, she's walking away from me and over to where Athena de la Peña is holding court with two guys and a girl I've never seen before.

As Savannah sits down, one of the guys turns toward her and gives her a smile. Am I proud of the fact I'm jealous as fuck right now? No. We haven't defined the terms of our very, very, very...okay, one more *very* fledgling...thing...yet, but I want to. I want her to be mine, exclusively. From now until always.

I hold up a finger to the two guys wanting to talk, but they've already lost interest and are chatting about the game to Tate and Scott. Scott has positioned himself to have an eye on Savannah and Athena. Does he have the hots for her too? I need to act quickly before my teammate takes it upon himself to move in on my girl.

I'd have to kill him and hide his body. Way too much work. And we'd need to find a replacement for him on the team. I shelve that thought for a hot minute and grab my phone from my pocket.

> Justin: Can I take you home?

> Justin: When you're ready I mean. Not right now.

Her body jumps upright in her seat. If I had to guess, she

has the vibrate function turned on, and her phone scared the crap out of her.

"Good game, Cap." Another stranger pats me on the shoulder and walks past. I smile and nod, feeling like a fraud. I don't feel like I've given any area of my life the time and dedication it needs lately and my spinning plates are starting to do that wibbly-wobbly thing they do right before they crash to the ground.

"You good?" Apollo steps into my line of sight. I don't want to make it obvious who I'm staring at, so I drag my eyes from Savannah to his face.

I put my beer on the bar and scrub my fingers through my still-damp hair. "Just disappointed in myself lately, that's all."

His sympathetic nod isn't particularly encouraging. Great. He's disappointed in me, too. Who else on my team is feeling that way?

"You have a lot on your plate, Cap."

The sinking feeling in my stomach turns to those free-fall feelings you get on a rollercoaster. I'm letting down my boys.

Something registers on his face, and he shakes his head. "You know that wasn't necessarily a criticism, right? It's a simple fact. You're pretty busy."

I sigh. "I know. I just don't know how people do it."

He nudges me. "Most of us don't play competitive college sports while simultaneously trying to get a full-time degree and launch our careers off the ground. Just chill the fuck out a bit. You're making the rest of us look bad." He winks as though he knows telling me to calm down will just wind me up further.

He doesn't get it. *Can't* get it. He was born into money, and while he didn't ask for it, he'll never know what it's like to hear your mom crying while your dad tries to juggle bills. He'll never know what it's like to have your grandfather tell your dad what a failure he is that he can't take care of your mom

while you're standing on his doorstep with all your posses-
sions in tattered suitcases and trash bags.

He doesn't get my "why." And that's okay. He doesn't
have to. We're not all motivated by the same things, and that's
okay too. But there's no way I can take my foot off the gas. I
have big plans for my future, and they don't involve pieces of
shit cars held together by duct tape or final notice bills coming
through my storm-damaged door.

I take another drink of beer, squeezing my phone in my
other hand. It hasn't vibrated yet, so Vannah hasn't replied to
my messages. I flex my jaw. I want to go over there, pick her
up, swing her over my shoulder and take her home to have my
way with her.

It's not the most gentlemanly thing I could do, and she
might not be ready, but it would show her for sure that I'm all
in. All. In. Preferably in her pussy. Assuming she's open to the
idea of course.

Apollo grabs my shoulder and gives me a shake. "Stop
being so hard on yourself, Cap. You're doing great."

I don't know how to stop being so hard on myself, but I
tell him I'll try just to get him to leave me alone with my
thoughts. And so he'll step the hell out of my way so I can
stare at Savannah again. Yes, it's creepy, but she's a beacon of
light in this on-the-right-side-of-dingy bar, and I want to soak
her in.

Her phone is sitting on the table in front of her when
Apollo walks away.

> Justin: I have something else to ask
> you, too.

She casts a glance over to me, and I tilt my head. Pick up
the phone. Talk to me.

> Justin: I want to take you out. A real date.
> Say yes, pretty girl.

She's nibbling on her lip, phone now in hand. Athena grabs the cell from her hand, and her thumbs move over the screen. After a second or two she hands the phone back and my hands vibrate.

> Savannah: She'd love to. But you gotta take her somewhere nice, Justin Ass. Or you and me are gonna have issues. Now quit distracting my girl. You can take her home in an hour.

It feels mildly like Athena de la Peña just stepped into pimp territory for her friend, and I can't help but laugh as I re-read the message. An hour. I can absolutely handle drinking with my team for an hour. Right?

Ares bursts into the bar with a bright pink, bedazzled leash clutched in his hand. Bacon—still dressed as a raccoon—leads the way. It takes less than a second for people to realize he's brought a pet fucking pig to the bar and people flock to him to say hi and love on our new mascot.

Our goaltender laps up the attention more than the damn pig does. Ares is not someone I'd ever call shy, and his charisma and ease in dealing with everyone is pretty impressive. He's a cocky fucker on the ice, but having seen some of the saves he's made over our last few games, well, he has reason to be.

I feel someone staring at me. When I look around, my gaze meets Savannah's. It's going to be a long sixty minutes, but then I get her all to myself for the ride home.

CHAPTER 17
Savannah

I'm going to puke. Justin took me home last night, and at the door to my building, he kissed the breath from my body until I felt dizzy and needed a time out. Today is our first date. Our first real, no parents, no team mates, no meddling best friends, no coincidences date.

Today, not tonight. Which is weird, right? You don't take someone you want to do naughty things to out in the middle of the afternoon.

Definitely weird.

And I'm crapping my pants. Figuratively. If it was real poop I'd at least have an excuse not to go.

It's not that I don't want to see him, but he didn't tell me where we are going, what we are doing, or what I should wear, and I'm nervous AF about spending time with him one-on-one. Are we in sexy-time date territory? Or does the fact we did those few weeks long distance change the dating trajectory?

My track record of alone time with Justin Ashe hasn't been great: Tears, panic attacks, and being cock blocked by his mother. It doesn't really bode well for us. I'm starting to wonder if these are all signs telling me I shouldn't get too close. Not to mention the almost concussions we keep having when we're in each other's airspace.

I've changed my outfit three times already. I shaved my legs and got my hoo-ha waxed this morning because Athena said it's better to be over prepared and not need it, than to be caught with an unruly forest between my legs.

The beautician had to use a freakin' ride-on lawn mower at my appointment. I left her a ridiculous tip because no one should have to deal with that first thing on a Sunday morning.

Sunday. Who the hell picks Sunday for a first date?

Thank fuck Athena's beautician does house calls. I'm pretty sure Hen has her on retainer in case of hairy muff emergencies.

I guess the Sunday date just sums Justin up, though. He's unconventional and constantly surprising me.

Athena's face lights up the screen of my phone. I'm lying flopped out on my bed, and she's going to kick my ass for not being ready yet, so I contemplate ignoring the call.

Hen: Pick up the G-D phone.

I call her back. Her brows shoot up the second the video call connects. "You're naked."

"Not naked, naked, just…almost naked. I'm struggling with what to wear."

"This is my shocked face." She deadpans pointing two fingers at her face. "If he didn't tell you to dress up, then I'd say go casual. He's picking you up at like four, right? So, again, that's not a formal attire for dinner kind of date. Either wear jeans and your nice wine-colored cable knit sweater or wear some leggings with your Uggs…and your wine-colored cable knit sweater."

"It's as though you like my wine-colored cable knit sweater."

"What can I say?" She shrugs. "I have good taste. Put clothes on. It's three thirty. He'll be there soon. I have a feeling he's one of those guys who shows up early and calls it on time. Unless you want to answer the door in your underwear and cut straight to the fucking, you're going to want to get some clothes on."

It's tempting. I've dreamt about it every single night since the day I saw him in the coffee shop. Every. Single. Night.

Some of the dreams were so lucid I was completely convinced they were real. I would roll over in bed, stretching my hand out and expecting to touch his chiseled abs only to find a cold and empty bed next to me.

We've being doing this dance around each other for long enough. I want to be his girlfriend, I want him to be my boyfriend, and I'm hoping that our busy lives and the holiday season aren't a bad omen for us moving this thing a little farther down the tracks.

Athena is right. Someone knocks at the door at quarter to the hour, and I'm still running around half dressed. I check that it's Justin through the peephole before I holler at him that I'll be out in just a sec.

I jerk open the door a few minutes later, and he's standing right there, looking all casual and sexy as hell in slacks and a shirt. There's nothing this man can wear that he couldn't make look good. Hell, I'm sure if he wore a T-rex costume, I'd still wanna jump his bones.

"I'm sorry. I...uh...fell asleep and only woke up when Athena called a while ago." I can't tell him I've spent the last ninety minutes flouncing around my room almost ass naked trying to figure out what the fuck to wear to see him.

He slips his hand into mine and the warmth skates up my arm. "You look beautiful." He kisses my cheek. "Ready to go?"

We make our way out of my building and onto the street, but I don't see his shitty car anywhere. Sounds mean, but it really is a piece of crap. I have no idea how it still runs.

"Are we walking?"

His ears turn pink. "I borrowed Apollo's SUV. Mine's in the shop."

He unlocks a shiny black SUV and opens the door for me to get into the passenger seat. I'm resolved not to cry hysterically at him this time. I want us to have fun, not for me to cover his shirt in snot.

He hums along to the radio as he weaves in and out of traffic and drives through the city. Though humming is a kind term for it, he sounds like the buzz of an electric toothbrush.

When we pull up outside a laundromat, I think I'm being punked. Maybe he has to run an errand before we go for our date. I scrunch up my face. Laundry is definitely not date level material. Nope. And I just did my laundry yesterday, so he can't even offer to do my laundry for me in some act of blissful foreplay.

What the hell is going on right now?

"Don't think I can't see that judgy look on your face, Savannah Jane."

A laugh reverberates around my ribcage. Mom middle names me when I'm in trouble.

"Trust me?"

It's on the tip of my tongue to make a quip about him cheating on Molly, but I don't want to get things off on the wrong foot between us. I'm trying to put that small voice in my head to bed and get past it, even if it's hard. I need to get over it. I know this.

"Okay." I nod twice, hoping that it's a convincing, reassuring nod.

I can tell from how he's drumming his fingers on the wheel that he's nervous, and my curiosity is on full alert right now. What could we possibly do at a laundromat for a date? Are we going to steal people's undies? Is that his kink? Getting arrested for underwear stealing would certainly be a memorable first date to tell the grandkids.

Huh. I guess I can see myself with this guy in the future. I don't have time to unpack that thought as he leads me inside, still holding my hand, to a door behind a long workbench that has a sign overhead: GTFO.

I mean, call me cautious Cathy, but I question the logic of going through a door that clearly tells you to get the fuck out.

There's nothing particularly impressive about the door. It could do with a fresh coat of brilliant white paint to cover the scuff marks. And the sign hanging over it looks like someone wrote on a piece of cardboard and stuck it up with crazy glue.

I'm not sure whether to laugh or run. If it wasn't for the comforting warmth of the room, the drone of tumble dryers, and a weirdly sweet smell permeating the air and making my mouth water, I'd definitely run. Or at least walk quickly.

"Are you sure we should be here? I feel like we shouldn't be here."

He squeezes my fingers, and with his free hand he opens the door. A gasp escapes me as we walk into a secret room. It's a hidden cafe of some kind. There are maybe a dozen brightly colored two and four seater tables with chairs around the homey space. Bookshelves to my left have a variety of well-loved books, and shelves lining the wall to my right house a collection of games, both board and card.

There's a small counter with a bright pink fluorescent GTFO sign overhead. The lighting is intimate, the smells incredible, and we're the only people that I can see in the space.

Justin pushes a button on the counter. It doesn't make a sound but he turns to the tables and leads me to one in the back corner, grabbing Scrabble from a shelf as he passes.

There's a large chalkboard on the front of the counter. It's got a savory pie of the week, sweet pie of the week, and book and game of the month written on it. The book for this month is the same book Justin gave me for Christmas which makes me smile.

Clearly the owner of this quirky establishment has impeccable taste.

Justin pulls out my chair, and I can't stop myself from looking all around the small space as I sit. There's so much to look at. Fairy lights, a shelf of succulents, a large glass lemonade dispenser on a stand. This might be my new favorite place on earth. I feel so at home here, so comfortable, so safe, that I never want to leave.

A giant of a man comes out from behind the small counter. He's probably taller than Justin, which is saying something, and his shoulders are twice as broad. He's giving me hot Hagrid vibes. His jet black hair is shorter than the groundskeeper's from Harry Potter, but not short. It's glossy and wavy, falling perfectly over his forehead.

He looks like he stepped right out of a commercial for conditioner. He's got a goatee, the palest skin I've ever seen, and he's wearing a Ted Lasso shirt.

I like him already.

"Savannah, this is Brian."

"With an I." The giant arches an eyebrow like he expects me to ask about Bryan-with-a-y and why he feels the need to distinguish himself from him. Brian has the most divine Irish accent I've ever heard. I don't know if he does audio work, but he needs to.

I'd listen to so many more books if he was the narrator of them, and I'd love an evening wind down podcast by him. Something to sooth my racing mind right before bed. He'd make a killing at guided meditation.

"I is *so* much better than y." I arch my brow right back,

except because I can't control them independently, both of them shoot up and I'm 100% sure I look like a surprised idiot now.

He nods like it's a given. I dunno who Bryan-with-a-y is, but he can't be this cool.

"Brian, this is Savannah."

"Huh." Brian doesn't say anything else as he hands me a laminated menu.

"Huh? What huh?" I accept the menu that says "Get the Fork Out" across the top of it, and hug it against my chest not looking at the offerings yet.

He ignores my question and gives Justin a menu, too, jerking his chin at the box between us on the table. "Same game, different date?"

Justin rolls his lips between his teeth and turns the color of ketchup.

"I guess you're just going to keep bringing new ones until you win?"

I can tell from Brian's tone that he's poking fun at Justin, but Justin doesn't seem convinced that I know the man is kidding as well. I fold my arms and play along. "You mean this isn't our special secret dating place?" I level him with a glare. "You bring all your conquests here for an intimate first date?"

"I...uh...I..." He heaves out a breath, rakes both hands through his hair, and looks ready to explode like a saturated rain cloud. "No, I don't. I swear. I..."

Brian and I meet each other's gaze, and I just can't keep it together. I burst out laughing, then it's my turn to be on the receiving end of Brian's disdain. He curls his lip. "You couldn't have hung in there a bit more? The man was near ready to cry."

His words are sharp, but his lilting tone is playful, and his eyes sparkle. I want to know everything about the man. What brought him to the US from Ireland? What made him start a secret pie shop? Where'd he learn to make pies? What products does he use to make his hair look so damn amazing?

"I don't need this." Justin hands the menu back to Brian. "I've been here before."

"Oh, I know you have. But she's more inclined to know what to do because she's a smart woman—except for the 'being here with you' bit."

I'm living for the pie guy snark.

Justin rolls his eyes. "I'll take beef and Guinness for my savory, and coconut cream pie, with lemonade please, Brian."

Brian grunts, and I can't tell if Justin's selection is met with approval or contempt.

"I'll take The Comfort please."

Polish sausage, potatoes, and a light cheese sauce sounds incredible.

"Then I'll have," I tap my finger on my chin as I scan the offerings. "Pineapple pie please, Brian. Oh! With a lemonade too, light ice please."

Another grunt and he's turning to leave. "I'd avoid that one." He tips the menus to point at the Scrabble box. "It's missing a few pieces, but I doubt he'll notice. He's not one to go for the full package." He makes a move to leave, but pauses. "Oh! And if you let him win, that's an automatic second date."

Justin is smiling, but his ears are still pink. "Next time you'll have to try the breakfast pie, it's orgasmic."

Next time. He's already looking forward to another date. I kind of am too.

CHAPTER 18
Justin

I probably shouldn't have eaten that much pie. I kind of gorged myself, and now I have regrets. That, and I really need to fart. I think Brian bakes something addictive into his pie crust that makes us mere mortals incapable of saying no, or stopping when we're actually full.

I can't fart, though, because I have Savannah next to me in the car, and I'm taking her back to her dorm. We had the best date—and I'm not just saying that because there was pie. Though I do fucking love pie.

Vannah went toe-to-toe with Brian and didn't let his snark bother her, she met his sarcasm with barbs of her own, and she never let me win a single game. I had to work for it. And even then I didn't clean sweep. We were very evenly matched.

I feel like that's the theme of our entire relationship. She's not open to giving me an inch, but any ground I do make with her, I seem to keep.

She takes my hand and pulls it onto her lap as I meander through the streets back to where I picked her up. Do I ask to walk her to her door? Will she think I'm pushing her into taking things further?

A girl got attacked on campus last week, and while UCR is taking it seriously, I'm becoming more aware of the dangers the females at college face. So I really don't want to make Savannah feel at all uncomfortable, especially since we're in a confined space.

At the same time, though, I don't want her thinking I'm disinterested, that I want to drop her off and tire squeal away from her. I need her to know I'm interested, but not pushy. I want her, but I'll respect her no. That's a fine balance, and I need to get it just right. One look at the hard on in my pants and she'll know I want her, but I don't want to pressure her.

I shouldn't have spent the drive running this over in my head, fretting over it, because as soon as I pull up she turns to me and asks if I'd like to come inside with her.

"Are you sure?"

She nods, curling her bottom lip between her teeth. I'd guess her cheeks are pink, but it's dark out, and I can't see them. My fingers itch to reach out and touch her, to tuck that stubborn stray piece of hair behind her ear so I can see her.

I hop out of Apollo's vehicle and hurry around the front of the SUV to open her door, releasing my gas before I get there. Praise the Lord. We're not at the "no boundaries" point in our relationship, and I don't want to make it awkward by popping out a toot on our first real date.

I reach my hand out to help her down from her seat. The warmth from her hand seeps up my arm and nestles in my chest.

"I think that was the best pie I've ever eaten."

I close the door and lock the car. While it's not a bad area, Apollo would kill me dead if his car got stolen—even if he has the cash to replace it ten times over. That's not the point, even if I'd love access to his black card for like, an hour, someday.

"Brian makes great pies. I try a new one each time I go, just to see if I can find one that doesn't make my mouth water. I haven't found a single one that I don't want to eat again."

She leads me to the door of her building. "Why doesn't he open a bigger place? Franchise it? Advertise more? I dunno... anything? I've been here for years and had no idea it was even there. I feel like he's missing out on a lot of business."

"He likes to keep it small. He prefers a more intimate customer experience, and he largely hates people. So going big is his own special kind of nightmare."

She nods. "Still. I feel like he could make a killing with those pies, especially since he stays open late. Think of the line out the door for pie at three a.m. from drunk and stoned college kids."

"I know. I've told him as much. The whole team has. He even has his back against the wall right now. Some big company wants to buy him out, bulldoze the building, and put condos or something there instead."

She stops at the door to her room and turns to me, her eyes sparkling even in the darkness. "Oh my goodness, he's Meg Ryan."

Laughing, I nod. "Yeah. He's Meg Ryan. Don't let him hear you say that though."

"I wonder if the person wanting to buy GTFO will be his Tom Hanks. Ugh." She claps her hands over her chest and swoons. "Can you imagine the tall, gruff, Irish man finding his happily ever after with the woman who wants to destroy his livelihood?" She sighs again, and I fall a little in love with her right there on the spot. "*You've Got Mail* is such a classic."

There's not much space in her dorm room. In fact, I don't think I've seen a dorm room this small before. I should have asked her to come over to the hockey house. My room is bigger, much bigger, but I guess there's also every chance the boys would throw a party around us, or walk in on us without knocking, or there'd be a gangbang happening in the next room.

Okay, that one's likely just to be Ares, and he has his own place for that. But I'd be lying if I said he's never come over to the house for a party and ended up naked and surrounded by a bunch of other naked people. Dude's loud AF too.

Despite the tiny cubby sized room, this is probably better. She has her own bathroom, but it's minuscule, too. I'm not sure I can even step in there and stand upright without getting concussion. Did she lose a bet to get stuck with this place?

When I turn back, she's watching me with cautious eyes. "I have soda, water, wine, snacks..."

At the thought of eating anything else, my stomach lurches. Sure, I let one rip when I stepped out of the SUV, and thank the stars it was quiet and not the pant-shredder I expected it to be, but I'm still fuller than full.

"I'm good, thanks. But out of interest, where do you keep them?"

"There's a shared kitchen at the end of the hall. But I have a mini fridge in my closet."

This girl is smart.

"I know it's tiny." She takes off her jacket and hangs it on a hook on the back of her door with her scarf. "Athena keeps offering for me to move in with her. I keep saying no. But the longer I spend in this box, the more I question why I keep fighting her on it. It's not like she'll give me a free ride or anything. It isn't charity. I can still pay her rent."

I kick off my shoes and leave them next to her tidy line of boots next to the door. "So...what's stopping you?"

She tilts her head and stares at me. I regret asking the question because her sadness is tangible in the air, and I hate that I led her there with just one question.

"You really want to know?"

"I really do." I hop onto her bed and pat my chest.

She doesn't hesitate to kick off her shoes and climb into my open arm, resting her head on my shoulder. "I'm afraid of losing her. My whole foundation feels unsteady right now. I'm still hurt my parents lied to me. I'm confused and don't really know where I came from. I can't talk to my birth mom. Athena's all I really have outside my family."

She winces against my body. "That sounds so pathetic, but it's kind of true. I mean, I talk to other people, I'm friendly, but I don't have a lot of friends, you know? Not good ones. I'm on the periphery of a bunch of friendship groups but I don't feel like I belong in any of them. No matter how hard I tried and tried... I've never had a girl squad, you know? There's just...Hen. And if I lost her..."

She falls quiet against me, but I can still feel her pain, her fear, her anxiety.

I plant a kiss in her hair. "You forgot someone, Savannah Banana... You forgot me. I'll be in your girl squad."

Her body tenses in my arms but she remains silent.

"I know we haven't really talked about labeling what we have between us yet," I say, "but since I saw you in the coffee shop, there's been no one else for me. I don't want there to be anyone else. I've been calling you my girl in my head for a while now, and I'm not going anywhere unless you tell me to."

"There's been no one else for me either. But I don't have a great dating history. My good guy radar seems to be broken. I don't want to mess this up either."

"And you can't trust me yet."

She flinches.

"It's okay." I run my thumb down the length of her bicep as she leans against me. "Trust takes time to build, and I'm here to build it."

I want to tell her that I never cheated on Molly or my test paper. But I'm kind of scared that even if I told her the truth, she won't believe me. Just like Dad. Trust needs to be built in both directions. That's not what stops me though. What stops me from sharing is that my mouth is suddenly busy.

Savannah cups my jaw as she kisses me, her fingertips curling into my skin. I guess we're done talking, which is fine by me. I kiss her back, softly, sweetly, but she doesn't seem to be into that right now. Her kisses are demanding, aggressive, and if she doesn't slow down I'm going to embarrass myself and come right there on the bed before she's even touched my cock.

My pants are uncomfortably tight. My dick is pointing her way like she's due north on a fucking compass, and when her delicate fingers unbutton my pants, I groan into her mouth. She tastes of pineapple and coconut. I let her steal some of my pie to try and the combination is almost as enchanting as she is.

I run interference at my crotch though, stopping her from opening the zipper. If she wraps her hand around my cock I'm going to blow. And I really don't want her to think I'm a chump. Luckily for me she's wearing leggings, so I slide my hand up the inside of her thigh and pause, waiting for permission.

Her nails curl into my shoulder as she grunts. She covers my hand with hers and shoves it higher up her leg so I'm cupping her pussy. Heat radiates through the fabric of her crotch, she's already damp.

Fuck.

"Don't stop." She pulls her head back and glares at me.

I don't usually dig taking orders, either in or out of the bedroom. It's why I prefer being captain to following someone else out on the ice. But something about her command drives me forward. I slip my hand under the band of her yoga pants, and her body softens against my side as my fingers trail lower.

She's bare, smooth, and absolutely fucking soaking. She

shivers against me as I slide my fingers through her arousal before withdrawing my hand.

She's panting and smacks my shoulder with a light flick of her hand. "I said don't stop. What are you—?" Her voice cuts off as my fingers touch my lips.

"I'm tasting you, pretty girl."

"Oh." The single syllable falls from her mouth on a sigh as her eyes stay glued to my lips. As soon as I've licked her juices from my fingers, humming in delight, she's tugging at me to kiss her again.

My hand finds its way back between her legs. She rolls her hips forward to meet my hand as I circle her clit.

"It's not easy to make me come." Her chest heaves, and her cheeks are pink. "I can..."

Is she serious right now? "You can what, Vannah?"

"I can finish myself." She shrugs like her words mean nothing. Like she's just told me she's all out of milk or something. The air deflates from my lungs like she's hit me in the chest with a battering ram. Hell fucking no.

She turns her head into my shoulder as I continue my endeavors between her legs. My fingers strum her clit like it's a perfectly tuned guitar. From her noises, she's definitely enjoying it, but after that statement from her, I'm wondering if she's conditioned herself to fake it, to make all the right noises just to please whoever she's with.

That won't fly with me. I don't need my ego stroked. I need my woman sated.

I'll be damned if I'm letting this beautiful woman either fake it or not finish. Hell fucking no. I don't know if she's ever had an orgasm from someone else before or not, but it doesn't matter. I'm going to make her fall apart, even if it takes all goddamn night.

"Savannah?"

When she doesn't answer, I stop my fingers in their tracks, and she whimpers.

"Savannah." My voice is harder, but this is something I need her to hear, really hear, and absorb.

"Please don't stop."

"I need you to listen to me right now. I will never ask you to finish for me yourself, unless we're both getting ourselves off together. Do you understand? It may take hours. I may need to use toys. But I won't ever quit until you come for me. Okay?"

She nods, but her eyes tell me she doesn't believe me. I don't know what her damage is with her exes but bet your ass I'm going to prove to her that I'm not full of shit.

I start circling her clit again in earnest. "Has anyone ever made you come before?"

She opens her mouth, and lets out a moan as my fingers pick up speed.

"Other than yourself."

"I... I don't know. I'm not sure. I think so? Maybe?"

Christ. This is tragic. If whoever she'd been with wasn't a selfish prick she'd have both come, and known she'd come.

"I don't care how long it takes. I don't want you ever to fake it with me, okay? And my goal is to make it so you never offer to finish yourself off again. Pull your pants down for me."

I don't want to stop touching her clit to undress her if I can help it. Her skin is flushed, her breathing short and rapid, and her whole body reacts when I'm touching her. She shifts her weight from side to side as she picks her hips off the bed and shucks her pants down her thighs.

I squeeze her clit between my finger and thumb, and her body ripples next to me so I do it again.

"Take off your sweater. I don't want you getting too

warm." And I want access to her skin without getting tangled in fabric.

She does as she's told, revealing a purpley-red lace bra that matches her sweater. I kiss a damp trail down her body, and when I get far enough down, I grab her leggings and panties, tug them off her feet and drop them over the edge of the bed.

My mouth goes dry, and my already painfully hard erection strains against the seam of my pants. I tear off my own sweater and shirt. I don't want to be fully clothed while she's spread out so beautifully underneath me. But I leave my pants on because I don't want her to think I'm presuming we're going straight to home base.

She gasps when I move into position between her thighs. "You don't have to do that, Justin." Her fingers are curled into my hair and she's pulling the strands so hard there's a bite of pain shooting across my scalp. I kind of love it.

"Do you like oral?"

She nods.

It's game on. I'm not letting her demons get the better of her. The second my tongue hits her clit she bucks her hips into my face. I hum against her, relishing the salty sweet taste of her in my mouth. I spread her thighs apart farther and finger her entrance.

Tongue lapping against her clit, I pump my fingers in and out of her, curving to reach the soft, sensitive spot against her wall, and I'm trying to hump the damn bed for some relief of my own. I don't care anymore if I blow my load in my pants.

Everything about her is goddamned delicious. Her body responds to me in ways I could only dream of, and I never want to stop touching her, licking her, *feeling* her.

Her fingers tighten in my hair again, and she locks her thighs around my head, bucking against my mouth with her pussy dripping and my name on her lips.

I could stay here all night, drink every single drop of

arousal she has for me, and push her buttons repeatedly until I make her fall apart over and over on my tongue.

She seems to have forgotten her hesitation to oral because she's now riding my face, both hands tangled in my hair, and her hips jerking back and forward as she moves. She's chasing her orgasm, her walls occasionally flickering around my fingers, and her ass cheeks and thigh muscles clench and loosen every couple of seconds.

She's close, and while sometimes I might be happy for her to do the chasing, this time I'm not. This time I want her O to crash into her and pull her into ecstasy.

I sweep my tongue around her swelling clit. Her walls pulse around my fingers as I pump harder against her g-spot, and my free hand slides up the length of her body, grabbing at the cups of her bra to free her tits.

Her pebbled nipple meets my fingers, and I brush my hand back and forth, enjoying the whispered sounds of her breathing out my name. "Don't stop," she chants over and over. "Please, Justin. Please don't stop."

I want to reassure her that I won't stop, I'll never stop unless she wants me to. But instead of breaking off my pursuit to make her body explode so that I can tell her, I lap at her pussy harder. Actions speak louder than words. My jaw is starting to ache, she's definitely harder to make come than other women I've been with, but that just makes me even more determined to push through and bring her over the edge.

"I'm s-s-sorry, I know...it's...hard. It's...taking...too long." This woman needs to get out of her own head. She needs to stop thinking she's a burden, or that having the honor of eating her out like this is some kind of hardship for me.

I'm not giving up. I'm going to make her come on my face, and when she does, if she lets me, I'm going to make her come on my fucking dick as well. I'm going to make her come until she realizes that she's not defective, or broken, that some people just take longer than others to come.

I'm going to fuck her until she realizes that the heroes and heroines in romance novels are created to appeal to the masses, but everyone is different. And that's not a bad thing. There are definitely worse things than being trapped between her tense thighs with her delicious pussy braced against my face.

I add another finger, now using three to press against her wall. My face is soaked, her juices trickling down my chin and throat, and she's still humping my face like her life depends on it. And by extension, my life suddenly depends on making this woman come for me, too.

CHAPTER 19

Savannah

A scream tears from my chest as my body convulses, every muscle twitching and spasming as I come. I'm pretty sure Justin is drowning in my pussy, but right now that's his problem, I'm too busy trying to keep my body from floating away into the sky.

Another orgasm crashes into me as he flexes his hand against my inner wall. Or maybe it's the same one, just lasting forever. I'd be totally okay if it never stopped. Vibrations threaten to pull me apart as I crest the wave. Every inch of my body is covered with a sticky film of sweat, and the guilt I felt at taking so long to come for him has been replaced by a feral need for him to do it again.

And again.

And then a few more times just to make sure it wasn't a fluke.

I'm boneless, trembling all over, sagging into the bed. My pulse skips so fast I'm not sure it'll ever slow down again. He hums against my swollen clit, sending a shiver through my insides. Yeah, I've definitely never had this before. And now any man who has ever had the privilege of being between my thighs is officially being dubbed a slacker.

Did any of them ever really care whether I came or not? I'd flip back through my sexual conquests to see if I can remember them ever asking if I came, or if it was good for me—or, worse still, if I led them to believe I'd come—but I can't. My brain isn't working. I'm not sure my body is either now that I think about it.

I need my limbs to report in. My legs are still there, right? Grinding the heels of my hands into my eye sockets, I force my breathing to slow but my body isn't listening to me. It's completely focused on Justin and how he's still nestled between my thighs with no sign of moving.

When he blows on my bare pussy, I whimper. As much as I've had from him, a mind-blowing, body-shattering, life-changing orgasm, possibly two back to back, I still don't know for sure, it's not enough. It's just...not. I've tasted the forbidden fruit, and now I want the whole fucking orchard.

The idea of chaining him to my bed and making him my live-in sex slave appeals, but too many people would notice if he went missing. And at least a few of them would know where to come calling to find him.

I've had his tongue, and now the needy little bitch I am can't wait another second to have his mondo dick inside me. I sink my fingers into his hair, scratching his scalp with my nails. I'm still numb from the waist down, other than my tingling toes. My heart's thrashing around like a caged animal, and if Justin can't hear it, he probably feels it. I feel its rhythm pulsating everywhere.

When he retracts his hand, and his fingers dance along my swollen slit, it draws a guttural moan from me.

I lift my head a little so I can see him. He's still lying between my legs like he has nowhere else to be in a hurry. Like his face isn't soaked enough by my wetness. Like he hasn't tasted enough of me. Without breaking eye contact, and with painstaking commitment to the task, he sucks his fingers into his mouth and licks them clean.

My entire being is on fire, and my pussy aches for him to touch me again. My cum is literally dripping from his chin, and he's grinning at me like he's just had the first plate from a Michelin starred menu. The hunger in his eyes tells me he's nowhere near sated, that he needs more, too.

We both yank off the remainder of our clothes, and he slides up my body before hovering his mouth over mine. When his lips capture me, it's not a slow kiss, not soft or tender. It's demanding, it's consuming, it's possessive. It's like now that we've broken the seal, neither of us can get enough. It'll never be enough, not anymore.

I scratch at his—very firm and delectable—ass cheeks with my nails, and he leans into me more. I rock my hips against his as though I can guide his cock to where I need him to be while he has me pinned on the mattress.

"Tell me what you—"

"Get the fuck inside m—"

We both speak at the same time, but there's no time to laugh about it because he's already lined up at my entrance, stretching my lips around his erection.

"Protection?"

"I'm on the pill."

"My last physical was clear."

Fuck. I often forget that birth control sometimes isn't enough. There are other things than pregnancy to protect against. "I haven't been tested...but..." My face heats like a solar flare. "It's been a while." Hence the forgetting.

He cradles my head like it's precious, slides my hair back from my face, and presses a kiss to my forehead. That small act has my body at odds with itself. Part of me wants to cry from the tenderness of the moment, but the louder, more demanding part needs him to get the fuck inside me.

"I'm going to take it slow, okay?" He dots another kiss on my face as I breathe him in. "I don't want to hurt you."

I can't say I've ever tried putting a pop can in my cooter, but I know it's going to pinch.

Nodding, I say okay and hold my breath as he navigates his tip inside me. That's not so bad, I can totally take that. I let some of the air I've been holding escape on a slow sigh.

"I know you're soaking, pretty girl. But if this hurts, or we need more lubrication, I need you to tell me, okay?"

I'm so focused on trying to stay relaxed so my pussy doesn't cock-block his entry that I don't answer. I know most women say size matters, and others say it's not the size so much as what you do with it, but I'm sure there's a point at which guys get self-conscious about the size of their member, too. I'm gonna guess that super-schlong here has given Justin some issues over the years, and I really don't want to make him feel any more uncomfortable than he might already be.

"Savannah?"

"Okay." I meet his eyes and nod again. "It's all right Justin." I dig my nails deeper into his ass cheeks, as tight as it is, it's not enough. Even with the sting of being stretched around him, I need more. I'm being teased with just the tip, but I know if we go too fast we'll both get more than we bargained for.

He eases another inch or so inside me, hooking his hand around my knee and using me to help steady himself and guide himself in. His teeth are clenched, and beads of sweat trickle down his forehead.

"So fucking tight." He pulls back an inch, pushes in two more as I stretch around him with a blissful sting. His expression doesn't suggest pain, but his features are strained. His self-control is admirable. I can't imagine how much restraint it's taking for him *not* to sink all the way into me on one thrust.

It's not a quick process, and I appreciate the fact he didn't ram right in and start pounding. I'm 100% sure I'd have had friction burns and probably pussy bruises. They're a thing, right? Dudes with huge dicks can leave bruises? Justin's lightsaber could definitely bruise my lady garden.

When he's all the way inside me, buried to the hilt, we sag against each other like we've just run a marathon. His mouth is next to my ear, and every time he breathes, the heat from his breath caresses my sweat-slicked skin sending ripples of goose-flesh over my body.

Now that he's fully seated inside me, I'm never letting him leave. I've never felt so delightfully full before, and even though there's a pinch and throb of pain from being stretched around him, it's not an entirely bad ache. He shifts his hips a little and pulls a moan from me.

It's possible I'm going to come from him just being inside me. The pressure is delicious, the angle is making my toes curl, and if he moves again there's every chance I'm going to explode on his dick.

We take a minute to catch our breath. "You okay?" The concern on his face sinks deeper into my skin. His eyes skim across me like they're searching for some sign that it's not okay for him to be inside me like this, that I'm hurt or uncom-fortable.

I scrape my nails up his back, pressing them into his shoul-ders. "Don't stop. I promise I'm fine."

From the first languid stroke I know I'm going to be walking funny tomorrow, but I don't care. And I get wetter just thinking about practicing with him over and over until we don't need to go slow and he can just drive into me and make me scream.

My mouth waters, my head lolls back, and I lose myself in

the dizzying euphoria. The scent of sex fills the air and my entire body is charged with anticipation. When his hips draw back from me, I suck in a breath as he pulls his dick out of me halfway.

When he sinks back inside me, my brain malfunctions. I'm mumbling incoherent words that even I don't understand as he pulls back and repeats the motion, thrusting painfully slowly until he's balls deep.

As much as I want him to go faster, I've had razor burn on my crotch before, I know that shit's not fun. So I just lie there and take it, letting him set the pace. Eyes rolling back in my head, I fight the urge to lift my pelvis to meet his. I know it'll get easier over time, but if his huge cock hurts me somehow, he'll never forgive himself, and this needs to happen again. Repeatedly.

"Savannah." My name is a pained whisper from his lips, skimming across my shoulder and tickling my ear. Is he gritting his teeth? Poor guy's probably terrified of hurting m—

"So...close." He grunts. Bracing his forearms on either side of my face, he pushes himself up. "I know you're not close, but will you be offended if—?"

I cut him off with a kiss, a deep, passionate, stop overthinking and just *do* kiss because we're clearly both all up in our brains over this, and we need to just be in the moment and *feel*.

He thrusts all the way inside me again, my body ripples against his. With each movement he takes my breath away, giving it back to me with his kisses. My inner walls flex around him, pulsing as his cock glides in and out of me in a rhythm that's gaining speed.

He's chanting my name in my ear with such reverence and adoration I really might cry. I've never had sex with someone and felt it everywhere, from the tiny hairs on the surface of my skin right the way down to my very soul. In this moment, my entire being is connected to his, and I never want it to stop.

Our pants and moans fill the air. His hands thread into my hair as he tips his head back and a roar rips from him like a wild animal. His cock stays hard inside me, and if it wasn't for the blissed-out look on his face, I'd question whether or not he finished.

He sags on top of me, dotting languid kisses across my collarbones and up the column of my neck. I feel like a priceless treasure as he caresses my skin with a feather-light touch, and I don't realize I've started crying until his finger sweeps across the highest point of my cheekbone, collecting my tears.

His serene face changes in less than a second. A frown claims his forehead, and the edges of his lips turn downward. "Did I hurt you, pretty girl?"

Shaking my head, I suck in a deep breath filling my entire body. In fact, he may have just saved me somehow. I don't understand it, but it sounds so fucking crazy inside my sex-buzzed head that I'm afraid to say it out loud in case he flees.

I'm not ready for him to leave.

"I'm just...emotional, I guess. I've never..." I suck in another breath, urging the traitorous tears to ignore gravity and go back into my tear ducts. "I just..." Another pant. I'd really rather not have an emotional breakdown on this poor guy right after we've just done...*that*.

His face softens, and he brushes his nose against mine. "Pretty special, huh?"

I nod, rolling my lips between my teeth and blinking rapidly.

He shifts his weight, but I grab him with both hands, my nails squeeze into his skin.

"Please don't move yet."

He doesn't. Instead he kisses me so tenderly my toes prickle. If he keeps this up I'm going to want round two. I already feel like I need to prove to him that I don't cry every time I have sex. But I'm not sure I can.

It's as though being connected in all the most intimate ways allows him to reach inside my very essence and pull out all the biggest feels. Maybe when you have sex with the person you're meant to be with, you can't contain all that emotion inside you, and you're supposed to cry. I have no idea. This is my first time getting so worked up and overwhelmed by my feelings that I'm low-key freaking out.

I'm going to need to ask Hen if she's ever cried after sex before. I already know she's going to crack up.

"Hey." He pecks my nose. "Where'd you go to?"

My body's already hot, but my cheeks heat even more. "I'm wondering how I'm going to casually ask Athena if she's ever had sex so great it made her cry without her making fun of me. I think I'm screwed."

His low chuckle vibrates through my chest. "Oh, you're absolutely screwed. But I'm not worried about your tears, pretty girl. I felt it too."

Welp. There goes my heart, like a shooting star into the atmosphere.

So. Fucking. Screwed.

CHAPTER 20

Justin

I had no idea that I went to bed with Cousin IT, but when the light teases around the edges of the curtains of Savannah's dorm room and draws me into the land of the living, her hair is *everywhere*. We both kind of passed out after round two, and I'm pretty sure from the bird's nest of tangles on her head and covering her face, she's going to be pissed she didn't at least tie her hair up first.

Last night was so unexpected, so unusual, that I'm surprised by it but also not. Those feelings inside my chest about Savannah had warned me that things between us would be special. I went in knowing that it would be different, but I had no idea it would be quite like *that*.

I wasn't sure she was feeling it too until she cried, at which point it took all my self-control not to cry with her. I didn't want to freak her out or embarrass her any more than she already seemed to be.

She twists her naked body into me, her hand splaying right over my heart and her leg hooking over mine when she settles. Instead of being awkward, it's comfortable. And despite the tiny matchbox bed, I'm not teetering on the edge of the mattress, I'm not too hot, and I got a decent night's sleep. That's a big win all around.

I don't know what time it is, or where I'm supposed to be, and right now, I don't care. It's as though I've been an incomplete jigsaw puzzle my whole life, and now that I've found her, I'm finished.

She's my missing piece.

That thought should terrify me.

We're both young, with things we need to do and dreams to reach. She wants to be a teacher, studying education and math—who the hell volunteers to study math? And who the hell chooses to surround themselves with a room full of snotty nosed kids that don't even belong to her?

Not all heroes wear capes.

I mean, I want to have kids of my own someday, but the idea of being surrounded by other people's kids and teaching them math makes my stomach hurt. That's way too much pressure for one person. Or at least for me. I couldn't even teach myself math.

The tiny voice of reason and logic in the back of my brain gets louder. *You don't have time for a relationship. She'll only get in the way.*

I want to have my cake and eat it too.

But lying here, tangled up in this beautiful woman who *sees* me, I'd trade every slice of that damn cake for Savannah Bowen without hesitation.

Warning lights flicker inside my head, but my naive, hopelessly romantic heart glows brighter, drowning out the beeping. Savannah's index finger trails down my chest, circles my belly button, and finds the edges of the lines of my iliac furrow.

As her gentle touch moves lower I focus on the different names women have for a guy's magic V so I don't shoot my load all over her hand. How can she bring me so close to the edge with barely a touch? It's not like I don't get off by myself and my dick's just grossly neglected or anything.

Aphrodite's Saddle. I hiss out a breath through my teeth as my already awake and ready for action dick twitches toward her hand.

Hercules's Girdles.

She ignores the demanding dick and stays on my line. I clench my teeth, flexing my jaw.

Adonis's Belt.

She runs her finger back up to the top and starts again.

It's delicious torment. There's a bead of precum snaking down the head of my dick, and it spasms again. My breathing has quickened, and my heart skitters against my ribcage.

I went to sleep perfectly sated, content, my heart full and my balls empty. But with her naked curves flush against my side and her hand so damn close to my junk, I'm needy, desperate, aching for her to touch me and bring me to release all over again.

I lick my lips hoping I can still taste her salty-sweet. I can't, and now I don't care so much about coming as I do about tasting her again. Making her hips shake against me as I press my face into her soaking wet pussy.

My mouth watering, I roll her onto her back. I don't know if she's okay with morning-breath kisses so I graze my lips across her forehead, down her temple, along the line of her jaw and down the front of her neck.

"Good morning." Her husky morning voice has a direct line to my crotch, and my dick strains again.

"Good." I kiss her breast bone, enjoying how her body arches into my touch. "Morning." I kiss the swell of her right tit, not missing the fact her dusky nipples are already standing at attention, begging for my teeth to say hello.

And who am I to turn down such an invitation?

I skim my teeth over the perfectly pert nipple, which sends

Vannah's nails cascading down my shoulder blade and back. She's a scratcher, and I'm totally here for it.

If she didn't leave marks on my ass last night, my shoulder this morning will make up for it. Tipping my head back, a growl reverberates behind my ribs as she drags her nails into my skin leaving a trail of delicious searing burn in her wake.

I clamp my teeth down on her nipple, enjoying her sudden intake of breath before teasing it with the tip of my tongue, making her wriggle beneath me.

"Justin."

Her voice alone might push me over the edge. My cock pulses with my racing heart. It needs to be inside her again, but I can't. I don't know if she's hurting from last night, or if not sore, at least tender. And I certainly don't want to make her any worse this morning. I lick my way lazily over to the other side, ignoring the pressure building in my balls.

"How are you feeling this morning?" My words are mumbled against her skin as I continue my journey down her body, exploring her plush stomach, and the squish of her hips. She's fucking perfect.

Perfect.

"Wet." Her word escapes on a sigh as she rolls her hips, her thighs falling apart just a little. "Soaking."

I shoulder her legs farther apart, pausing a moment, taking in her glistening lips. I'm probably drooling, but I don't care. The memory of her taste, her scent, her reactions are overpowering me right now, driving me to nestle between her thighs and make her soak me with her cum once again.

"Sore?" My higher brain function has deserted me. I'm not capable of forming complete sentences. My inner caveman is in control, and at this point, he's just grunting words.

She arches again, curving her spine so her pussy lips graze the tip of my nose. "Justin...please..."

The caveman swings his club against the bars of my

ribcage, but I can't bring myself to dive in until I know for sure she's not hurting.

"Sore?"

Her pussy flexes right in front of my eyes. She did that. She made it clench to tease me, sending memories of those muscles twitching and gripping me straight to my dick.

Fuck, I'm going to ruin her sheets.

"No." Her closed fists slam against the bed on either side of her body, and I can't help but grin at her impatience. She pushes her hair off her face, blowing at it and shoving it out of her eyes. "Justin, please. Just..." She waves a hand toward her crotch. "Do...*something*. Please."

Her cheeks and chest are flushed, and part of me is tempted to lie there and tease her until she can't take another second of it. But the other, *smarter* part of me knows that if I dare tease this woman for a single minute longer, she's legitimately going to kill me, or at the very least claw my eyes out with her perfectly manicured nails.

My eyes fall closed as I trail the tip of my tongue along the slick seam of her pussy. She's every bit as delicious as I remember from the night before, and I hum so she knows just how tasty she is. I tease her lips apart with the end of my nose, dragging my tongue from her entrance all the way to her clit.

Her little bundle of nerves isn't so little this morning. It's swollen and clearly sensitive as hell because she's already writhing underneath me, and her fingers are clawing at my shoulders as she bucks her pelvis against my face.

Sliding my fingers inside her, I stretch a little, checking to see if she's really not sore at all, or if she just told me she's not in pain because she's as needy as I am and so fucking desperate to come. I stretch a little more as I suck and nibble on her clit. My free hand walks up her stomach before cupping her lush breast, palming it around, squeezing and tugging.

Her body is every bit as responsive as it was last night, and then some, but I'm not fool enough to think it's going to be any easier for me to make her come this morning.

I don't care how long it takes, I'm ready for the challenge. I brush the flat of my tongue against her clit, enjoying the little shivers it sends through her muscles. She rests her calves on my shoulders, and I slide my fingers inside. I tap on her g-spot with a single finger, in time with the sweeps of my tongue against her pussy.

"Just...in... Justin..." She's panting my name in time to the beat of my mouth and hand. "More. More fingers."

I murmur against her, my eyes fluttering open to see her head tip back as she moans my name again.

"Fill me."

I can't help the grin that spreads across my face. She had my dick twice last night, and she feels empty this morning. She wants it again.

I've never had that before.

I've had girls bitch about how uncomfortably big I am, how they can't fit me in their mouth or pussy, how I've butted up against their cervix, how I need to sort myself out with my hands.

But Savannah, my pretty girl, can't get enough.

"Justin, more." It's a command and a plea as her hips roll.

I ease all four fingers inside her, enjoying her purr as my fingertips press against her smooth, warm inner wall. She squirts at me, and I stay there, moving my fingers in tandem with my mouth as I work to stretch her, readying her for my cock.

Her body tenses as I tuck my thumb to move it inside, but she demands I don't stop. She grunts as my whole hand curls into a fist inside her.

"Y-yes. Y-yes. More. Harder, Justin."

I love that my girl is so fucking vocal, telling me what she wants, what she needs.

I move my fist, slowly, letting her adjust to the presence of my whole hand inside her. Her walls flutter against my knuckles, gripping me like she might never let me go. I'm okay with that.

She's soaking, my face is soaking, my arm is soaking, I'm sure the sheet under her ass is probably soaking too, and her breath is coming in sharp pants again. That's when I know I have her.

"Harder, Justin. I'm not fucking fragile."

I snort into her pussy. Fragile is not something I'd ever have called her, but knowing she wants more from me makes it really hard to hold back. I thrust my fist in deeper, enjoying her mewls and moans as her hips lift off the bed. I lap at her like a man starved, but it's not enough.

I can't take it anymore. I need to be inside her. I need those rippling muscles to clench around my dick, not my fist. I try to ease my hand out without hurting her, but I'm wobbling on the edge of my patience, and I just need to act.

She whimpers when her squelching pussy releases my hand, but before she can suck in a breath to protest, I'm upright on my knees, her heels on my shoulders, and my cock is halfway inside her.

She reaches a hand down toward her pussy, but I swat her away.

"If you want to play with something, play with your nipples. Your pussy is mine."

I'm pretty sure she says "fuck" but I'm too busy reaching for her clit. It's not easy and I might have to dislocate my shoulder to make it work, but I'm not letting this woman bring herself over the line while I'm inside her. Not this time at least.

It's less than a minute before she detonates like a grenade with the pin pulled. She didn't come on my cock last night so I didn't have the exquisite pleasure of feeling the vise-like grip of her pussy around my dick when her release hit. She squirts again when she comes, I feel it, I hear it, I see it, but only for a split second because I'm pretty sure the muscles of her pussy are controlling the flow of oxygen to my brain.

The base of my spine tingles. She's twisting her nipples, pinching them between her fingers and thumbs, eyes rolled back in her head and meeting me thrust for thrust as I smack my hips against her, bracing her against me with my forearm banded across her shins.

My body goes limp as I come, my orgasm rolling through every muscle. The anticipation of my own demanding release was consuming, but now that I'm spilling inside her, I realize it was her orgasm I was chasing far more than my own.

It took every bit as long this morning to make her come as it did last night, and it was every bit as worth it, too.

She smiles up at me. "You okay?"

I've never seen a more beautiful woman. Her cheeks are rosy, her chest is pink and flushed, and her eyes are heavy like she might fall back to sleep despite the fact her legs are still bolt upright in the air. Her hair is wild, and her skin has a sheen of sweat glistening in the morning light.

I'm breathless. This woman has literally stolen the oxygen from my body. How can I tell her how I feel without sounding like I'm a stage five clinger? Her pussy still hasn't released my dick. And while I'm not complaining, we're locked here, just staring at each other. I find myself wanting to crawl inside her mind to see what she's thinking right now.

She has to feel this too, right?

It's so out of the norm for me that it can't be one sided. She parts her legs and drops them onto the bed with a soft thud. When I pull my hips back, she narrows her eyes. "Don't you fucking dare. Not yet."

"Yes, ma'am." I give her a quick salute before leaning over her body and stealing a kiss from her. Her position on morning breath no longer matters because I need to kiss her. I need to pour some of this emotion welling inside me into her so she can feel it too. If she doesn't already.

Her arms don't move to wrap around my neck or shoulders. Her legs are now flat on the bed, not on my shoulders or curled around my waist. And she's not digging her nails into my butt cheeks as we kiss, so I pull back, searching her face for signs she's not okay. She's lying like a limp starfish, her hands and feet hanging off the edge of the bed.

Her sheepish smile softens my hardening insides. "I don't have the use of my limbs quite yet." She jerks her chin at me. "Continue, though."

I burst out laughing. My girl is bossy as fuck even when she can't move. Should I tell her I'm falling for her? Right now, with my cock still buried deep inside her velvety prison? Her legs don't work so she can't haul ass and run away from me.

Until her muscles stop contracting around me and let me go, I'm stuck right here. Do I risk having that awkward moment hanging over us while waiting for her pussy to unlock and release my dick?

She covers both ears with flat palms. "Can you keep the noise down please? Your thoughts are hurting my delicate sensibilities."

My chuckle shifts my dick inside her, and she moans. I feel like she might need an ice pack for her vagina. Do they make those? Are there enough dudes out there hung like in those monster porn books that would require such a thing to exist?

She's still staring at me as I lower myself to kiss her again, but she shifts her head so my lips graze her cheek. "You wanna talk about it?"

I heave out a sigh, and her nipples skim my chest. Fuck. I can't get enough of this woman. I don't want her pussy to let go of my cock. Ever. I live here now.

"That's what I've been trying to decide."

She flexes her muscles around my dick, and it's my turn to moan. She's milked every single drop of cum from me, and I'm damn near ready to fill her up all over again. I want to cover her skin, to come all over her stomach. She's like a sun-kissed blank canvas, and I ache to paint her with my release.

Maybe later. She's staring at me expectantly. I need to say something before she assumes it wasn't good for me.

I drag a hand through my hair and lean up, making us both shiver when my cock moves inside her again. "I...don't know that this is the right time."

She curls her arms behind my neck and pulls me to her for another kiss. "Tell me anyway."

"I think I'm falling for you Savannah Jane. I think I'm falling for you hard."

I feel her lips curve into a smile against my shoulder before she dots three kisses along the space where my neck and shoulder meet. "Good. We can fall togeth —aaaaaaaaaaaaaaaaaaaaaaaagh."

She bolts off the bed, our foreheads colliding as she sits upright.

Fuck. That's not quite how I thought that would go.

CHAPTER 21

Savannah

Pain rips through my abdomen, and I can't fight the wail that falls from my lips. I've never had trapped gas so bad in my entire life, and I don't want Justin to be here when it finally breaks free.

"You should go."

His face morphs from concern, probably that he broke me with his huge dick, to straight up mad. "I'm not leaving you." He shakes his head.

"But..." I can't force the words from my mouth. Even the thought of saying the word fart in front of him is making me perspire. "I think it's just gas." My voice is barely a whisper, and I want the ground to open up and swallow me. It's not gas making me feel sick, it's the mortification of telling Justin I need to let one rip.

Another sharp pain tears through my body, and I roll to my side, tucking my legs as close to my chest as I can.

His warm hand meets my back and rubs in circles like I'm a baby. It's kind of nice. "Then you should feel better pretty quickly. A couple of farts and you'll be good as new." His voice says he doesn't believe me, but he doesn't push it. At least not yet. "You want me to get some Pepto?"

"I have Tums in the bathroom."

The mattress shifts as he stands and circles the bed, grumbling something about my tiny bathroom, and another wave of pain passes through my body. I don't think this is gas. And once the urge to puke passes again, I'm wondering if I might need to get rid of Justin so I can hit up the Urgent Care a couple blocks from my dorm room.

I must fall back to sleep. Stabbing discomfort in my gut wakes me up, and I curl into as tight a ball as I can. Justin's back on the bed with me, still rubbing my back, shushing me and telling me that it's all going to be okay, but it's time to go see a doctor.

I don't think I can argue with him.

"Vannah, you've been moaning in your sleep for over an hour. I really don't think this is gas."

I nod. My skin is clammy. I'm not convinced that I'm safe from puking or crapping my pants in front of this man. If I get to Urgent Care and they tell me I need to go home and fart, I'm going to be so fucking mad.

"As someone who has farted on this earth for almost twenty one years I can safely say, it's never looked like that. Want me to call your mom?"

I shake my head, clutching my stomach like it might fall out of my body if I don't press against it.

He helps me sit up in bed, brings me clothes to put on, and when I get light headed from bending down to put my shoes on, he does that for me too. Even in my agony-haze I'm aware of how sweet and amazing Justin is being, and if I wasn't using all my energy to keep from throwing up, I'd kiss him where he stands...or rather crouches in front of me like Prince Charming putting Cinderella's glass slipper back on.

When I stand up, the pain gets worse. I want to lie back

down on the bed and not move. Moving is bad. Very bad. It's like I've been winded, and as he leads me to the door, with his solid arm banded around me, I'm consciously forcing breath into my body to try to breathe through the pain.

Justin grabs my coat and purse on the way to the door. The level of consideration and attention he pays to me would make me weep if I wasn't already weeping. I cling to him as we make our way outside. Fuck, it hurts.

When I stumble, he catches me, and those forearms flex making my mouth water. I know it's not the time, but there's nothing swoonier than a hot as hell guy taking care of someone, and when I'm that someone... Well, let's just say that between stabs of pain in my abdomen, I'm wishing to go back to bed.

I frown at him when he stops at the car and jerks the door open. "It's only a few blocks, we can wa—agh." I fold over at the waist and clutch the offending part of my body. What the hell is wrong with me? Is this how death feels? Did he break me with his penis?

He doesn't even grace me with an answer, just a look, a look that says, "Don't fight me and get in the damn car, Savannah Jane."

So I do.

When he pulls up outside the emergency room a few minutes later, I shift in the seat. This isn't urgent care. I want to argue with him and tell him it's not this bad, but it totally feels this bad. I want to tell him to leave, that I've totally got this by myself, but he's already out of the driver's side and running around the car.

He helps me out, and we're facing each other on the sidewalk. I open my mouth to tell him to go but his finger lands on my lips. "Don't. Just don't. I don't want to leave, and I don't think you really want me to either."

He's not wrong.

When we're inside, we get checked in, and I'm handed a clipboard. Justin surfs on his phone while I fill in the information and try to swallow my howls of pain each time a jag of pain strikes. I know I'm not pregnant, but could this be what labor pains feel like? If so, I'm tapping out right here before it ever happens. This level of pain isn't for me, even if you do get a bundle of joy on the other end.

"Want me to distract you?"

I nod, sliding down in my seat, still clutching my stomach, and rest my head on his shoulder. I'm cold, in more pain than I've ever been in my entire life, and too fucking stubborn to call my mom. She's going to be pissed at me for not telling her I'm sick, but it could still be nothing, and I don't want to worry her.

That's what I'll tell her. That I didn't want to worry her over a little stomach pain. I almost snort at my own lie. It feels like someone's stabbing my insides with a red-hot poker, and I don't even fully understand why I don't want to call my mom in this moment.

Is it because I'm still upset at her for keeping my adoption from me for so long? Is it because I don't want to give her any reason to unadopt me?

Is unadopting a thing? Can they put me back on the shelf like a defective toy?

Fuck. I haven't been the best child to them since I found out over the summer, and ultimately, I'm officially an adult so I'm supposed to be strong and capable and able to make it out in the world by myself.

Fly, baby bird, fly.

I struggle to wear matching underwear, never mind adulting like a real grown up, and I'm supposed to fly solo?

What a terrifying fucking thought.

"You wanna talk about books?"

I smile through my misery, giving him another nod. We

spend the next twenty five minutes playing something Justin calls the three books game. I think he made it up just to distract me which just makes me swoon even harder.

So far we've each picked a book that we love and want the other to read. And we've also picked a book we think encapsulates the personality of each other, something we think the other would enjoy reading.

Justin's keeping notes on his phone, I'm pretty sure he's dropping the books into his Amazon cart as a reminder to pick them up at work, or order them if we don't have them when he's next on shift.

We're on the third thing, each picking a book to buddy read together, when my name is called. The hard stare Justin gives me suggests he's not going to let me tell him to leave, and I'm torn. The strong, independent, twenty-year-old-boss-bitch wants to push back and tell him I'm fine and can do it all by my big girl self. But the rest of me could cry with relief because I'm not completely sure that I can.

What if something's really wrong with me?

The doctor examines me and sends me for an ultrasound. The ultrasound tech makes a joke about the carb-heavy dinner I must have had the night before, and my simmering embarrassment rears its head again.

Justin makes jokes about how much he loves pie while the very nice nurse lady gives me a shot of something to take the edge off. Turns out she doesn't just mean the pain, the meds take the edge off *everything*.

The whole room gets a little fuzzy as the cool liquid injected into my arm spreads around my body making me care just a little less about *everything*.

I think I'm slipping in and out of consciousness. My nose is itchy but my fingers don't care enough to scratch it. Did she cure my pain with that shot? Did I just need some morphine and now I'm good?

I'm staring at Justin, wondering if he's a figment of my imagination. Is that why he's being so amazing? Because he's the book boyfriend dreams are made of, conjured from the depths of my own mind?

His smile is strained, concerned, I guess he was hoping I needed to fart, too. His smile widens and I realize I spoke out loud, but I think I'm too buzzed to care right now.

He shifts his chair closer to my bed and strokes my hair. "Yeah, pretty girl. I was hoping you just needed to fart. I don't think you realize just how much it sucks seeing you in pain." He rubs at his chest like he's the one with indigestion.

That's sweet. I make a mental note to come back to that when I'm not in a drugged haze. I suck in a deep breath, expecting the stabbing to start over in my belly, but it doesn't. Are we sure she gave me morphine and not some magic potion? She did kind of look a bit like Ginny Weasley.

Justin smiles again like he can read my thoughts, but my mouth is moving so maybe I'm mumbling them all out loud and making it easy for him. I'm still not sure I care.

I dunno how long I lie there dozing, but when I wake up to the doctor making his way into the room Justin is typing frantically on his phone. What the hell is he doing? Writing a damn novel? I'm not sure I'd want to be on the receiving end of the text making him frown so hard.

He tucks away his phone and stands when the doctor approaches. That's weird, right? Is he just being polite? I tap the tip of my tongue against my lip, just to make sure it's still there. The doctor's talking to me, and I should probably listen to what he's saying but now that I know my tongue is still there, I just want Justin to kiss me.

From the redness splotching his cheeks I'd guess I said that out loud again. I'm probably going to care about that when this truth serum wears off.

A different doctor comes in and tells me I have gallstones,

and an inflamed gallbladder and need surgery to remove it. Not right this second, but within the next week or so. He also says I don't fit the typical four-F profile for someone to get gallstones, I'm not fat, over forty, or fertile—as in having recently given birth to a child, though I am the fourth, female. So he's going to run some more tests to make sure there's nothing sinister or underlying.

Sounds good to me. I mean, right now he could tell me he's taking a chainsaw to my stomach and I'd nod and smile. Those were some damn good drugs.

He gives me a business card to call and schedule my surgery, but Justin reaches out and intercepts.

"I'm not sure we should let you operate heavy machinery just yet, pretty girl."

I do love it when he calls me that.

The doctor also gives me a script for Vicodin, because even if the pain goes away for a while, he says it'll come back. He also said not to wait too long to schedule surgery because sometimes the gallstones shift and can block my bile duct and make more of a mess.

That's not at all scary, nope.

Justin asks if I'd like him to call to schedule the surgery for me, and by the time he gets me back to my building, I have an appointment for Friday, four days from now, and he has picked up my prescription from the drive through pharmacy on campus.

Except I'm not back at my building. The car is idling outside the hockey house. Why are we at the hockey house?

"You're staying with me tonight, Vannah. And I really need you to not fight me on that. I want to take care of you and make sure you have everything you need overnight. I can bring you to Athena's if you'd rather, but you're staying with someone."

Hen's penthouse apartment is really high up, and while

there's an elevator to save me from the five million stairs, Justin's bed is way closer right now and that's a lot more appealing than driving across town.

Hen. Oh, fuck. She's going to kill me for not telling her I'm sick.

"What's it going to be, pretty girl?"

I can't stay with him for four days and nights. I'm going to be in pain, and grumpy, and I'm going to be not so fun to live with. At this point I'm not even sure I can squat to use the restroom.

But his bed is *right there* just a short walk inside the building.

"Can I stay today with you and maybe I can move to Hen's tomorrow?" I sag against the seat. "I'm just so damn tired, Justin."

A single nod is the only reply I get. He taps the screen of his phone, and a few seconds later one of his teammates comes outside pushing a wheelchair with a pig tottering along behind him.

I'm not sure if I'm hallucinating the pig, or the chair, maybe both, but I can't help giggling at the bizarre sight. Justin doesn't even let me try to get out of the vehicle by myself—he sweeps me up in his arms and sets me down with care and precision.

As he walks, he's saying something about how there's almost always someone injured and they have a whole hoard of medical equipment on hand if I ever find myself needing a wheelchair again.

I really should just go back to my dorm room, but that's future Vannah's problem. Right now I just need to lie down and sleep until things aren't quite so fuzzy.

The hockey house is eerily quiet as Justin pushes me through the foyer. He carries me upstairs, ignoring my protests, and I'm kind of glad about that because that was way too many stairs for me to amble up. I'd probably have broken something else.

The drapes in his room have been pulled closed, there's a lamp switched on next to the bed, and there's a bottle of cold water sitting next to a menu.

"I didn't have time to track down some soup yet, but if you want to pick something from the menu I can head out to The Sandwich Squad and grab it."

Is Ares de la Peña offering to get me soup? I have to be making this up in my head. It has to be a dream, because Ares de la Peña doesn't even get himself soup. He has minions to do that for him. Many, many, usually very naked minions if the reports are accurate.

Justin tucks me into bed, tugs his quilt right up to my chin, and drops a kiss on my forehead. I don't know if he plans to leave or not, but I grab his hand and try to ask him to stay before I pass back out.

CHAPTER 22
Justin

"Ares says there's a beautiful woman in your bed." Scott offers me a beer despite the fact it's not after 5pm anywhere in the continental United States. I nod and accept it, but don't take a drink.

"So why are you down here in the den while there's a beautiful woman in your bed?"

"She's sick. I was up there for a couple hours, but she had her pain meds and crashed. She's going to be out for a while. I needed to eat and call Athena."

As though speaking her name summoned her through a portal from another dimension, the door to the house squeaks open and the femme fatale de la Peña appears, the winter sun already setting behind her.

Apollo is in the foyer kicking a soccer ball back and forth with Tate. The siblings look at each other as though they're both out of place, which is kind of true. Neither of them live here, and while all three of her brothers can often be found in the hockey house, this is one of the few times she's ever visited.

"Are you looking for me?" Apollo's confused head-tilt morphs right there in front of me to wide-eyed fear like he's racking his brain for whatever it is he's done to deserve a house call from his sister.

She might be the only de la Peña sibling without a peen, and the boys might be beyond protective of her, but she can chill the blood in your veins with only a look.

She barely shakes her head. "Justin."

I know I'm not in trouble, but my balls shrivel up at her mention of my name all the same. Apollo jerks his chin toward the den and follows his sister toward me.

"Where is she?"

I bounce up to my feet. I dunno why, but standing eye to eye when you're talking to someone has always been deemed polite where I come from. "She's upstairs, out cold on pain meds. She had some chicken noodle soup earlier." For some reason I feel like I need to give props where they're due and not take the credit here. "Ares picked it up for her."

Yeah, that twitch of surprise she barely manages to smooth away from her features is exactly why I mentioned his name.

"He did?"

I nod.

"Why didn't you bring her to my place?" She waves an open palm toward the now six hockey players standing around us both. I bet those fuckers came in 'cause they thought she was going to barbecue my balls for something and they wanted a rink-side seat. "It's hardly quiet here."

This was the question I'd been waiting to be asked. I'm not sure if Vannah has told her best friend we're a thing, and I haven't yet told the guys. Not for any bad reason, I was just giving us time without inflicting an entire hockey team of protective big brothers on her shoulders. They can be a *lot*.

Why are my palms sweating?

I don't break eye contact. Athena can smell fear, and when she does she goes straight for the jugular.

"I wanted her close."

Her eyes narrow.

Heaving out a sigh, I shrug. "I just didn't want to take my girlfriend all the way across town, okay? I'm worried about her, and I figured we have lots of hands to help here at the hockey house if she needs something. And at least four of us have your number in case we needed to call you."

No one moves or speaks, I'm pretty sure all my teammates are holding their collective breath. She pulls a business card from her purse. What college kid carries a friggin' business card?

She hands it to Tate and tells him to put it on the refrigerator in case anyone needs to call about Savannah. Then she makes sure to warn anyone in ear shot that if her number ends up on a bathroom wall, or being used for something that isn't reporting on her best friend, heads will roll.

Athena folds her arms and takes a measured step toward me. "What are your intentions with my bestie?"

There's a snort, likely from Apollo or Ares, glad his sister is directing her attention to someone other than him for a change.

What are my intentions? My heart is lying upstairs next to her in bed, but I have no fucking clue how to make it work when the other pieces of my life are so demanding. Her surgery is already slated for game day. How can I tell her that I need to leave her in the hospital by herself to get cut open while I go play a game?

My heart crosschecks my brain and takes the lead. "I love her, Athena. I'm in with both skates."

That draws a slow eye roll from her, but she's smiling. "You know if you hurt her..."

My head is already bobbing up and down. "You'll kill me, I know." I'm acutely aware that Athena de la Peña probably has the connections to make me disappear forever without so much as chipping the paint on her nails.

"I don't care if my brothers love you. I don't care if you're team captain. If you break my girl's heart, I will break you." She's pointing her index finger at me now, and I'm pretty sure my teammates, my brothers in arms, my ride-or-die friends have all taken a very large step back from me.

Assholes.

Still trapped in some intense stare-down with the eldest de la Peña, I chance a blink or two, then a third. "Athena, I have no intention of hurting your best friend. The opposite in fact."

Her eyes narrow again like she wants to say something else but isn't sure she should.

"Whatever it is, just say it."

"I've heard things." The finger is wagging at my face now.

I fold my arms, determined not to let that old hurt break open in my chest again. "They're not true."

She jerks her head back. "Does she know that?"

My face burns. I still haven't gotten around to telling her my side of the story yet. I haven't really known how to approach the "Hey, your high school bestie was wrong" discussion.

"You might want to deal with that." She regards me for what feels like a solid twenty minutes, but it can't possibly be more than a few seconds 'cause that would just be weird. "What's your plan for when she wakes up?"

This question I'm ready for. I've spent every free minute I've had since her diagnosis at the hospital earlier Googling what the hell to do to make her feel better. "Rookie's on his way back from the store with provisions. We're going to set up this room like a theater and watch a couple of her favorite movie adaptations from books."

I hadn't gotten around to telling the guys this yet, but I already know none of them will mind. "The guys can hang out too, if Savannah is okay with it."

Athena hasn't slapped me yet, and she makes a "go on" gesture, so I take that to mean I'm not going to die just yet.

"Raffi's going to cook her something low fat for dinner. The guys are going to have pizza, so they're going to have it while she's asleep, or in another room, so she doesn't feel like she's missing out. If she wants movie snacks, we have fruit and popcorn, again low fat so it doesn't hurt her too badly."

"You've done your homework."

That might be as close to a compliment from Athena as I'm going to get, so I just nod. She's such an impressive woman that on one hand it's hard to fathom how she's not in a relationship yet, and on the other, she probably terrifies potential suitors. Few people could stack up to her family name, but add in, well, *Athena*, and it's an impossible task to scale for anyone.

"What are your movie options?"

This is like a pop quiz. Which is ridiculous because if I wanted things to be long-term with Savannah I should have probably expected the inquisition from her best friend.

"I have a short list. *Me Before You, Twilight, Fifty Shades.*" I know my girl is a sucker for sparkly vamps and kinky billionaires. "*The Hating Game* and *After.*"

"And if she wants to stay upstairs?"

"Scott has a tray for her to eat dinner in bed, and I'll play the movies on Raffi's laptop 'cause his is faster than mine. She doesn't have to move." Am I sweating?

"How does she get downstairs if she's in pain?"

"Same way she got up there." It's possible I puff my chest out a little.

"You carried her? That's kind of adorable. I'm sure she loved that. What if she wants to leave?"

I can't help but snort. "She's not a prisoner here, Athena. I want to take care of her, not chain her to the—" Oh God.

Her eyebrows shoot up and more than one of my teammates are fighting back laughter. Someone mutters, "At least not until she's recovered."

I'm going to kill them all.

Athena purses her lips as though fighting back a smile. "I have an elevator." She says that like it's the answer to all of Savannah's problems. "And I live closer to the hospital where she's getting her surgery."

"Are you prepared to have a hockey player come live in your apartment for a while?" It's really the only option. If she wants to claim best friend privileges and move Savannah into her penthouse, then I'm going with.

Someone around me sucks in an audible breath.

She nods. And something in my chest cracks open. I feel like I've won big, and the urge to dance out my victory is strong. I mean, living with Athena de la Peña isn't exactly on my bucket list, but knowing she's cool with it is all I need to hear.

Her focus on me is laser precise. "Did you call her parents?"

Fuck. Checkmate. I shift my weight from one foot to the other, finally drawing my eyes from her piercing glare. I'd like a different question please.

"Huh." She drops down onto the couch and indicates for me to do the same. This isn't good. It means she's not leaving yet, and there's only so much grilling I can stand up to.

"Did she ask you to call her mom?"

Don't move, don't breathe, don't give her any reason to think you—

"You went behind her back to tell her parents?" She groans, then her shoulders start shaking and the couch vibrates. She throws her head back, laughing so hard tears are literally spilling down her cheeks.

It's not like her assumptions are wrong. I texted the

Bowens from the emergency room and kept them up to date with Savannah's progress, even though she asked me not to.

"Does she know you told them?"

More silence from me, more laughter from her, and one of the guys releases a slow hiss. Yeah, he knows I'm fucked, too.

"Are they coming here?"

They said they'll be here Friday for her surgery. I might even have helped them sort out accommodation close by. Yeah, I was pretty busy while Vannah took her first of twenty cat naps earlier. And of course Athena knows despite me keeping my mouth shut. Dammit.

"You were doing so well." Athena sits up and pats my chest. "It's been nice knowing you, Justin. You might want to say your goodbyes to your boys, because when she finds out about this, I'm going to be the least of your problems."

My stomach sinks. So Savannah said she didn't want to tell her parents, but that's what we all say, right? We don't want to bother them with something small. Except abdominal surgery isn't small, and by the time she's being wheeled into surgery and decides she wants her parents by her side, it'll be too late to get them here in time.

I needed to act. I know she's upset with her folks for keeping the truth from her about her adoption, but creating more space between them isn't going to do any of them any good.

I did the right thing. I did.

"Did you, though?" Athena's expectant face softens with sympathy? Pity? Something that doesn't feel great.

I must have said that last part out loud. I'm clearly spending too much time with Savannah and her habits are rubbing off on me. I nod, firm in my decision to contact my girlfriend's family without her permission. "I did. Surgery isn't a small deal. I read up on this one, the potential complications... And while chances are she'll be fine, there's always the possibility that things could go wrong on the table."

"You should probably tell her you told her parents and they're coming."

"You're not going to tell her?"

Athena rolls her eyes again. "If I wanted to destroy your relationship, sure. I'd go tell her you ratted her out to her parents. But she likes you, and she was starting to trust you. I don't want to be the one to ruin that for her, for either of you. You need to get ahead of this, and tell her when she wakes up."

I don't know if this is an olive branch from the ice queen, or if she's toying with me and this is some kind of blood sport so she can watch Savannah pull my body apart with her teeth.

"Can I at least wait until after the popcorn?"

It's the worst trope in the book. Miscommunication. I know in my heart I should have been upfront with her, about my past, about my career, and now about her parents. It's like a snowball gathering size as it rolls downhill, and the only way to stop it is to lie in its path and let it crash into me.

How did I even get here? Reading miscommunication tropes in romance novels is so frustrating that I try hard not to write them. Yet here I am living the damn thing.

When I read it, it seems so easy. *"Just tell her,"* you scream at the pages, wanting to smack the hero's head with the girthy paperback of their love story. But here, now, living it, breathing it? I get it. The fear of putting your truth out there for the person you love, to see, is fucking terrifying. Especially when it directly contradicts everything she believes about you, or has the power to destroy everything you've built between you both. Yeah, I totally get it now.

Athena's glare cuts straight through my chest. She doesn't need to answer. "I'm gonna split, but I'll stay local in case she wants to leave."

My stomach sinks further. This really isn't good. I kept

the truth from her, about my career, about her parents, about everything. She's already mad at everyone else in her life, and she's not going to care that I didn't technically lie to her.

It no longer really matters that I love her, because all she's going to hear when I tell her the truth is that I lied to her, just like her parents did.

And then I'm going to lose her.

CHAPTER 23
Savannah

I need everyone to join me in wishing a huge get well soon to one of our own this week, Trash Panda fans. Tittle-tattle tells me that the girlfriend of our beloved captain, Justin Ashe, is having surgery today while the team heads to Kansas City for a double header against the Cyclones. We're all thinking of you, Savannah. Hit me up if you need anything!

I don't know whether I'm honored to be mentioned in this week's *Trash Can Tattle with Tabitha,* impressed at her sleuthing skills, or grumpy at the invasion of my privacy. But now anyone who reads the weekly column by the secretive hockey journalist knows I'm going under the knife. It's not a bad thing that people know, it's just, I kind of wish she didn't make it sound like I was getting a nose job, you know?

I assume it's a "she" anyway. In reality I have no idea, none of us do. We could be being cat-fished by one of the team, or even an opposing team for all we know. "Tabitha" could be anyone, and while her weekly column gives me serious Lady Whistledown vibes from *Bridgerton*, I'm not thrilled to be mentioned in it. As helpful as it is for hockey newbies with all the technical information they need to learn the game, it's a gossip column, and I hate being the subject matter for *tittle-tattle*.

I groan. It's not *Tabitha* I'm grumpy at, it's myself. I told him I'd be fine. I had no idea just how not-fine I'd be until just this second. I mean, I had my suspicions of course. I'm sitting in a hospital bed ahead of my "very minor and every day surgery." While a laparoscopic cholecystectomy might be an everyday procedure for the surgeon and the surgical team, it's *not* an everyday occurrence for me.

I'm not too proud to admit that I'm freaking the fuck out right now. Until today I couldn't even spell cholecystectomy. But there was nothing else to do other than tell him I'd be fine. I couldn't exactly tell him, "Hey, Justin, can you abandon your brothers, your game, and your life's work to sit at my bedside and hold my hand this weekend because I'm a big fat scaredy cat?"

I mean, I wanted to. Obviously. And right now I'm kind of wishing I had. But I shouldn't have had to, right? I mean, surely if he wanted to stay and hold my hand he would have, no matter what I said to him. Because that's what people do for the people they love. They're there for them when they need them most.

I know I'm going in circles. And I hate it.

Anxiety brings out the worst in me sometimes, and while I'm often aware of the cycle I'm caught in, there's often no way to stop it all from rolling around inside my head.

I don't like being scared. I don't think horror movies are the shit, I hate being home alone in a dark house, and sometimes I manage to scare the crap out of myself even if I'm the only one around. I have an over active imagination which loves to play tricks on me. Even the Goosebumps books gave me the creeps as a kid.

It's why I read romance novels and not psychological thrillers. I read a Patricia Cornwell novel once, followed by a

Kathy Reichs book the next day. Then I didn't sleep right for almost a week. I was tempted to light the books on fire to purge the scary from my life, but instead, after a brief book time out in my freezer, I just donated them to a women's shelter to let someone else deal with the bad guys.

I'm acutely aware of all the things that could go wrong in my surgery, and all the traits and genetic conditions I could have from my birth mom. I Googled. The list of possibilities is endless, every single inherited disease, disorder, anomaly, and mutation. This list could fill a notebook.

"Savannah?"

I'm pretty sure they haven't given me the good drugs yet and those two people standing in the doorway of my room are my parents, but I blink a few times just in case I'm imagining they're here.

"Mom?"

She nods and shuffles just enough inside the room that Dad can close the door behind her.

"What are you doing here?" I fold my arms. I'm not sure if it's to hide the fact my hands are shaking or to let her know I'm still sort of mad at them right now or even to stop myself reaching for her. Maybe it's all three. Inside my chest the anxiety and tension I've been holding for days unfurls just a little and I'm kind of mad about that, too.

Her face scrunches into a frown like my question makes no sense. "You're having surgery, honey. Why wouldn't we be here? Planes were grounded or we'd have been here sooner."

I huff out a breath at her confronting me with logic right now. I'm torn inside. I want my parents here for this big scary thing, sure. Of course I do. But there's a part of me—a really big and potentially irrational part of me—that is super pissed at them.

What else might be wrong with me? I know nothing

about my genetics, my birth parents, their family history, or what health skeletons lie in that closet.

I've spent my life thinking that Mom's anxiety, Dad's mom's high blood pressure, and my mom's great grandfather's diabetes were the only things I had to worry about getting when I'm older. And now I'm faced with a black abyss of uncertainty.

"How did you know I was having surgery?"

They both blush. I know exactly where they heard it from. Athena wouldn't have called them without my express consent, and now I'm not only pissed at Justin Ass for not being here, I'm pissed at him for ratting me out to my folks.

Seems I'm pissed at pretty much everyone.

Pissed and scared.

Scared and pissed.

I hate it. I'm usually a pretty live-and-let-live kind of girl. I mean, other than the years of hate I harbored in my heart for Justin breaking my girl Molly's heart, I'm pretty chill. With Athena as a best friend there's only so much space in our friendship for savage, and she makes up like 92% of it.

Right now, in this pre-op moment of terror, I'm a ball of negative emotional energy, and I have no clue what to do with it.

Dad shifts his weight, reminding me they haven't answered where they heard about my surgery.

"Mom?"

"He was only trying to help."

"He." She clearly doesn't want to say his name, like somehow that'll make me madder, or make his betrayal worse. I don't know whether to laugh or cry, though I'm hysterical enough to do both so I bite down on my lip to avoid both.

I open my mouth to chew them out, to let go of some of the anger that has my insides tangled up in knots when the door opens and an attractive nurse walks in with Athena behind him.

"Sorry I'm late, I got caught up." She waves a scrap of paper which probably has the hot nurse's number on it, like it explains everything. "Mr. and Mrs. Bowen. You're here!" She steps forward and hugs Mom, casting me a wary glance over Mom's shoulder, and when she hugs Dad, she mouths the words "not it" to me.

I nod and mouth back that I know.

I was ready to lay out my issues with my folks, but the hottie nurse is here to take me to surgery and suddenly I don't really care about all that crap anymore. I could die in surgery, and the dramatics have kicked in.

Fine, there's a less than one percent chance of me dying in this surgery but that's still way higher than I'd like it to be. So I give both my parents a hug, reassuring my tearful Mom that I'll be fine and she shouldn't worry, and I tell them both that I love them. Because I really fucking do.

Hen snaps a selfie from the foot of my bed with me in the background. I'm scowling at her and have a mesh bonnet over my hair for surgery. Ten bucks says that picture is for future bribery purposes.

I'm whisked away into the operating room, and my stomach clenches when they tell me to breathe the anesthesia in deep and count backwards from ten.

Ten.

I tell myself I'm going to wake up. Twice.

Nine.

When I do wake up, I'm going to hug Justin for calling my parents, and then smack him for doing the same.

Eight.

Justin is so pretty.

"Are you sure you're going to be okay here without us?" Mom gnaws on the nail on her index finger.

I nod and shift myself higher in the bed, letting out a low groan.

"She'll be fine here, Mrs. B." Athena pastes a reassuring smile on her face. She's good with parents.

I'm still not sure how I got from the car up to her apartment after my surgery on Friday. I feel like she has minions who might have carried me, but I can't be sure. It's kind of hazy.

"I'll take good care of her. I promise to call if there are any complications."

Mom nods. It's the third time we've been through this. She doesn't want to leave, and honestly, I have no idea why. I've been nothing but bitchy to her since I woke up. We haven't talked, and right now I don't want to.

I don't want the words that fall from my lips to be impacted by the pain searing through my body, or made blurry by Vicodin.

"Justin gets back today, right? He'll probably call to check if you need anything."

It seems that at some point since I started dating Justin, Mom and Dad discovered that the sun shines out of Justin's ass. They know he cheated on Molly, and they put it down to being a dumb adolescent in high school. They think he's changed, and it's all part of growing up.

I think that's part of why I haven't confronted them about keeping my adoption secret for all this time. I don't want to hear some lame excuse about how they thought they were protecting me somehow.

I sigh, even that hurts. "Yes, Mom. Justin will be back in a few hours." I press my hand against my collarbone. It's as though there's a knife lodged under it, and I don't know why since my gallbladder and my collarbone aren't even close to each other. "I really will be okay."

I'm in a penthouse apartment with a woman who thrives on taking care of those she loves. There's a reason I call her Hen, and it's not just because it's in her name. Though she denies it, the eldest de la Peña sibling is a mother hen. The biggest problem we'll have over the coming weeks is arguing over which of her favorite bougie cafes to order chicken noodle soup from.

After another painful squish from Mom and a kiss to the forehead from Dad they leave, taking a chunk of my anxiety along with them.

"Time for meds?" Hen holds out two Vicodin and a glass of water.

"That bad, huh?"

"I mean, I'm not saying you're a bitch, but two of my neighbors have put their apartments up for sale because of the crabby lady on the eighteenth floor of the building."

I clutch my midsection as I laugh. "I'm sorry. I just... I don't know how to talk to them right now. They kept this huge thing from me, and I'm scared about what that means. I don't even know if Sophia knew before me. And I know they don't treat us any differently but all these thoughts are playing around in my head."

Hen gestures her hand at me again. "Let narcotics take the edge off for now, and when you're better we can look at getting you someone to talk to. A professional."

She's right. I can't pick through this emotional dumpster fire all by myself. I swallow the pills with the entire glass of water and try to get comfy before sleep takes me.

When I wake up, it's dark out. I don't know how long has passed. The blinds are still open and the apartment is quiet. I haul myself out of bed to brave the bathroom. There's a fresh bottle of water by my bed and someone plugged my phone in to charge.

I smile to myself at Hen's hen-ing as I shuffle into the bathroom, the pain in my body still dulled from the meds and grunt as I maneuver myself onto the toilet.

By the time I'm done I'm sweating and praying for death. I don't want to stand up again, but I don't want to call my best friend to help pull me up off the shitter. I suck in a few steadying breaths and bite the inside of my cheek as I pull myself to standing.

I'm sticky with sweat and lightheaded, but I know if I don't eat something I won't be able to take my next round of meds before bed, so I have to dig deep and put my big girl panties on to brave the kitchen.

As much as I love Athena, and as much as I know she'd be at my beck and call, I don't want to summon her to bring me food. Plus, the doctor told me it's good to move, even if it hurts like a motherfucker.

It takes me twenty five days to make it into the open planned living space.

Snails are moving faster than me right now, and I'm pretty sure there's sweat in my butt crack. I'm kind of regretting having my gallbladder removed. Would an inflamed gallbladder and some gallstones rolling around my insides have been worse than this?

Okay, fine, that was some serious pain that brought me to the emergency room.

There's a light on in Athena's study and the door is open, but the rest of the apartment is dark. She must be working. Maybe she could do with some soup, or grilled cheese, or a PB&J, too. I don't know what carries me to the room but when I get there it's not the back of my best friend's head I'm staring at, it's my boyfriend.

He's sitting at her desk, typing frantically on his laptop.

He's got three drinks in various states of empty around him. He has what seems to be notes to his left, with numbers scrawled down the margin, then his head is hanging in his hands like he's despairing at something.

When I inch forward I take a peek at his screen, my breath catches. The document has the same title as the book I have on preorder. And Justin isn't reading it, he's writing it.

CHAPTER 24
Justin

S avannah's gasp behind me gives her away, and my stomach sinks. Not because she's interrupted any great stream-of-consciousness of writing or the perfect climax to my book or anything, but because she busted me before I found time to tell her.

I swivel around to face her in Athena's fancy office chair. It probably cost more than my car is worth, and it's comfy as hell. I wonder if she'd notice if it went missing and magically appeared in the hockey house a couple days later. She's rarely at our place so it's not like she'd see where it ended up. It's tempting, but she'd probably rip my balls off and feed them to Bacon before I could even explain myself.

Best not.

Ashen, face twisted in pain, and hands on her hips, Savannah scowls at me from a few feet away. But before she can utter a word, I'm up on my feet and sliding my arm through hers, banding my forearm across her back to steady her and take her weight.

"Let's get you sitting down."

She grunts, but otherwise stays quiet as she lets me lead

her back through the corridor and into the living room. I ease her onto the couch, prop a couple of throw pillows—that probably cost more than my hockey skates—behind her, and pull up the footstool so I can sit within arm's reach of her.

Stupid? Possibly. She has a few things she probably wants to slap me for, but right now she's clearly in so much pain, and all I can think about is taking it from her.

"We'll talk. I promise. But right now I just need to help you, okay?"

Her face says she wants to fight me, that she wants to tell me to go fuck myself and figure her shit out by herself. But then her mask falls, and she's back to pinched features and hissing through her teeth.

"Meds?"

She shakes her head and presses the palm of her hand to her chest. "It's not time yet." She mutters something about her collarbone, and I know how to make things even a fraction better for her.

"Your collarbone hurts?" I just want to make sure she's feeling what I think she's feeling.

Vannah nods. "I know it's crazy. My gallbladder isn't up here. My incisions aren't up here. But I swear, it's like someone's jamming a knife into my collarbone. It's driving me nuts."

"It's not crazy. It's a thing. The gas they use to inflate you during the surgery travels. They may only make three small holes in you, but they puff you up like a balloon so they can see what they're doing. Dad had the same surgery a couple years ago, he said the collarbone pain was worse than any of the rest of it. Like way worse."

She nods, grimacing. "I agree. How did he make it go away? How do I fix it?"

"Ibuprofen and ice are your best shot. It'll go away by itself eventually, lots of farting out that excess air." I throw her an exaggerated wink, hoping to draw a smile from her, but her cheeks darken instead. "But we can try ice and meds for now." I don't let her protest before I'm on my way to Athena's master bathroom, where I correctly assume her over the counter meds are stashed. Armed with ibuprofen, a bottle of water, an ice pack from the freezer and a towel to wrap it in, I head back to the living room.

"I'll make you something to eat in a sec, but let's try to get you comfy first, okay?"

She nods, accepting the meds and open bottle of water. "Thank you." The pain laced around her words pinches my chest so hard I have to force in a breath. I don't have time to dwell. I add another pillow behind her, and she uses my shoulder and bicep to pull herself into a position that hopefully brings her some comfort.

I need to feed her. "Toast? Grilled cheese? Fluffernutter sandwich? Cereal?" I might just keep listing things I know how to make until she nods at one but she's very clearly not in the mood for bullshit right now. "There's soup in the fridge I can heat up, and Athena said I can order just about anything you're feeling and get it delivered to the door."

My breath comes somewhat easier when she returns my smile. It's a small win, but I'll take it.

"PB&J sounds good."

Phew. That I can make without screwing it up or burning the house down. I spent an hour on the phone to Mom earlier asking for her recipe for mac and cheese, and for the special ingredient to her grilled cheese sandwiches. I can't help it— I'm a feeder like Mom. Except I haven't taken the time to learn many of her secrets. I need to fix that so I can treat my girl to all of Mom's delicious food. I know Vannah pretty well, but in the blind panic of having to take care of another human being, I drew a blank.

Athena assured me Vannah loves cheese as much as I do, so

they felt like safe enough dishes to make, but I'm too nervous and worried about her to cook anything complex right now. She looks pretty green.

Part of me also doesn't want to have to clean up her mac and cheese puke. I love her, but I'm not sure I'm at puke-clean-up level love just yet. Something plainer is probably a safer bet.

"Can do. Be right back. Don't go anywhere, 'kay?" I toss her an easy smile and another wink before hitting the kitchen.

Ten minutes later, it's possible I've made a few too many PB&J sandwiches. They won't go to waste by any means, but I think six sandwiches between the two of us *might* just be one or two too many.

Guilt stirs in my chest as I plate them up and grab a soda from the fridge for myself. I'm going to miss the deadline with my editor. It's par for the course these days. But if I miss it by too much, I'll have to cancel my preorder and push back my next release. The thought alone makes my stomach churn. I should be writing, but my heart won't let me leave the woman I care for on the sofa in terrible pain.

I already feel guilty enough for leaving her to go play hockey in Kansas City—the less said about that hot mess express the better. I can't leave Savannah now just because my characters are being dicks and not doing what I tell them to.

"Did you use the whole jar of peanut butter?" She cocks an eyebrow, and I can't help but laugh. Still sassy, even when she's in pain.

"Not quite. I figured whatever you don't eat, I'll finish off."

She smirks and rolls her eyes. It's true, hockey players have big appetites. We work out a lot, we eat a lot, and we work out some more. It's just who we are. I once saw Raffi put away eight grilled cheese sandwiches by himself. Dude has one hell of an appetite.

She moves the ice pack from her chest to the coffee table and accepts the plate, taking a huge bite of the sandwich and closing her eyes. "Comfort food. Thank you."

"I make the best PB&J in the Midwest."

Her eyebrow curves again.

"Okay, fine. Maybe not in the entire Midwest, but definitely the best in the UCR hockey house. I usually grill them, and add a pinch of sea salt."

"You're so fancy." She takes another bite.

I wave my triangle of sandwich at her. "Damn straight. And they have to be cut in triangles. Rectangular cut PB&J should be against the law."

Her body shakes with a giggle and then she grimaces. Shit. No laughter. Got it.

"So you write spicy books?"

"I'm sorry. I didn't know how to tell you. I wanted to. I almost did, the day I saw you in *Bitches Brew* with Athena and my book. But you seemed a bit..."

"Pissed? Embarrassed?"

"Yes?" I take another bite and let her process the information.

"You know you're my favorite author, right?"

Warmth spreads through my entire body at her compliment. It's hard to believe I'm anyone's favorite author, but my girlfriend's? That's pretty fucking special. Not least of all considering the fact I'm not all that well known yet.

"Given how much you read, that's a huge compliment."

"Does the team not know? Is that why you didn't tell me? You're embarrassed?"

I half snort, half choke on my mouthful of deliciousness. "No. Not embarrassed. My brothers all know. My parents know. I mean, it's not public knowledge by any means, but some people know. I just...honestly, I have no reason why I didn't tell you about it. There just didn't seem to be a good time, and I didn't want to make it a thing."

She chews in silence for another moment or two. "I'm a little butt hurt you didn't think you could trust me with that kind of information yet, or that you didn't make time to tell me. But I love your books. Big love. You're so fucking talented, Justin. I have every book you've written since you started." She levels me with a hard stare. "You're going to have to sign them all for me."

The laugh that escapes me unwinds some of the tension in my shoulders. "I can definitely manage that. So you're not mad I didn't tell you?"

She shakes her head before picking up another triangle of sandwich. "Not as mad as I am that you called my parents." She takes a bite, and there's that stare again.

My stomach clenches, and suddenly the idea of peanut butter and jelly sandwiches is a terrible one.

"It wasn't for you to decide that I needed my parents." She bites again, her tongue darting out to pick up the tiny droplet of jelly at the corner of her mouth. "Even if I did need them. I know I didn't come right out and forbid you from calling them, but I feel like I was pretty clear. And you knew I'd be pissed."

I'm already scrubbing at my neck with my palm. She's not wrong. It's not my place to decide what's right for her, even if I think she's being an idiot.

Just as I open my mouth to apologize again, she holds up a hand. "I'm glad you called them though. I might be pissed as hell at them for keeping my adoption a secret all these years, but I'm happy they were here for the procedure."

She definitely didn't seem like she was happy they were here.

She smiles like she knows what I'm thinking. "Even if it

didn't seem like it. It was nice having them around." She puts her sandwich back onto the plate and turns sad eyes my direction. Fuck. I'm a goner. Whatever she's about to ask me for, she can have it. Bone marrow, my right lung, my still beating heart for a transplant, it's hers. She can take whatever she needs from me.

"I just need you in my corner. I don't want to have to worry that if I ask you to do, or not do something, you're going to go behind my back and do the exact opposite. I need to be able to trust you, Justin."

And there it is.

The root of all our problems. She still doesn't trust me.

"I never cheated on Molly." I hold her gaze but put the remnants of my food onto the plate and set it aside. "I know what it looked like. But I didn't. I saw that girl crying in Applebee's and sat down next to her. I tried to console her, talk to her, to see what was wrong with her. I swear to God, Vannah, she just pounced on me right at the minute the Morrisons walked into that restaurant."

Her jaw drops and her eyes widen. "Why did you never say anything?"

I shrug, my collar suddenly feeling tight and my skin hot. "I tried, but no one ever gave me the chance. One minute this stranger was macking on me, the next I was being dragged outside and getting my shit kicked in by O'Brien. Add in the term paper scandal and..." I just shrug again. There's nothing much else to say.

"Did you...?" She doesn't finish the sentence, and she doesn't meet my stare either, but the accusation is heavy in the air between us.

"No!" I capture her chin and make her look at me. "I never cheated. Not on my test, not on Molly. I know. I know." I rake my hands through my hair. "I know everyone said I did. They assumed the worst in me. Even," I swallow like there's broken glass in the back of my throat. "Even my own dad didn't believe me."

Tears well up inside me as I try to push down those memories, those feelings bubbling in my veins. "Just because no one believed me, doesn't mean I'm not telling the truth."

She cups my face with both hands. "Oh, Justin!" Her eyes are glassy, too. "I can't believe you just let me...let me..." She slaps both hands across her mouth like she can't bear to say it out loud.

"Hate me?"

She nods. "Because of a *lie*!"

I hold up two fingers. "Two lies." I'm being flippant, but we both know it's not at all funny.

"Justin." Her voice is muffled because her hands are back over her face. "I can't believe you let everyone believe those lies. For *years*. Why didn't you stand up for yourself?"

"Why bother when everyone had already made up their mind about me?"

I want to tell her that those who knew me best didn't believe the bullshit, but I can't, so I just sit in silence. Her eyes are roaming my face, like ants crawling under my skin. Does she believe me? Is she searching for signs that I'm lying?

She might feel like she needs to be able to trust me, but nowhere near as much as I wish she did.

CHAPTER 25
Savannah

I'm pacing back and forth in Athena's living room while she hides out in another room, giving me space to have this monumental showdown with my parents via phone call. I'm far enough post-op that I can pace, but not far enough that I don't feel it with every step, but this brewing storm in my chest needed to break free either way. So I'm pacing.

My parents have been great for the past week. Too great. They've checked in every day, sent food to Athena's apartment, they even offered to come back to Iowa and spend the weekend. But it's too nice, it's too civil, and it's far too much avoidance for my hurt and angry self.

So I kind of lost it.

And now I can't put the toothpaste back in the freakin' tube. I'm not sure I even want to.

Mom's crying, Dad's shushing her and telling her it'll all be okay, and so far, all they've given me is that they weren't sure what to say, and they kept my adoption from me for my own good. No matter how much I rack my brain I can't figure out what that good might have been.

"Are you ashamed of adopting me? Or of me being adopted?"

Mom hiccups, and Dad shoots me down right away. "There's nothing wrong with adoption. It bears no reflection on you, or your birth parents for that matter."

"I know that. I was just checking that you guys know that."

"We just wanted to protect you."

"From what? Feeling unwanted?" I smack my thigh with my free hand clipping the table and making my phone judder against the wood. "Not telling me I'm adopted cements the idea that I was unwanted by my birth parents, like it's some dark and dirty secret. How many times have you guys told me that the best way to deal with something is to work tirelessly to normalize it?"

Tears stream down my face. The facts in front of me—that my amazing, supportive, accepting parents kept this from me —don't line up. There has to be a why. There has to be a reason they kept me in the dark.

I move my phone from my ear and pull up a website where I read how important it is to tell your children they're adopted.

"*Many adoptees who found out they were adopted as adults feel betrayed and lied to by their adoptive parents.* No shit."

I turn on my heel and walk back over Hen's plush cream rug, still reading.

"*Talking to your child about adoption from an early age will help them trust you and feel that they can come to you with their feelings about adoption. Keeping their story a secret from them will only hurt them.*"

It's hard to put into words exactly what I'm feeling, but if I don't try to do it now, this conversation will have to happen again, and I'm not sure I can make Mom cry like this again. Hurting her is hurting me even more, and while I don't understand their decision to keep such a huge thing secret, I may have to accept that I'll never understand their decision.

But I'm not ready to accept that just yet.

"Being adopted isn't my whole story. I know that. It's not all that I am. But it's still a big part of me, and you still withheld a vital piece of information from me. I had a right to search for my birth parents if I wanted to." I sniff, my tears coming faster than my words. "I had the right to grieve my adoption if I needed to. You made this huge choice about my life for your own benefit, when I deserved to know who I was and process that however I needed to."

Silence.

I guess there's not much they can say to that because I'm right. I knew that already, but my righteousness doesn't begin to undo the hurt that's engulfed my entire being.

I'm sobbing now—heaving, shuddering, ragged breaths being sucked into my body but I'm not feeling the benefit of the oxygen in the air.

"You had no right to keep this from me. I don't know how she died. I don't know what illnesses ran in her family. Did she leave any other family? Did she leave a diary with my birth father's name on it? I... I thought I knew all this stuff about myself, my past, my potential future, and I don't. You took that from me. You kept it from me."

"Honey..." Mom has stopped crying now but she's still sniffing. I'd guess between us we've used more than a box of Kleenex on this call alone.

"No!" It's possible I'm screaming now. Athena has burst into the living space, her face pale and her brows pinched into a frown.

"You have no good reason for keeping this from me. Now I just need to figure out if I can forgive you for it." I hang up. I can't hear their pain anymore. Their pain is not my problem.

Their pain is not on me, it's on them. They did this. They kept secrets.

As the call clears from my phone's screen, a message from Justin appears, telling me that he can't come over tonight and asking if I've had a chance to read his manuscript yet. His text fans the flames of ire in my stomach.

He kept secrets just like they did. And if I hadn't burst in on him writing his damn book, how long would it have taken for him to come clean and tell me the truth? Would he have let me believe he cheated on Molly forever, too?

I wasn't really mad in the moment when I found out. I had other things to keep me occupied, like wounds in my belly and a devastating pain in my collar bone. Plus, I was pretty high. But the longer it's stewed inside me, the more pissed off I seem to be getting. What other secrets is he keeping from me?

Secrets are fucking exhausting.

I know Hen keeps secrets, but I also know no matter how much I ask, she just won't talk to me. She says they aren't secrets about me. Something happened to her while I've been staying with her that's made her light dim just a little, and I don't know what it is.

I thought I was seeing things at first, that the meds had made me loopy. But it's there in the tightness of her jaw, the sadness in her eyes. When she's ready to tell me, she'll tell me. I hope.

What is it about me that means people can't tell me things? Do I come across as untrustworthy? Or loose lipped? Try as I might, I can't find understanding, and the more it all whirrs around in my head the angrier and betrayed I feel.

Athena's just staring at me, eyes narrow, face impassive. I know my emotions freak her out sometimes but she always lets me feel them freely.

She walks right up to me and grabs me by the shoulders. "Don't feel guilty about this, Vannah. You have every right to feel these feelings, even if it has been months, even if your folks don't like it. It was their action that caused this reaction. You've done nothing wrong."

I'm not sure I believe her, because it kind of feels like I have. I feel dirty, and the tiny voice that's been whispering in my head that I was given up for adoption because I'm unlovable is getting louder and louder with each breath I take.

Am I unlovable?

If my birth parents loved me, they'd have kept me, right? And if my adoptive parents loved me they'd have told me this huge freakin' thing about myself, right?

Logic and irrationality swirl around in my head, clashing every few seconds. I'm exhausted, starving, and probably dehydrated from all the crying.

Athena just watches me quietly. She's stoic and strong, and some days I wish I could manage my feelings the way she seems to. But I'm so fucking glad she's here right now.

She cants her head. "Tacos?"

My stomach grumbles.

"I just so happen to have a line on the best tacos in the state."

She's not wrong. And Abuelita de la Peña will know what to say to make me feel better about everything.

It takes us less than thirty minutes to get out of our pjs, dressed, and over to *Guac n' Roll*. Since it's not a game night, there's little risk of the team landing post-game for a feed. There are three girls I recognize from UCR sitting in the center of the restaurant sipping on 'ritas and nibbling on chips and dips. A group of guys are close but not too close, and a pink haired girl with her back to us is sitting at the bar next to what looks like Athena's youngest brother, Ares.

In the next room there's a large party of middle aged women, each person has a gift in front of them and there are more fishbowl margaritas on the tables in front of them than there are women to drink them. I'm kinda jelly.

One thing's for sure, this place is never empty.

My favorite server, Claudia, is working. I love being in her space—she radiates joy, and she's so down to earth that being here always feels like coming home. She always remembers my order, too.

Drowning out the background noise of my life with tequila isn't usually how I handle my problems. And considering I don't know if I come from a long line of alcoholics or not, it's probably not my smartest move either.

But I'm not taking meds anymore, I'm well along the road to recovery, and the warm and comforting burn of the tequila as it slips down my throat makes me feel better. Before our food is even placed on the table, we're onto our second margarita.

Over tacos and margs I tell Athena everything about Justin. She doesn't seem in a chatty mood, but she's always been a great listener. She already knows all about my parents, and that's not a conversation I want to have—again—right now. So instead I talk about Molly, about the test paper, about Justin's dad not believing him, and about the fact that Justin not only writes dirty books, but he writes my favorite dirty books.

I've only had a few margaritas but I'm feeling them, and Abuelita sent us home with an entire tres leches cake that is probably not going to last the night.

I know I'm supposed to be on a low-fat diet post-op, but I think my body will understand. You can't *not* have the famous tres leches cake from *Guac n' Roll*, especially when you're gifted an entire sheet cake.

I'm sure it'll all be fine. And if it's not, I'll just eat more cake until it is. I'm convinced it has healing powers baked into its deliciousness.

When I finally hit my pillow I'm drunk, so full I feel kinda queasy, and still pissed as hell at almost all of the people I love the most.

Crying didn't cure me, yelling didn't cure me, and tequila didn't cure me.

Maybe this is something that just can't be fixed.

CHAPTER 26
Justin

Trash Panda fans...you guys aren't going to believe this. I've learned SO FREAKIN' MUCH this week that I'm not sure that there's enough page space in Trash Can Tattle with Tabitha to tell you everything I need to.

I'm beside myself with just how sweet all this tea is.

Sit down, kick back, and get ready to sink your teeth into some salacious gossip about none other than our very own UCR captain, Justin Ashe.

My blood is cold, my muscles tense, and my friends, my teammates are staring at me as though they're expecting me to explode at any moment.

I won't lie, it's possible.

Rumor has it that our very own Captain America isn't so squeaky clean after all. He hauled ass out of Minnesota like his feet were on fire to attend UCR in a bid to leave his past behind him, but Trash Panda fans, we all know that your past never stays there. It always catches up to you in the end.

My chest tightens. Did Savannah do this? Did she learn all my truths and then run off to her computer to pound it all out into The Internet? Is *she* Tabitha the tattletale? It feels a little out of character to blame her so quickly. I've never had questions about her loyalty or ability to keep secrets before this, but she's the only person I've told recently. The only new entity in this situation.

This reporter heard stories about our beloved captain cheating on more than just his girlfriend in high school.

What the hell? Tabitha has never gone this far across the line before. She's always been cheeky, brazen, sometimes even a little risqué, but outright trashing someone like this just isn't her style. The article goes on to out my freakin' pen name. I can't believe this.

It has to be Vannah. She has to have told the wrong person. I hate to be *that guy*, but this totally stinks of a woman scorned. I wonder who she might have told. Or maybe she *did* do it herself.

But why? I told her the truth. I told her that I didn't do the things I was accused of. Doesn't she believe me? Or does she just not care? Has this whole thing been a ploy to get close to me to destroy me for something I did when I was a teenager?

Fuck.

Dragging my fingers through my hair, I look up from the article on my phone to the expectant stares of my team.

"None of this is true."

Someone folds their arms, and another clears his throat, but so far no one has yelled bullshit or started punching my face, so I'm taking the win.

"I was accused of cheating... On Morrison's sister and my term paper, but it wasn't true. I let them believe it was true 'cause it was kinda hard to explain myself with O'Brien's fist crunching my orbital sockets. Plus, when your girlfriend doesn't believe you and your dad doesn't believe you, like right off the bat, then what's the point in even trying to explain? But it wasn't true. I swear."

Cold fear trickles down my spine. What if they don't believe me, like my friends in high school, my teammates. My own fucking father?

How can they play under a captain, a leader they can't trust?

"We believe you. At least I do." Scott's face is firm, his nod resolute. His eyes tell me that for him there is no doubt in his mind that I'm telling the truth. Something uncoils in my chest, and I suck in an unsteady breath.

"I do, too." Apollo holds my stare before I move my eyes around my team, my family, searching for the disbelief, the uncertainty, but I don't see it. I could cry. I might cry. I know they wouldn't care. But in this moment, their support means more to me than I know how to put into words.

"After Finn kicked my ass when he saw what he thought he saw, I was quietly shoved out of social circles. Hockey became hostile, and I couldn't get a single girl to hang out with me, not even to study, let alone go on a date with me. It was like I had a scarlet letter inked on my forehead, and no one wanted anything to do with me."

I rub my stomach as the memories assault me from those days. It was awful. I ate lunch alone, I hung out alone, and even if I scored a hat trick at games, my teammates always had that look in their eye as though they were always waiting for me to betray them somehow.

The more they dug their heels in, determined to believe the lies, the harder it got to find a way to clear my name. Especially with the term paper thing. The Molly situation was something that started out as a simple misunderstanding, but it caused an emotional reaction from someone I'd considered to be my friend, and it spiraled out of control.

Someone grabs my shoulder, pulling me out of the past, and I'm damn near nose to nose with Raffi. "We believe you. And even if you did fuck up in high school—which I'm not saying I think you did—we wouldn't hold it against you. That's not who we are, it's not what we do. Everyone does stupid shit when they're young and thoughtless. It's how that shapes us into who we are today that matters. We know who you are, Cap. Down deep, in there." He pats my chest, and it takes all I have not to let the tears welling in my eyes escape and course down my cheeks in front of my boys.

"We've played with you for years. One bullshit rumor from your past isn't going to undo the years of skating by your side." I don't know who said that, everyone's kind of blurry, and I'm trying to swallow down the lump in my throat before I fall apart. I know for sure some of those pesky tears have already escaped and are making a bid for freedom down my cheeks but no one says a word.

"Tabitha has gone too far this time." Artemis's face is taut, and his nostrils are flaring. Dude is piiiissed. "I get freedom of speech, but this hurts one of us, and that's a step too far."

"Yeah. Not cool," someone else murmurs.

It's on the tip of my tongue to out my girlfriend, but the more I think about it, the less I believe it was Savannah. Even if she's pissed at me for keeping secrets from her, there's no way she'd do this. None. She'd never betray the anonymity of my pen name to the public like this. I know in my gut she wouldn't. But that begs the question how someone who isn't my girlfriend has information that I only gave to my girlfriend.

I scan the faces in front of me, landing on the twins. Is this a de la Peña problem? Girls talk, and I bet my girl told her best friend. Did Athena do this? Did the guys? What reason would they have to stab me in the back like this?

I scrub my jaw. I can't see it, but that doesn't mean she wouldn't if she thought she was protecting Vannah.

Ugh. I need to slow my roll. I can't afford to let this incident plant seeds of mistrust between me and my brothers. Like Raffi said, it's not what we do. We're ride or die. I don't think it's anyone on the team, I don't think it's Savannah or Athena, so the burning question of whodunit fizzles deep in my stomach. Who would do this to me...and why?

CHAPTER 27
Savannah

My hand trembles as my phone threatens to tumble from my hand onto Athena's fancy kitchen tiles.

I live here now might be a common pop culture reference but in this case, it also happens to be true. Hen made me move in with her. In fact, I'm pretty sure she kidnapped me.

She paid up my dorm room for the rest of the year and asked the university to gift the room to someone who needs it and can't afford it. Then she had her minions haul my shit across town to her apartment while I was happily buzzed on narcotics.

I didn't stand a chance.

And while this is technically my home now, I can't afford to replace her shiny black floor tiles, so I grip my phone-holding hand with my free hand and urge it to stop trembling.

I want to throat punch Tabitha. Whoever the fuck she, or indeed he is. In fact, I want to junk punch them. Vag or peen, I don't care. I want to make them hurt like they're hurting me right now.

I'm sweating so much my shirt has stuck to my back. I might puke.

There's no way my relationship with Justin will survive this huge breach of trust. Even if I didn't do any of the breaching. There I was being all "yadda yadda...I can't trust you...yadda yadda...you cheated on my friend..." to him and now look. Someone took his story and printed it in black and white. Okay, hunter green and white, right there on The Internet for everyone in the whole universe to see.

Do aliens have The Internet?

Fuck. This really isn't funny. But maybe the aliens would let me join them in outer space and escape my life, even just for a little while until I get all my ducks back in a row.

Dammit. They outed his pen name in the article, too.

I don't care so much about the rest of it. Tabitha can print a retraction for publishing bullshit about his high school life. But the pen name... It's out there now, and it can't be taken back. He might not be a big deal right now, but when he gets big—and I have every belief he'll be the next Pippa Grant or Lucy Score level big in the indie world—it might be a big deal. He has kept it a secret for a reason, and now it's just...out there.

He's going to think I did this, right? He's totally going to think this was me. I mean, it was me. I spoke about it to Athena over Mexican food.

I'm one of only a few people who know his pen name, and he'd just talked to me about what happened with Molly and the test in school. My chest rises and falls faster and faster. I haven't spoken to my parents since our huge blow up on the phone but I was starting to work on my trust issues with Justin so we could move forward.

And now this.

Shit. Fuck. Fuckety fucking fuck.

This isn't good.

"You're making me dizzy, walking in circles." Athena stares at me from the dining room table. Her concern is radiating from her as she kicks out another chair and jerks her chin at it for me to sit down.

I can't sit. Now isn't the time to sit. I need to act. I need to fix this.

"Do you know who Tabitha is?" I jab my phone toward my best friend.

She throws her hands up with a derisive smile. "Nope. I already told you, I don't."

"And you swear it's not you?"

Her brows shoot up before smashing down over her eyes. "You think I'd do this to him? To *you*? Betray your trust like this?"

She's right, I know she would never do that. I don't even know why I'm accusing her.

She shakes her head, her loose dark hair falling forward over her face and blows out a breath. "This isn't me. I didn't do this, and rational Savannah-llama knows that. So I'm going to just go ahead and pretend you didn't just accuse me of stabbing you in the back, right to your face."

"Quite the contortionist."

"I don't know who Tabitha is, Vannah. And after this, she's made so many people so very fucking mad that I don't know how she'll recover from it. My brothers are out for blood." She waves her phone at me. "They're pissed. No one messes with their dumb hockey fam."

Knowing the team has Justin's back and isn't believing the lies Tabitha wrote in her article warms my chest. Would Molly have done this? Would she have been so pissed at Justin for breaking her heart, and me for going out with him that she'd trash him online? Or send it to Tabitha to trash him? Does she even know he writes smut?

"I'm sorry. I know it wasn't you. I do."

"I know you do. You're just reacting, and that's okay. You're going through a lot right now. Though I need you to know that no matter how hard you push, I'm staying right here."

I swallow down the lump in my throat. "You live here, Hen."

She rolls her eyes, and I can almost see her straining the muscles in her face. "You can deflect all you want, baby girl, but I mean it. I'm not going anywhere."

Her reassurance that she's with me hits hard. I know my parents said they'll be there when I'm ready to talk to them again but a piece of me is scared they'll give up waiting and just let me go. My stomach fills with lead. I don't want my stubbornness to lose me my family, but at the same time I really do need some space to figure things out. Where's the balance?

Hen whistles through her teeth. "I don't know who Tabitha is, but someone definitely did her dirty at some point. This reads like a seething girlfriend."

"That's why I thought it could be Molly."

I grab my phone and drop Molly a text, just to be sure.

> Savvyanna: I don't mean to be all accusatory, but is there any chance at all you told our local sports reporter about your history with Justin?

> Molly: I was just texting you. I saw Tabitha's article. You know I like to keep my pulse on the happenings in other teams and go a little further with my investigative journalism than the rest.

> Molly: But no. This wasn't me. Though I can see why you'd think it was.

It's on the tip of my tongue to ask her if she knows who Tabitha is when my phone chimes again.

> Molly: And no. I don't know who the real Tabitha is.

>> Savvyanna: Thanks, Mol. And I'm sorry for accusing you, things are just a bit... tense here at the minute.

> Molly: It's all good, I get it. I heard you and Justin are together though. Does he make you happy?

My chest expands.

>> Savvyanna: He does. And I know you don't want to hear it, but he isn't who you think he is.

> Molly: Let's get together when you're both in town. The four of us, a double date. We can clear the air between us, and he can tell his side of the story.

I like that idea a lot and tell her as much. I really hope the four of us can be friends, even if her boyfriend beat up my boyfriend a few years ago, over her. Oof. Okay, maybe friends might be a stretch.

"I could be wrong, but I don't think this is Molly." Athena takes a drink from her wine glass, but I'm pretty sure there's something stronger swirling around in there. "I don't even think this person has a grudge against Justin. She just feels...angry. It has to have been someone at the restaurant. I can't even remember who we saw that night."

Nodding, I agree. It's not Molly. "I need to go to him, though, tell him this wasn't me. That I didn't spill his secret."

Tapping her chin with her phone, she nods. "Agreed. Get out ahead of it instead of hiding out here and waiting for him to come to you. Meanwhile I'll set the record straight with Tabitha." She's already pounding the screen with her thumbs. I wouldn't want to be on the receiving end of whatever scathing email she's penning right now.

I grab my purse and head for the door.

"Wait!"

Spinning to face her, I sigh. "What?"

She jerks a thumb toward the living room. "Look outside, dumbass. It's pouring down out there. I get that you're a hopeless romantic and all, but hypothermia isn't sexy, boo."

Pulling a rain jacket from the coat rack as I pass, I ready myself for a show down with Justin. He's going to be mad, and I'm going to have to find a way to make him believe me when I say it wasn't me that ratted him out to Tabitha.

Sucking in one last breath and tucking the jacket under my arm to put on when I get out of the building, I jerk the front door open and am ready to face Justin Ashe.

Which is just as well really, since he's standing right in front of me, rain water still sluicing down his face and dripping from his sodden body. My jaw falls open as I step back from him. His UCR tee is stuck to every ridge and muscle on his chest, his hair is pasted to his forehead, and there's a puddle forming around his sneakers.

He must have left a water trail into the lobby. There's probably a pool in the elevator where he rode up to Athena's apartment. Athena. She had to have given him the code to get in, and I care, I do, but... I can't tear my eyes from his body.

He might be wearing dark colored sweatpants, but I can still see his...uh...outline, so I'm glad he didn't run out into the rain in pale gray sweats or he'd have a line of really wet women waiting behind him, too.

Wait.

He couldn't have gotten up to the penthouse unaided, which means my bestie is complicit.

"What are you doing here?" My heart's hammering. I'm not ready to lose this beautiful, loving man.

Searching his face for anger, all I see is warmth despite his shivering.

"We need to talk."

Regardless of where this conversation goes, I still need to go out to pick up my freefalling stomach from the ground floor. No conversation that starts with "We need to talk" ends well.

Shit.

"It wasn't me."

"I know it wasn't you."

We speak together, awkward laugh, and he shifts his weight which makes his wet shoes squeak against the floor. I should really invite him in.

Athena's voice comes from behind me. "Told you hypothermia isn't sexy."

I turn just in time to catch the towels she has launched at me. "Invite the man in before he freezes to death. The neighbors will talk." With that, she disappears, and when I turn to hand Justin a towel, he's already peeling his soaking shirt from his body.

That is one fine as fuck man right there.

He shakes his head, and where I'd look like a golden retriever shaking off after a fall into a muddy lake, Justin looks like a deity of some kind, flinging away water droplets in slow motion. I'm struggling to remember the panic, the fear, or anything other than my sexy parts right now because hot damn, I want to lick every droplet of rain off those abs.

He tilts his head when I meet his eyes again and flashes me a cheeky grin.

The boy knows what I was thinking. Am thinking. Because his abs are bite-able.

He reaches out a hand. "You gonna give me one of those so I can come in?" He's kicked off his shoes and moved them to the side with his wet feet.

I hand over the towel so he can dry his hair and pat down his chest as Athena appears behind me with a mop and bucket.

"Make sure he doesn't bring all that," she points to the puddle on the tiles, "in here."

It's kind of comical. We all know Justin and I need to talk, but the logistics of him having been caught in the downpour outside haven't exactly lent themselves to making it easy for us. He's tugging off his pants and wrapping a towel around his middle while I mop up the pool around his feet.

Hen holds out an empty basket and collects his clothes. How he managed to shuck his boxers without the towel falling, or flashing us both *Mjöllnir*, Thor's Hammer, is anyone's guess.

Athena runs off to throw his clothes in the dryer, and I take another step back to let him in.

"This didn't exactly go how I'd planned it in my head." He wraps a second towel around his shoulders and follows me into the living room. "It was supposed to be romantic."

While Athena had a real, open fire installed in her living room, it's not lit, but the heat is on and there's a box of blankets at the end of the sofa in case his shivering escalates and he can't get warm.

"Are you here to break up with me?" The words are out before I've given a second thought to their meaning. I don't know that I even want the answer though.

Athena's feet squeak to a halt behind me. "Uh... That's my

cue to..." She flees from the room, her bedroom door clicking shut as she leaves us alone.

I twist the hem of my shirt. "I mean, I'd get it. I'm a hot mess right now. I'm still kind of pissed at you for withholding things from me, and I know you said you don't think I told Tabitha all those things about you, but do you believe that?" I try to drag my hand through my hair but it gets stuck, and I cuss under my breath. "I didn't. I mean, at least not on purpose. I told Athena, and I think someone overheard." The more words tumble out of my mouth, the more I realize my righteous indignation isn't so righteous. Oof. This is so on me.

I suck in another deep breath. "So just tell me, are you here to end things?"

As he steps toward me, the towel falls off his shoulders onto the floor. "No."

"No?"

"I made an executive decision shortly after I read Tabitha's tattle."

"Is that so?" I idly fold my arms across myself. I'm not sure what he's going to say, and even though he says he's not ending things between us, it's as though my body knows I need to protect myself in case it's not good.

"I decided we aren't going to have a third act break up. No gross miscommunication, no dark night of the soul, no catharsis. The information was bound to come out eventually, you say you didn't do it on purpose, I believe you. And I'm not willing to let it come between us."

He's lost me, and from the slight stitch pinching his eyebrows, he knows it. Stepping toward me again, he tries once more. "You read romance novels just like I do. You know how at like seventy or eighty percent of the way through the book one of the couple does something stupid, or the other person *thinks* they did something stupid? There's a huge fight, they break up, and then they mope around for a few chapters before someone close to them smacks them upside the head with common sense?"

I get it now and nod.

"We aren't having that, Savannah. I've decided. I know I've been shit at communicating with you. I know we have baggage between us, and we have some things to work out for sure. But if it's okay with you, I want to skip over all the break up part so we can work through it all, together."

"You're breaking up with the third act break up?" I quirk a brow. "How progressive."

"Yes. I am." He nods and a few droplets of water from his still semi-wet hair course down his cheek.

"Can you just...do that?"

He shrugs with that lazy smile that lights me up, and if it isn't the cutest thing I ever did see. "The author can do whatever they want to, Vannah. And this, what we have? This is our story. We're the authors. We can write our story however the hell we want it to go. And I don't want to let some stupid miscommunication or in the moment reaction ruin what we're building. So yeah. I decided we're changing the rules." He pauses, reaching out a hand to cup my chin and stroke my cheek with the side of his thumb. "If you want to."

I'm acutely aware that the only piece of clothing he's wearing is a towel wrapped around his middle. And I'm almost sure that Athena has her ear pressed against her bedroom door listening to every word we're saying.

"What's it going to be, pretty girl? Are we writing our story how we want it to go?"

I lean into the warmth from his hand cupping my face. "How do we want it to go?" My voice is barely a whisper.

Some painfully insecure part of me needs to hear him say it out loud. That he's not leaving, that he's choosing me over the chaos, that he wants to be with me. That I'm not unlovable.

"I love you, Savannah Jane."

I'm pretty sure my heart stops, and I'm holding the breath that the heroine in romance novels always forgets she's holding.

"I love you, and I want to be with you. Probably forever, but I don't want to freak you the fuck out right now so we'll just leave it at 'I want to be with you' and call it good, okay?"

"Yessss!" Athena's gleeful voice hisses through her door before there's a thunk. "Fuck. Shit. Ouch."

Hopefully karma bit her in the funny bone for eavesdropping on my conversation, and I'm a little smug about that right now.

Rolling my lips between my teeth so I don't laugh out loud, I nod. "I love you too, Justin."

He shakes his head. "Not finished."

I bite down on my lips again and swallow the giggle bubbling its way up into my chest. "I like it when you're bossy."

He winks. "I'll have to remember that. I wanted to add that I'm here for you, however you need. If you want to spit into a tube and find out your genealogy, I'll hold the tube. If you want to go to libraries and research your birth parents and their family tree, I'll get paper cuts from turning the pages. And if you need a buffer to go visit your parents until things feel better between you, I've got you. I'll even drive so you don't have to get back on a plane any time soon."

Whatever I did to deserve this amazing guy, I hope I keep doing it. Tears course down my cheeks as I nod, and a couple things happen all at once.

Athena bursts into the room offering hot chocolate and grilled cheese to warm us up and celebrate our not breaking up, lightning flickers across the sky and illuminates the lamp-lit living room, and Justin's towel falls to the floor.

CHAPTER 28

Justin

"Oh my, Justin! What a big...*big* dick you have. I mean, I've heard the rumors, but they don't do you justice. Is it staring at me? I feel like it might be staring at me."

Savannah bursts out laughing, Athena joins her, and I'm pretty sure Athena's eyes are about to pop out of her head. As a hockey player I don't tend to care all that much when people see me naked, but as a well-endowed dude, when women see my junk they do that embarrassing double take like they don't believe they've seen what they've actually seen.

Athena hasn't done a double take, she's still on the first. And she's not breaking eye contact with my trouser snake.

Vannah and I bend to grab my towel at the same time, cracking our heads together. Again. I feel like our life is destined to be filled with face bruises and headaches. We both reach for her head while mine stays swinging in the breeze, which only seems to serve to make Athena laugh harder.

"Dude. Does that thing have its own zip code?"

I'm definitely blushing now, despite my bone-deep chill,

my skin flares hot. Savannah shoots Athena a warning glare who just throws her a casual wink. "I totally get it now."

I don't think people understand just how much of a fucking pain it is to have *such* a giant dick. Big dicks, sure, chicks dig that. And everyone claims size matters—it totally does, no dude wants a small cock. But even though everyone *thinks* size matters, when it comes down to it, no one wants to climb this particular tree trunk.

I get the impression Savannah understands how complex this piece of my anatomy is, and how self-conscious I am about it. I abandon my bid to check how Vannah's forehead is and opt instead to cover my joystick. I really, *really* don't want to be on the receiving end of a beating from the de la Peña bash brothers for swinging my cock around in front of their sister. Even if she is the oldest of the gang and could slice it off with one of her icy glares.

Towel securely back around my waist, I check Savannah's forehead.

"I'm good," she assures me. "Are you?"

Nodding, I release a slow breath. Hurting her is literally the last thing I ever want to do. The idea that I might have bruised her gorgeous face feels like something sharp sliding deep into my nail bed.

"Did you run here?" Savannah's eyes linger on my damp and unruly hair as Athena mutters something about making hot chocolate for real this time and leaves again. If she doesn't deliver on her promise I might stamp my feet like a toddler, 'cause I'm cold into my freakin' bones, and I mean, who doesn't love hot chocolate?

"No. I drove. But I might as well have walked in that rain. There were no spaces outside Athena's building so I had to run a couple blocks in the downpour."

She sighs, giving me a wide grin. "So romantic."

I pinch her chin between my thumb and forefinger. "You

know it." I pull her to me, skimming my palm up her spine and splaying my hand across her shoulder blades to get her as close to me as I can.

"You're very, very naked right now."

Even in the low light I can see her pink cheeks. If I didn't think Athena was either listening in to our conversation, or getting ready to bring me my damn cocoa, I'd get Savannah just as naked as I am and bend her over the white sofa to have my way with her.

Brushing my nose against hers, I take an extra beat to stare at her before I kiss her. "We'll both be very, very naked soon enough."

She makes a satisfied noise against my lips as she presses her mouth to mine. Her tongue demands entry, but I'm all too aware that she's barely two weeks out from major surgery, and I'm not even sure she's allowed to have sex yet.

"You assholes better not be leaving bodily fluids on my pristine couch. I don't hear talking. I hear kissy kissy noises." Athena crosses the open space, she's got mugs of hot chocolate topped with whipped cream, sparkly sprinkles, and mini marshmallows in her hands, and a pair of sweats and a shirt over her shoulder.

"I've seen as much of your nakedness as my derelict lady garden can handle, Captain Ashe. You can borrow these until your clothes are ready."

I really don't need to know that my teammates' sister isn't getting any, but it also doesn't surprise me. She's renowned for being the model child and never putting a step wrong. It must be exhausting, the weight of the family name on her shoulders, but she doesn't seem to let it bother her.

The ass cheeks on the sweats she has given me are bedazzled, the legs too short, and I think the wide-neck t-shirt is supposed to be an off-the-shoulder number. But when you are *all* shoulders, it doesn't really go anywhere, and clings everywhere. Savannah snorts behind her hands as I get dressed.

"You don't like my bedazzled butt?" I shake my behind in her direction, and she smacks it.

When I turn to face her, she's fanning herself. "You know I love it when you bring the alliteration."

Athena groans and takes a sip of her hot cocoa. When I settle on the couch next to Savannah, she shuffles closer to me. Whether it's for her sake, or because I'm still shivering, I'm not sure, but I also don't care. Closer is definitely better.

"So you're the infamous J.R. Blake?" Athena eyes me over the top of her mug. She's got some whipped cream on her nose but I'm not sure I want to tell her. "The author who sets Vannah's girl parts alight?"

"Yup. I guess now that it's out there, I can't really deny it."

"And how is authoring as a career?"

It's as loaded a question as her stare is. A warning flickers in the back of my brain, but I'm not sure what it's warning me against.

"I do okay. I work hard, but I'm finally starting to see some traction with my royalties. It's taken a while."

When Savannah points to her nose, Athena snakes out a lizard tongue I had no idea she had holed up in her mouth and licks the tip of her nose. To be honest I'm not sure if I'm impressed, horrified, or turned on right now. As though sensing my surprise, Savannah giggles.

"How long have you been publishing?"

"Coming up on three years."

"How many books?"

Savannah's head bounces back and forth between Athena and me like she's watching a ping pong ball in a game of table tennis. But she stays quiet, sipping on her cocoa and making yummy noises with each taste.

I didn't think my girl could be more adorable, but sitting

here bundled up in an oversized sweater, hair falling freely around her shoulders, cheeks pink and cradling a giant mug of cocoa with both hands...damn. If I wasn't already a goner for the woman, I'd fall for her right here and now.

Athena clears her throat before rolling her eyes at me like my getting lost in her best friend's beauty is an interruption to her day. "How many books?"

"I'm about to publish number ten, I think? It's all a blur. I have a signing at the bookstore next week now that my name is out there. Frieda said there's been a lot of buzz and people requesting a meet and greet. I can't really say no."

"Better that than your puck bunny entourage grows with book bunnies." Savannah grins.

"Book bunnies aren't a thing."

She raises her eyebrows like she knows something I don't. After a giant sip of my drink, I think I might be in the clear from the de la Peña inquisition.

"And you make a decent income?"

No such luck. The questions from Athena keep coming.

She arches her eyebrow like she's judging the contents of my bank account from across the room. "Your car is a piece of shit, J."

"Why don't you come right out and ask me what you want to ask me."

Savannah shifts next to me, but still says nothing.

"You want to know whether I'm solvent enough to take care of our girl, ask me. Otherwise, don't talk about my piece of shit car. She's a family heirloom."

That makes both girls laugh.

I sigh. "Sorry. I just..." How to tell a rich person that not everyone is wealthy? "I don't like spending money unless I have to." I clear my throat, washing away the dryness coating my mouth with another gulp of the rich, creamy hot chocolate.

"We've never had a lot of money. My parents, well, they declared bankruptcy a number of years ago, and we had to move in with my grandparents. They've never really recovered. They tell me they still live there for my grandparents' sake, but I know it's because they're afraid of losing everything they have all over again." I snort. "Hell, my grandparents have a better social life than I do. They're barely ever home."

Athena's face has lost all trace of humor. She might have come from money, but I know she knows the value of a buck. She works hard, and unlike at least one of her brothers, she doesn't throw her family wealth around or rub it in people's faces, despite her fancy car and lavish penthouse apartment.

"I drive a shitty car so I can save every penny I make. I work in the bookstore because I don't like relying on my author royalties. And I study to have a college degree to fall back on if I get injured playing hockey, or don't make it to the big leagues. I do okay, but the market could change, or the industry could change, and I could be out on my ear before you can say 'one click.'" I drape an arm around Savannah and give her a squeeze.

"I know I'll need a new car soon, I just want to drive the old one into the ground first. Ultimately, if it wasn't for my hockey scholarship and living at the hockey house, I couldn't even afford to go to college." I shrug, and my mouth is dry again. There's an awkward silence hanging over us, so I keep talking just to fill it.

"I don't want that for my kids. I want better, more. So I work my ass off, at school, at the bookshop, at hockey, at my writing... I guess I'm covering all my bases in case something goes wrong along the way and I need to pivot."

Athena's staring at the inside of her mug like she's evaluating it. "That's..." She huffs out a breath.

Savannah sniffs and sweeps her fingers across her cheek.

"Wow. That's a lot, Justin. Not gonna lie. It's heavy."

Athena drags her finger around the rim of her mug. "It's too heavy for a college kid, I know that for sure. But we both know with my family name, I know all about heavy, too."

Savannah's hand lands on my thigh, and she gives me a reassuring squeeze.

"Smart, strategic planning, but heavy as fuck." Athena's pensive face is almost more terrifying than her assessing face. "You're right. I just wanted to make sure our girl was taken care of. But I'm also just nosy as hell. I have no idea how lucrative a career as an author is, or can be."

I shrug. "It can be as lucrative as you want it to be if you're willing to do the work. And it's a *lot* of work. Doing absolutely everything by yourself can be...draining."

Savannah's spine straightens as she bolts upright. "Oh! Oh! We could totally be a publishing powerhouse couple. I could learn to do some things to help you out."

It's a great idea. I know of at least a dozen authors who have supportive spouses who work right alongside them to grow their literary empire. And it would certainly allow me to spend more of my time writing, creating books, rather than fighting with ads, social media, marketing, accounting, and aaaaall the other business-y shit that my right-sided brain struggles with.

"I'd love that. But you really don't need to give up on your dream just to help me with mine."

"¿Por qué no dos?"

I almost forgot Athena was here too. Almost. But her piercing stare cuts through the room, and if I'd committed a crime I'd be running to the police station to confess. She's...intense.

"Hen is right. Why can't I do both? And who knows? Maybe your dream can be my dream too. The thing about dreams is, they're flexible. You're not restricted to just one. And you can change them if you want to. Sometimes you don't know what your dreams are until you learn about them, until someone shows you what's possible."

She nudges me. "I have no plans to lose myself just so you can find yourself. But there's no rule that says I can't help you up the mountain a little."

I kiss her hair, enjoying the warm buzz rolling through my veins. It's definitely something I'll think about, though there's a seed of doubt laying roots in my stomach since I still haven't told her that my next book is about her, about us, our story.

My editor has thankfully taken it from me in chunks, so I can keep writing. And sitting here, slurping on the marshmallow sludge at the bottom of my mug, I know how it needs to end. I think she'll be happy, surprised, sure, but she won't want to beat me to death with the hardback copy. At least I don't think she will.

Though if she does, I know for sure that Athena will help her hide my body. Those two are as ride or die as my hockey brothers and I. There's no escaping the fact that I'm not only in a relationship with Vannah, but her best friend as well.

It's nice to know I'm not the only one looking out for my girl, even if I'm pretty sure it'll be Athena, and not Vannah's dad I'll need to talk to when I need to get someone's blessing to marry her.

CHAPTER 29
Savannah

I feel like I'm living someone else's life right now. Tabitha printed a retraction, or rather, a correction. She interviewed Justin over email—because God forbid she let anyone know who she really is over a face-to-face interview—and printed his side of the story. While she couldn't take back outing his pen name, she's announced that she's going to spotlight one of his books every week and even offered to advertise his growing male-only romance book club. When she'd asked him why he didn't tell people about his pen name from the get-go, his answer fragmented my heart into a bazillion pieces. He told her he was afraid people wouldn't accept him.

Male author writing romance.

Jock writing romance.

Guy accused of cheating writing romance.

Apparently he had big feels, which, Tabitha reported, just made her feel even worse about outing him the way she did. Good. She should feel bad. What she did was pretty unforgivable in my book. It wasn't her truth to tell.

My phone pings as I towel off after a shower. It's an email

telling me that Justin has a new book out today. Huh. No shit. Like I could forget. Today is his first ever in-person signing, and while it's tempting to bring my *entire* J.R. Blake collection to get signed, I'm not sure my lower back could take it. Plus, I already convinced him to sign all of them a couple of days ago —to work on his in person signature and small talk.

The truth is I'd really rather not have to fight off a throng of book bunnies to keep my stack from their hungry hands and end up on the local news for beating other women to death with a book.

I don't know anything about this new book other than it's already downloaded into my Kindle app and the title. *Crushin' at the Cafe* wasn't on his release list for the year, and it's got me all kinds of curious. I was going to wait until I picked up the paperback copy at the signing today but it's burning through the phone in my palm and scorching my skin.

Wouldn't hurt to take a peek at the first chapter, right?

An hour later, my hair has half-dried itself and I'm still wrapped in a towel, curled up on my bed, gripped. This is our story. He's written a book about our very own romance, our journey to being together. Okay, so he's taken some creative license here and there, but I'd recognize it anywhere. And I love it.

If I couldn't tell from the story, the dedication of the book is a dead giveaway. It was written to me.

To Savannah

It might not be a perfect story, but it's ours, and I wouldn't change it for the world. I love you more today than yesterday and can't wait to see how much I love you for each of our tomorrows.

P.S. Thanks for not breaking my arm on the plane so I could type this book.

S-w-o-o-n.

Even Hen clucked her tongue and made barfy noises as she read it over my shoulder before heading out. She's meeting me at the signing. Or at least, she's supposed to be, assuming I can put this book down and get my ass out the door on time, anyway.

Speaking of the succubus, she's blowing up my phone with texts telling me to put the book down and to "get the fuck ready." It's almost like she knows me or something. I text her back my go-to phrase in situations like this.

> Savannah: Just one more chapter.

I toss in a winky emoji just for fun, knowing she's not going to believe me for a second.

Just as I'm dressed, booted, and ready to head out the door Justin's weekly newsletter email arrives in my inbox.

Today's the day! If you're local to Cedar Rapids, feel free to come by The Book Bin in downtown Cedar Rapids to pick up your paperback copy of Crushin' at the Cafe, get it signed, and snap a picture.

I'm forever grateful to you all for your support. Without you, none of these characters living in my head would have a voice of their own.

A little known tidbit about this particular release of mine, dear reader, is that I've been living in something of a romance novel myself.

My skin prickles, and my muscles tighten. I'm paused right behind the front door to the apartment, knowing I should move, but my feet are not complying.

I fucked up along the way to us being together. Actually, I fucked up a couple times, mostly by not being transparent and honest. But thankfully, my beautiful girlfriend forgave me, and this book is kinda-sorta based on her. That's not why I'm writ-

ing, however. I'm sending this newsletter not only to encourage you all to buy my new release, but to confess that I'm a guy.

I know some of you might have preconceived notions about reading romance written by a dude, but I wanted to come clean and let you know my most authentic self. Even if it's somewhat terrifying. I've learned that no matter how scary it is to be yourself, there's no better person to be. So...this is me. I'm sorry I wasn't more up front about it from the beginning, but fear makes us do some seriously dumb shit sometimes and that's the only excuse I have.

I've never felt such an overwhelming rush of emotion—which is saying something considering I often feel like a walking ball of feelings. I can't imagine how scared he was to send that email, and I can't wait to give him a huge hug and tell him how proud of him I am for owning his truth.

It takes me about fifteen minutes to get to work. The place is busy and the line for Justin already snakes outside the door and onto the street. I spy a few of his hockey buddies, whether they're here from his book club, or just to support their teammate, I'm not sure. I'm just glad to see people showing up to support him.

I should have brought pocket hand warmers. It's absolutely fucking freezing in line, but I'm not going to use the girlfriend card, nor the "I work here" card, to cut the line. I'm going to wait to see him just like everyone else. Even if it costs me my fingers and toes.

By the time I get to the front of the line, the tail of people behind me is still weaving its way outside. I guess Tabitha and Frieda both put the call out for the student body to support one of our own, and it worked. Grabbing a book from the pile at the edge of the table I slide it toward him.

He hasn't looked up yet, he's probably exhausted from all the peopling. Even though he's a raging extrovert, his little empathetic heart can get overwhelmed sometimes, too. And

I'd bet a week's salary that he's had at least a dozen marriage proposals, because damn, my guy looks downright edible sitting behind the signing table.

My bestie stands off to the left behind him, deep in conversation with one of the twins—I think it's Artemis, I have a hard time telling them apart now they're both sporting similar haircuts—and one of the other players. That at least explains why she hasn't texted me back. I don't think she's noticed me yet, but it kind of looks like she's scolding at least one, possibly both of the men so I'm just gonna leave her to it.

"Can you make it out to Savannah, please?"

Justin's head snaps up at my voice, and he's out of his seat before I can blink. Before I know what's happening, I'm encased in his arms and breathing in his scent. This is literally the best feeling in the world, and I'm happy all the way to the tips of my toes.

I'm not thrilled that there's a table between us, and it seems neither is he, because he's moving us around it and pulling me tighter to him. The world stops spinning when he kisses me. My whole body heats from the grumblings and muttered complaints of at least half of the women in the line behind me, but I don't care.

"I'm so proud of you, Justin."

He barely pulls back from me enough to let me speak, which makes me giggle.

"You know people can see us, right?" My voice is now muffled against his shoulder, he's hugging me tighter.

"Don't care." He gives me one last squeeze before allowing some space between us. His cheeks are pink, his eyes are bright, and he's grinning at me. "Thanks for coming."

"Like I'd miss this. Hen has your gift, though. I'll give it to you later. Do you need anything? Water? Snacks? A getaway car driver?"

He snorts and takes his seat again, uncapping the Sharpie

next to my soon-to-be new book. "You didn't need to buy me a gift." He scrawls my name. "And I'm good, thanks. The guys are making sure my bottle never runs empty. And Frieda keeps bringing me snacks."

"She's good like that." I accept the signed copy and hug it against my chest. The throwback to how we reconnected at *Bitches Brew,* how angry and bitter I was at him when I first saw him at the counter is not lost on me in this moment.

I wanted to hate him back then, hell, I even tried to, but I just couldn't. I guess there was a part of me that recognized he wasn't a bad person, even when I secretly wanted him to get gonorrhea from that girl he cheated on Molly with.

"Mom?" Justin's voice tugs me from romance straight to gross.

"Uh. No? Savannah. Remember?" Has the smell of success gone to his head? Oh crap, does he have a Mom kink? Is that even a thing?

He laughs and points to my right. His parents are both standing off to the side, his mom is giving him a shy wave. They're not in the signing line, but she's clutching a copy of his new book against her chest, just like I am, and it warms my heart.

Justin gets up from the table again and tackles his mom in a huge bear hug that draws "awwws" and dreamy sighs from his adoring readers. His dad pulls him into a gruff hug, and despite the din in the small space I hear his voice cut through the noise.

"Even though I thought you cheated, it didn't make me love you any less, son. I'm sorry."

Wow. The statement hits me in the solar plexus, and I don't know how Justin isn't in the fetal position on the ground crying his eyes out.

Even though I thought you cheated.

Does that mean he doesn't think that anymore?

It seems Justin has the same thought as he searches his parents face. "What? I..."

His mom rubs his arm. "We get Tabitha's newsletter too, Justin. We read it all."

Justin pales, his frown suggests he's not thrilled that his parents are reading the 4-1-1 on his team from a gossip column, but his shoulders fall just a little.

His dad pats him on the back. "We'll talk more later, but I needed to at least say that much."

His mom is dabbing at her eyes with the corner of a scrunched up Kleenex. I feel like I just witnessed a moment I had no business being a spectator to, and from the look in Justin's eyes, he's going to need help unpacking what just happened.

Athena finally notices me and makes her way over to where I'm standing next to the Ashes. I introduce her to Justin's parents, trying to keep an eye on him while he makes his way through the long line still in front of him. Chatting, signing, smiling for pictures, more chatting. Frieda places a steaming mug of coffee in front of him and the grateful smile he tosses her says it all. He's spent.

Every now and then, he glances over to where his parents are chatting to Athena and now some of his teammates, too. It's like he's expecting them to be gone every time he checks. What his dad just said in the middle of the bookstore is a pretty big deal, and Justin probably has a lot to say about it, but he's doing a great job at staying relatively focused and getting shit done.

It's a couple hours later before we're leaving The Book Bin to have dinner with his folks. I offered to let them eat together and hang out with them later but Justin asked me to stay. He's the one who needs a buffer with his parents this time.

Watching them talk to each other, really, openly talk, about things that have upset and hurt Justin for years is cathartic for me. I can only guess how therapeutic it must be for him. But it also makes me sad, and miss my family.

I feel like that means it might be time to go make amends.

CHAPTER 30
Justin

What a fucking day. My arm hurts from signing all the books, but the bookstore has never been more popular, and Frieda promised to bake cookies for me. Not oatmeal raisin, either, real cookies, with chocolate. Maybe even monster cookies with various kinds of chocolate.

I told her while she didn't need to bake for me, I definitely wouldn't say no to cookies. And neither would my hockey brothers. They're bottomless pits when it comes to homemade treats.

Savannah is in the bathroom brushing her teeth, and I'm tucked up in her bed waiting for cuddles. I'm emotionally drained, physically exhausted, and mentally worn down. Mom and Dad are in a local hotel, and they're staying for another day. I'm so glad they made the trip and we talked things out, but today was definitely a lot.

"You okay?" Vannah leans against the doorframe. Her bathroom is bigger than my entire room in the hockey house. I'm so glad Athena managed to convince her to move into the apartment with her. Though reports vary on how the end goal was accomplished, Athena says Vannah moved in, while Savannah insists she's being held hostage in the luxury penthouse. She doesn't seem mad about it, though. I wouldn't either, Athena has fantastic views of the city, and I'd kill my own dad for a TV that big. Okay, I wouldn't, but I'd maybe think about it.

Concern swims in her eyes as she makes her way toward the bed. She's wearing a UCR Raccoons tee that comes down to her thighs which has my dick praying it can finally slip inside her again tonight.

Due to a longer recovery than expected from her surgery, it has been weeks. Weeks. Weeks that have felt like months. Ugh. Generally speaking, I'm not a horn dog, and I have nothing but respect for my girl. I do. But as I drag my gaze up her toned thighs, roving over the curves of her hips and her beaded nipples pressing into the shirt, my self-restraint is wavering.

I'm glad the blanket is covering my pulsing hard on leaking pre-cum into my PJ shorts.

As though she senses what I'm thinking, her lips curve into a smile. "I asked if you're okay." She plants her hands on her hips as she stands just out of arm's reach.

I scrub my jaw before tucking a hand behind my head. "I think so. It was a long day, and talking through things with my parents has left me kind of raw. And tired."

"Too tired?" She waggles her eyebrows. I'm living for her lack of subtlety right now. I love that she feels she can be her honest self with me, that she feels safe to just tell me how it is.

"We don't have to do anything." I don't want her to feel pressured, or as though I can't wait. But at the same time I'm hoping she'll understand if I blow my load all over her quilt.

"I want to." She grabs the hem of her shirt and drags it, painfully slowly, up her body.

I think it falls to the floor in a pile, but I can't take my eyes off her naked body to check, and I don't care if I never see it again as long as she stays bare. She tugs back the blanket and eyes the wet spot on my shorts with a knowing grin before licking her lips.

Dear God please let this woman suck my dick.

She climbs onto the bed, settling herself between my legs and tugs down my shorts, dragging her tongue down my length as she undresses me. It's not the first time she's given me a blowjob. She was very clear that while her broken body was out of commission, there was no reason I couldn't still enjoy myself.

Fuck.

I've died and gone to heaven. I tuck my other hand behind my head and sink into the bed. Her tongue caresses my head, picking up the trail of pre-cum that has coated the tip. I know I don't have a reasonably enough sized dick that I can grab her head and fuck the back of her throat, so I just let her do her thing. And enjoy every sweep and swish of her tongue against my sensitive skin.

When she cups my balls and sucks hard on my cock, I groan. Then she squeezes just a little, and I can't help but pick my hips off the bed, encouraging her to take me in her mouth just a little deeper. She does, and gags, her spit coursing down the underside of my cock.

What is it about a woman you love sucking on your dick that makes you feel like a fucking king? She looks beautiful. Part of me wants to throw her onto her back and lick her until she can't feel her legs, but she seems intent on sucking me off, so I'm going to lie here and be selfish and let her.

She's got both hands gripped tight around my shaft, and her mouth covers the end. Her hands and mouth move in tandem as she slides up and down my cock. Fuck, this woman knows how to take care of me, my entire body is responding.

She brings me right to the edge, my toes curling, heels

digging into the mattress, before withdrawing her mouth with a loud pop. "You ready for me?"

I nod like a freakin' bobble head doll, unable to make my mouth and brain work together to say a simple "yes" in response.

She giggles as she moves up the bed and hovers her pussy right above my cock. It twitches, like a heat-seeking missile searching for its target. I need her. I ache to be inside her. My muscles are taut and tiny prickles of sweat are breaking out across my body from holding myself back.

Dragging her wet pussy along my dick, she licks her lips one more time. Again, I want to roll her onto her back, pin her hands above her head and sink so deeply inside her that she loses her breath. But she giggles as she grinds herself back down my length, toying with me, and the delicious taste of anticipation in the air stops me from taking control of the situation.

She angles my cock, lining me up so I'm grazing against her opening. My whole body is tense with expectation. She doesn't break eye contact as she lowers herself onto my tip. Though she's barely touching me, the feather-light ripples of her muscles around the head of my cock already have me losing my mind.

Sinking lower, she pushes out a low whoosh of breath as she rotates her hips, first one direction and then back again. Her eyes roll back as she takes even more of me inside her. Her inner walls flutter and twitch around me, and I'd be lying if I said I'm going to last much longer.

When she starts rocking her hips against mine, I'm ready to blow, but I want this to be good for my girl, so I fight the tightening in my balls and the tingling at the base of my spine.

Her tits jiggle as she rocks, moaning and clenching around my dick. Reaching one thumb to her clit and another to her hard nipples I'm fucking thrilled to find her soaked, dripping for me.

Fully seated, she breathes out again like she's relieved I fit inside her, or relieved I didn't hurt or give her a friction burn on her pussy. Now that she's recovered from her surgery, we'll be able to work on stretching her out for me a little, and hopefully reduce our giant-dick-sex-anxiety.

She rolls her hips forward as I flick and rub her clit with my thumb. She's tightening around me, panting pleases, and I'm glad to know I'm not the only one desperate to come.

Picking up her hips a little, she pulls herself off me—not a lot, but enough that my dick feels cold and sad as fuck at her absence—before dropping back down. She's clearly gaining confidence and starts to ride me harder. Head tossed back, hair wild, and tits bouncing as she moves, I couldn't stop spilling my load in her even if I wanted to. She's in complete control as I empty myself inside her.

I'm still pretty hard, and it's not long before I'm all the way hard again. Her hips buck against mine as she chases her own release. When I pinch her nipple between my thumb and forefinger, her fingernails dig into my side with a bite. She's chanting my name over and over, and I might come again when she falls over the edge because she's squeezing me so fucking hard my soul might pop out.

I see stars as she screams, unbridled through her orgasm before collapsing on top of me in a heap. I'm still inside her, semi-hard, and I'm okay with that. In fact, I never want to leave. The pulsing clench of her soft, velvety, hot walls around me as we come down from our high feels amazing.

Eventually, she rolls off me, but snuggles into my side, planting her face on my chest and heaving out a sigh. "Sleep or talk?" Her breath tickles my skin.

"Sleep. I don't think I have any emotional spoons left to talk."

She drops a kiss on my chest, another on my shoulder, one more on my jaw. "I get that. It's totally okay. I'm here whenever you're ready. Can I ask you something before we go to sleep?"

I nod and brush my lips against hers. Part of me wants to take her all over again, but my traitorous body has given up. My muscles are soft and relaxed, my brain has shut up shop for the night, and the rhythmic stroking of her fingers across my stomach is sending me straight to sleep.

"Will you come home with me to see my parents?" she asks through a yawn.

I nod again and assure her that I have her back. I'll go with her into the fires of hell if she needs me to, and I'll cover myself in gasoline if it keeps her from going up in flames.

~

It's been almost two weeks since my signing, but people keep patting me on the shoulder and talking to me in public. I was already well known, easily identifiable due to the fact I play hockey and sometimes lose my teeth, but people on campus, especially the girls, well, they're getting in my space a little. I don't tend to suffer from claustrophobia, but I find myself hoping it all dies down soon enough so I can go back to being one of the lesser known hockey players.

I dunno how the de la Peñas handle their rockstar level attention.

I walk into *Bitches Brew* and cast a glance around. It's early, only eight, so I'm not expecting to be accosted by anyone. But that also doesn't mean that no one's around. My girl should be here studying, but instead she's parked right up at the counter chatting away to Taryn. Taryn's hands move animatedly as she talks, and her bright pink high pony tail swishes back and forth when she laughs at something Vannah has said.

Taryn jerks her chin at me and starts making a drink behind the counter.

"You ready to go?" I'm picking Savannah up to take her on a road trip back to Minnesota to see her folks, and mine, but yeah, mostly hers. They have no idea we're coming, and I didn't want to risk my circulation, or my girl's mental health, by taking Vannah on a plane again.

I have a curated playlist, a giant bag of snacks, and a cooler full of picnic food for lunch, and once Taryn hands me a coffee the size of my head, we'll be ready for the road.

"Ruth Bader-Brewsburg?" Taryn questions Savannah over the top of the coffee machine, I'm guessing she's already made a start on my Whoopi Gold-brew. I texted her before I left and told her I was on my way.

Yup, as a hockey player we have some perks around campus. One of them is a direct line to the caffeine. Since the tacos we get at *Guac n' Roll* are free, the caffeine comes second in the perk standings, but it's pretty handy to be able to just text in your order.

"Actually, I'm going to have the Queen Latte-fah today." My girl sounds confident, sure, and only for the stunned look on Taryn's face I wouldn't know she'd probably spent the past twenty five minutes talking herself into ordering a new drink from the menu.

Taryn doesn't ask if she's sure, she simply gets to it behind the coffee bar while I plant a kiss on my pretty girl's temple. "Hey, you ready to roll?"

Savannah picks up a plastic packet from on top of the bar in front of her and waves it at me. "Got my ear plugs, so yeah, I'm good." She cracks up laughing, drawing stares from the early morning patrons scattered around the coffee shop.

I laugh with her. I'm so fucking proud of her for stepping out of her comfort zone and ordering something new from the menu, but I don't want to make a big deal of it. She likes her routines, she has her favorite things, and straying from those is something she struggles with. It doesn't have to be a thing, even if I want to celebrate it. I don't want to risk her changing her order before she's had a chance to try a new drink.

"I have something for you." She's going to lose her mind, but I can't wait another second to give her the pages in my bag. I present the spiral bound dumpster fire mess that is half of the first draft of my next book. This one has put me on the struggle bus, and I'm hoping that she can cast her eyes over the catastrophe that it is and maybe help me out of the hole I seem to have dug myself into.

I'm nauseous. The idea of *anyone* seeing one of my drafts in such a state is enough to damn near give me hives.

I don't even let Mom see my drafts this rough, though. I've probably misspelled my heroine's name and forgotten how to use basic punctuation and grammar. But I trust Savannah. She won't be unkind. And she could help, that's the important thing to remember. I need to get over myself enough and let her.

I wave the manuscript in front of her face. "One condition."

Her eyes light up as she reads the front page. "Name it."

"You can't read it on the drive and leave me with nothing else to do but sing to myself."

"If you're singing on the drive I won't be able to concentrate enough to read it." Nudging me, she lays one on my cheek, and the tingles rush all the way to my toes.

Taryn hands me my coffee, but instead of taking that first, precious sip, I hand it over to Vannah. "Try this one. I've decided I'm going to work my way through everything on the menu and let you try each and every one."

Taryn smirks, nods, then goes back to making Vannah's

drink. Savannah sighs, her shoulders loosening before she takes a sip. "You're the best."

"Did you like it?"

Her head bobs up and down. "Not as good as Ruth, but this isn't bad." She steals another taste.

"Shit. Okay, I lied. Two conditions."

She curves her brows and widens her eyes like I'm pushing my luck, but waves her open palm at me, indicating I should continue.

"Don't tell Mom you got it before she did."

CHAPTER 31

Savannah

J ustin and Sophia are in the next room playing what sounds like *Go Fish!* I'm sitting at my parents' dining table, an untouched mug of coffee in front of me, too busy twisting my hands together in my lap to drink it.

I haven't been here in a while. My stomach is churning, anxiety chewing on my raw nerves, and I'm grinding my teeth to fight the tears welling, but my jaw is so tense a headache is forming behind my eyes.

Mom and Dad sit facing me, quiet, waiting. They're letting me take the lead in this discussion, and I appreciate that, but I really don't know what to say. I've been kind of a brat, and while I feel like I've been justified in my reactions and needing time to process my feelings, I want to put it all behind us, move on, go back to normal.

But I'm not sure what normal is anymore. I know that ultimately nothing has changed, but on some level, it feels almost as if everything has changed.

"I'm sorry for being an ass." It's the only thing I can think to say in the moment, and those few words make my tears spill down my cheeks. I look at them through blurry eyes as the hot, thick droplets course down my face. Helplessness swamps me. I don't know how to fix this. I don't know how to move forward, and I don't want to move backwards, even if I could.

Mom throws herself at me, curling her arms around my neck and squeezing me tight like she's pushing all my fractured bits back where they're supposed to be.

Dad reaches onto the seat next to him and places a flat-ish box on the table in front of me. It's an Ancestry DNA testing kit. Something tight and painful unwinds in my chest as I pick it up and stare at the box, turning it over in my hand.

"We're sorry we kept this from you, Savannah." Mom's crying now, too. "We truly are. And while we can't go back and change how we handled the situation, we can help you try to find out about your roots, where you come from, if you have any family left..." A muscle in her cheek feathers at the mention of family.

This must be so hard for her, too. I'd bet a part of her expects me to look for my birth family and flee. But I've only ever wanted somewhere to belong. And I have that right here. It occurs to me just how lucky I've been to have had it this whole time.

The alternative, being alone, going into the system, maybe never getting adopted by a family like mine... Well, it tastes bitter in the back of my throat. I can't imagine never having my parents around me, or Sophia. I'm so fucking grateful that they picked me.

"I have my family right here, Mom." I place the kit back onto the table. "But I think I need to know my backstory. Not just for my sake, but for any kids I might have in the future, too."

Dad's eyebrows practically jump off his forehead. "Are you...?"

"No!" I snort through my tears, glad Justin's in another room and can't see this snot-mess-express ugly crying right now. "But if there are things in my genetics I need to know, I want to know them now. So when I do have children, if they ask, I have the answers."

Dad winces, but nods like he understands. He reaches down onto the chair again and picks up some papers. "We did a little digging. We still can't find your birth father, but we have some information on your birth mother if you'd like to read it. We haven't exhausted all avenues yet. We were thinking if you wanted..."

He tosses an unsure glance at Mom before passing the pages across the table. "We could hire a private detective to look into it. To see if he can find out who your birth father was, or if he can find anything else about where you came from."

"You did all of this for me?" Thick, sticky, heavy emotion lodges itself in my throat and no matter how many times I swallow, I can't make it go away.

"We'd do anything for you, baby. You're our daughter. Nothing we dig up, no history, no DNA test, no living relatives can ever take that away from us." Mom's escalated to ugly crying now. "You're right. You do need to know any pertinent medical details and that's not something we thought about, or know off hand, but we can help you find it."

Dad picks up Mom's hand with both of his. "And if you'd like to pursue a relationship with your birth family..."

Mom sniffs. "We'll support that too. Whatever you need, we're here for you. We love you so much, Savannah."

"I know. I love you both, too."

In all my reading about being adopted over the past few months, one thing has come up time and again. While there are various and endless reasons why people choose to adopt a child, most people want to provide a loving home for children who otherwise wouldn't have one. That shows such great kindness and love that sitting here, now, staring at both of my parents, I find it hard to remember why I thought I was ever unlovable.

They picked me, they kept me, they loved me. And no matter why my birth parents surrendered me for adoption, whether it was because they loved me, or they didn't, I can't deny that my Mom and Dad have loved me fiercely ever since.

It's not long before Sophia bursts into the dining room complaining she's hungry. A bashful Justin stands behind her, rubbing his neck. "Sorry. I tried to keep her busy for as long as I could."

I give him a watery smile. "It's okay. I think it's time to bring Sophia in anyway." I raise questioning eyebrows at my parents, and they both nod.

Justin moves to stand behind me, placing a strong, supportive hand on my shoulder while Sophia takes the empty seat next to dad. We talk about my origin story, and answer the questions she has, but she doesn't understand why Mom and I are crying.

To her, I get to be a part of something wonderful, the best family in the world, and no matter why my parents gave me away doesn't matter to her, because someone amazing found me and loved me. And that's the most important thing. She's not wrong.

A few hours later, the Ashes are on their way over for dinner, without Justin's grandparents once again. I'm starting to think they're imaginary at this point since he was right, they're never home. Since our first trip back together and that fateful flight, Mom and Mandy have been hanging out more. Sophia says the Ashes come over at least once a week to eat, and she even heard the moms talking about me and Justin getting married someday.

I'm peeling potatoes at the kitchen window, overlooking Justin playing street hockey with a dozen of the neighborhood kids. The laughter and joy radiating from the boys and girls in the middle of the freakin' road is contagious.

"You okay?" Dad's voice from behind makes me jump.

"Yeah." I rinse a potato and place it into the pot. "Just watching Justin causing havoc out there on the street."

"He's grown up to be a good man." His voice is heavy, laced with meaning. *He'd make a fine husband* is the unspoken message, and I almost giggle.

My parents got married super young—they were both nineteen. I think sometimes they forget that just because I'm a senior doesn't mean I'm an old maid that needs to be put out to pasture. I'm cool waiting for a while before anyone puts a ring on it.

But as I stare at my hot hockey boyfriend out the window, I can't help but imagine him in ten or even twenty years. Salt and pepper hair, strong shoulders, and still out in the cold, playing hockey with the neighborhood kids in the middle of the street.

The sound of breaking glass draws my day dreaming to a halt. Out the window, a couple of the kids flee in all directions, but cracking the window open just a little, I hear Justin reassuring the kids that it'll all be okay.

The door to the house across the street swings open and a huge, red-faced, angry as fuck dude comes stomping out onto his lawn. He's yelling, waving his hands, and even from this distance I can see the vein popping in his neck.

Justin leaps into action, putting himself between the kids and the raving lunatic pissed that his window has been broken. Justin raises both hands, and Dad, who was standing next to me just a second ago, is crossing *our* lawn and making his way toward the ruckus. He stops just short, though, and I'm grateful to him for letting Justin have the opportunity to handle this himself.

Justin takes full responsibility for the break. He's a college hockey player, so there's literally no way I believe he was the one to have broken the window. He has better aim than that, I know this because I've seen him play, but he says he is to blame. He says he'll cover the cost to replace the window, but the neighbor—a recent addition to my parents' street—doesn't visibly simmer down.

Before he can turn to leave, Justin grabs his arm and gets all the way in the guy's face, still speaking loudly enough for me—and all the other parents I just know are craning their necks out their own windows to listen—to hear. He tells him to check himself next time he barges out on the street to confront a group of elementary and middle school kids, no matter what the scenario is, no matter how much of a fright it is to have your window broken. The angry man nods, mutters something, and turns, stomping back into his house.

Justin spins to face the huddled group of little kids, crouching in front of them. "If that ever happens again, I want you to go to the Bowens house and tell someone in there." He points at my house to his left. "They'll let me know, and I'll make sure you don't get into trouble, and I'll cover the cost of any puck-induced damages, okay?"

I'm pretty sure my heart is now taking up 92% of all available space in my chest. It feels like it might explode. I'm not sure I can take so much adorableness all at once. Who is this man? And how the hell did I manage to convince him that he loves me?

The kids nod, some look over their shoulders, presumably to their respective houses to make sure their parents aren't storming out to yell at them. After a reassuring nod to Dad, Justin restarts the game.

"He's a good man." Mom must have turned on that stealth mode only parents seem to have, and I squeal.

"I didn't hear you come in." I cover my chest with both hands like I can control my racing heart.

She laughs and tips her head toward the window. "You were too busy swooning, darling." She nudges me. "He really is a good man, though."

"I'm hearing that a lot tonight."

"Mandy and I are already making plans."

My eye roll meets the Athena-level Olympic standard. "So I hear."

"I'm just saying." She bumps my shoulder with hers. "I wouldn't be mad if you made an army of little hockey playing babies with that man."

My face is on fire, but it's Dad who answers as he returns to the kitchen. "And I wouldn't be mad if you waited until you've at least finished college." He kisses the side of my head before pulling Mom into a hug.

It's over an hour before Justin comes inside. He stays out in the street until the very last kid is called in for dinner, leaving no one without someone to play with. He's so good with the kids, and before the group breaks, he promises to play again the next time he's in town.

His parents have arrived and we all enjoy a home-cooked meal, a few drinks and cupcakes from a local cupcakery. It's run by the partner of one of Justin's ex rivals from the home team—the Minnesota Snow Pirates—someone named Quinn. I can't recall a time when I've tasted cupcakes this delicious. They're melting on my tongue, the frosting is the perfect blend of cream cheese and sugar, and if I ever move back home after college, my waistline might be in danger.

Sophia announces we're watching a movie, and while she

and Dad bicker over what to choose, Justin and I claim the loveseat and I curl myself up on his lap to get comfy. Almost everyone I love is here in this room, and I have to say, it feels pretty fucking nice. I can't wait to see what the future holds for Justin and me, and if my gut is right, it's going to be epic.

Epilogue

(Two years later)

"Can you believe we came full circle and are back in Minnesota?" Justin sips on his ice cold bottle of Spotted Cow as I try not to gulp my margarita.

Shaking my head, I sigh. I can't. I always thought I'd stay in Cedar Rapids and build a life there, but the tug of home was just too strong for Justin and me to ignore. We even live in my parents' neighborhood. One of their neighbors moved out a few months after we graduated, and they gave us a great deal.

The house needs some updating, minor repairs here and there, and we have big plans to revamp the back yard to put a deck and grill out there, but as far as first homes go, we definitely did well for ourselves.

"Are you trying to distract me from your anxiety about the bestseller list with nostalgia?"

"Is it working?" He flashes me his movie star grin, and I roll my eyes.

"Nice try, hot shot."

Mom and Dad have been texting all day, and Justin's

parents haven't been much better, either. We're waiting for all manner of phone calls, and the anxiety is so thick in the house that you could cut it with a knife.

Justin is waiting for news of this week's bestseller list, and we're waiting to hear whether our application to foster a child, or children, has been accepted.

Mom: Any news?

I know she means well, but every time my phone chimes, I think this is it. If it's not news of Justin's latest release, it's someone going to tell me that we get to be parents. Or that we don't.

Justin is on book number sixteen. His readership has grown steadily with each release, and he's just signed a contract with a publisher for his paperback rights. He's going to be on the shelves of major bookstores not only across the country, but across the world. He's transferred his back catalog to all wide platforms, so his books are available on all major book sales platforms, and we're working on translations and audio.

He's thriving. I am so fucking proud of him, proud of us. We are turning into every bit the publishing power couple that I predicted we could.

I can't say it's been an easy ride. And learning to run his day-to-day operations, the advertising, the marketing, the formatting, the social media accounts, essentially everything that isn't the actual writing itself, well, let's just say it was a steep learning curve. Real steep. Like...off the sheer edge of a cliff kind of steep.

We've had his Facebook ad account disabled—and rein-stated—twice. He's had his Instagram account hacked and permanently locked so we've had to start a new account on the 'gram. And with his second to most recent release, his main sales platform inexplicably canceled his pre-orders meaning we wound up doing a live launch—boy was that fun. Not.

I'm constantly learning, and his business is constantly growing despite the shifting landscape of indie publishing. Despite pirates, fierce competition in the genre, and a constant need to pivot to keep up with the latest trends, my man is not only meeting expectations, he's excelling.

I'm still his biggest fan, though these days I get to read the rough draft, the word vomit that spills from his fingers into Scrivener before it's polished. I read it again when it comes out the other side of the machine, too.

Sophia has started to learn how to format his books. We pay her a fair wage for her time, and I'm hopeful that it'll be a nice side hustle for her when she goes off to college. If she doesn't spend it all on ice cream and board games first.

"Penny for your thoughts?" Justin's rumbling low voice permeates my thoughts.

"Just thinking about how far we've come." I'm well aware of just how fortunate we are to be able to afford to buy a house, Justin has traded in his old crappy car for a much nicer —though still preowned—upgrade, and we have a two week, all-inclusive vacation to Costa Rica planned for a couple months from now.

As much as we've both worked our asses off for the success, we've also been blessed with more than a little bit of good luck along the way as well.

His phone chimes, and I snatch mine off the table in front of me, almost sending my margarita flying. It's not my phone ringing, but what if the chimes from his phone drowned out my own ringer?

Yeah, I know the logic isn't there, but there isn't much rational thinking when it comes to something you want so badly you can almost taste it.

While Justin reads his message, I check his book's ranking

on his dashboard. It's been in the top fifty books of the entire US store since it released a couple weeks ago, getting all the way up to top ten for a few days, too.

He just keeps staring at it like he's seeing things. I don't blame him—it's a pretty huge accomplishment and even though it's amazing, I can see the wary hesitation in his eyes, the reluctance to fully accept that he has "made it." The caution with which he accepts his monthly paycheck, and the unwillingness to look beyond the bottom line being made each month. In this industry, you can't rely on consistency, you have to create it, and it's hard as fuck.

"We hit the list." My jaw hangs open.

I'm on my feet and squealing so loud the neighbors might call the police, but fuck if I care. He picks me up, banding his arms around my middle and swings me around. "We did it, pretty girl. We did it."

Tears stream down my beautiful man's face as he sobs enthusiastically. My own tears follow as I hug him tightly against me. This has been a dream of his since he started writing, and to be here to witness it is an honor I can't put into words.

"I told you it was your best book to date."

He shakes his head against my shoulder as I cling to him even tighter. "Sometimes it's not the best book that *does* the best. You know that. Some of my favorite books in my backlist are duds, some of my best written books are my poorest sellers, and sometimes people resonate with books you might not have thought would have done well."

I nod, knowing only too well that he's right. One of his author friends had a book in his backlist go viral from a social media clip, it shot the book straight to the top of the charts and stayed there for a whole month. The author had been stunned. It was a three-year-old book, sitting pretty in the top 100 of the store. For weeks.

"Congratulations, baby. You did it. You hit the list!"

"I hit the list." He's staring at his phone like it's a rare Pokémon, and he's afraid it'll evade capture. "We hit the fucking list."

Peeling him off me, I make my way to the fridge and dig out the $200 bottle of champagne I picked up and poorly hid to celebrate this exact moment.

"Wait." His hand shoots out, making me pause. "Let's wait to see what we hear back about becoming foster parents first."

He has a point, so instead we finish our drinks, grab another round, and spend the next hour calling our parents and answering texts and calls from almost everyone we know. Even though Justin no longer lives or plays in Cedar Rapids, Raccoons both old and new are deeply invested in his author career.

They're almost as excited as we are right now. Almost.

Since we moved, his *Get Lit* book club has continued in his absence. Frieda reports in every month from *The Book Bin* to gleefully tell him that the book club has grown, or they've added another meet up for a new book she can't wait to talk about.

Frieda texts, demanding an in person appearance in The Bin to celebrate his new status as a bestselling author. She says we'll have cupcakes, a book signing, champagne—no expense will be spared. I think she's been an integral part of Justin's journey to bestseller. There were a few times he was tempted to quit, but she never let him waver for long.

I grab him again, hugging him breathless. "I really am so proud of you, Justin You deserve this. Soak it in."

He kisses me, slow, tender, and deep. Pouring every beautiful emotion his overwhelmed self is feeling, into the kiss. His fingers skim my arm as his tongue presses at the seam of my lips. They part on a sigh as goosebumps spring under his touch.

He tastes of watermelon and beer, and when my hands roam up the length of his arms, his muscles flex, the definition of his biceps straining underneath his fitted shirt making my core spring to life.

"We should get married." The words are out of my mouth before I can stop the half-formed thought in its tracks. I've come close to saying it a few times lately, but every time it bubbles up inside me, I just bite it down and wait for the feeling to pass.

We've been together for two years, and I know we're end game. I feel it all the way down to the core of my being. We're going to be together forever. I don't mean to rush Justin, but sometimes that feeling, the blissfully warm and all-encompassing love, gets so much that I can't *not* ache for him to be mine forever. It threatens to overflow, kind of like it just did.

He jerks back away from me, eyes wide and blinking. And for what feels like the first time ever, his face seems unreadable. Should I laugh it off? Take the words back? Curl up under the dining room table until the embarrassment clawing at my skin fucks off? Move home with my parents?

Without a word, he turns away from me and makes his way to the laundry room through the kitchen. What the fuck just happened?

I drop my hands to my sides with a sigh, hoping I haven't read our entire relationship wrong this whole time. I'm not sure I could live with that level of mortification. Maybe I just caught him off guard, maybe he needs a minute.

He comes back a few seconds later with his hockey kit bag slung over his shoulder. He plays for a couple of local rec leagues a few times a week, though tonight isn't one of those nights. Does he need his pads to tell me he doesn't want to marry me?

He has already dumped the duffle on the table and is elbow deep in the bag, digging for what, I don't know. My face is hot, embarrassment souring my stomach and making it hard to breathe.

When he finally pulls his arm out of the bag, he's holding a small, black velvet box which takes my breath away. "Justin."

He holds up a finger to shush me, his eyes still red-rimmed and watery from our crying over hitting the bestseller list. My guy is a fucking bestseller!

"We *should* get married." He drops to one knee and presents me with the most beautiful teardrop-shaped diamond ring I've ever seen. It has two smaller, dark, almost black stones flanking the diamond on each side.

My hand flutters to cover my wide-open mouth. "H-h-how long have you had that?"

He grins at me. "Since we graduated? My grandma gave it to me when Mom told her I'd met the woman I was going to marry."

"And you keep it in your kit bag?"

"It's the one place in the house I know you'll never volunteer to go."

Scrunching my nose up, my head bobs. "Damn straight. It stinks."

Another smile, this one warms me all the way deep into my bones as he cants his head. "I talked to your dad about a year ago."

My brows twitch as my eyes flex wider.

"It took me a little longer to find my balls to talk to Athena. But I fed her liquor and pleaded my case, and she eventually relented and said I had her blessing. I feel like she faked it for a while just to make me buy her more drinks."

That makes me laugh, the vibrating amusement juxtaposing with the tears spilling down my cheeks. If I thought I was a hot mess before, it didn't have nothin' on me now. I'm pretty sure I'm going to snot on this man if he comes near me. In what's supposed to be a magical, romantic, timeless moment, I'm ugly crying and braying like a goddamn donkey.

I should really pull myself together, but I think we both know that's not going to happen.

"I've tried three times to ask you, and three times I've been interrupted, or something happened to make it so I couldn't. So this ring has lived in my bag for over a year when it should have been on your finger."

I sniff, brushing my tears off my cheeks with the heels of my hands.

"I've been trying to wait for the perfect moment, but it seems it doesn't exist. Or rather, every moment is the perfect moment and I was just being dumb about it. And I fully admit I've taken way too long to ask you this question, but I love you, Savannah Jane. I love you with every fiber of my being. I love you when I wake up to your bird's nest hair and drool covered pillow. I love you when you make fun of my tone deaf singing. I love you so much that some days I don't know what to do with all this love I have for you."

The sincerity on his face hits me like an arrow to the chest.

"Marry me. Be mine forever."

It's not really a question, more a demand, a plea, and I don't care because I've been his for so long now that I don't ever want to think about being with anyone else. If he'd said no, I'd have been begging and pleading too. We belong together.

With no ability to talk at the moment, I nod enthusiastically, and he bolts to his feet to pick me up and swing me around once again. Joy consumes my entire body, and I'm not sure how my overly emotional boyfriend—ha! Fiancé—is containing all his many big and messy feelings in his body right now because I'm close to my limits.

Happiness overwhelms me. Electricity buzzes through my

veins as he slides the ring onto my finger before kissing each of my fingertips and leaving a trail of kisses up the inside of my forearm.

"We need to call everyone back again to tell them the good news." I'm staring at my ring over his shoulder as he holds me, mumbling sweet nothings in my ear about how he'll always make sure the dishwasher is run before we go to bed, and how he'll never let my ice cream supply run empty.

As though it heard me, my phone chimes, and we both freeze.

Could we be three for three today?

"Are we making it a hat trick?" Justin echoes my sentiment as he hands me the phone without looking at the screen. His eyes never leave mine as though sending me unspoken waves of support and steadiness.

We have talked about our plans to start a family time and again. We want to foster, foster to adopt, and to have biological kids of our own as well. We want a big family, he wants enough kids to have his own hockey team, but I think I've talked him down to the right side of six.

I think four is a good number, one for each of our hands to hold onto when we're out in force, any more than four and we're going to start needing leashes. I think that's frowned upon. A shame, really. A few more leashes at my local grocery store wouldn't be amiss, and I don't even mean for the kids.

My insides warm at the idea that the message waiting for me on the phone could be the beginning of making our family. I glance at the "stuff" drawer in the kitchen. Everything my parents and the private investigator found out about my birth family is in an envelope in there. I read it from time to time, but I haven't felt the need to do anything with it. I'm not sure I ever will.

They never tracked down my father, but my birth mother

has a sister who is married with two kids, and a few cousins from her dad's side.

Other than diabetes on my birth mother's father's side, nothing came back in the reports to suggest anything sinister in my future.

"You've got to look at it, pretty girl."

The words swim as I cry for the third time in less than an hour. Not only has our application to become foster parents been accepted, but our newly assigned case worker says we might have an emergency foster child with us in a few days, maybe even as soon as tomorrow. She's calling me in an hour.

"We're going to be parents." My words out loud confirm the words on the screen of my cell. Surely this is a dream? How can this much good happen to two people all in one day?

I show Justin the message, and he picks me up, tossing me over his shoulder like I'm as light as a kitchen towel.

A sharp smack and the ensuing sting makes me stop wiggling in his hold.

"If we're getting a kid tomorrow, we need to take advantage of the quiet house and being able to do what we want, when we want, where we want."

I'm picking up what he's putting down, and by the time he tosses me onto the bed I've already shucked my shirt and bra.

"Wow. It seems my fiancée has some upside down stripping skills I didn't know she had."

"Shut up, get naked, and make me scream."

Click here to join my mailing list for an exclusive bonus epilogue.

Pulling the Goalie
Chapter 32
Eloise

I hate sports.

And I'm not just saying that because my dad's back in town and dragged me damn near kicking and screaming to the UCR hockey game tonight, though that might be a contributing factor. I'd rather boil my head.

It's cold. I'm cold. All the way to my size five feet. Can your bone marrow be cold? I feel like as a nursing student I should probably know the answer to that question, but I'm only a freshman. Maybe you learn that particular answer in your sophomore year.

Whether or not it's possible, it's happened. Maybe I'm the first ever person to have cold bone marrow, but I'm cold all the way through. I'm pretty sure I'm going to get frostbite in my fingers and nose. Though I guess if my nose turned purple, or black, people would have a reason other than the jagged scars to stare at my face.

I shiver, more from the memory than the cold, and on instinct my hand drifts up to where my vibrant pink hair falls to just below my chin level. I have it cut such that the bangs typically hide the remnants of the worst day of my life. I can't ignore the stabbing in my chest, the lump in my throat, or the welling of tears in my eyes as Mom's dying face flickers into my mind.

I can't cry at a hockey game. From the looks of the swinging fists on the ice, there's no crying in hockey. Plus, if I let myself cry, I'm pretty sure my tears will freeze my eyes shut. And that's just inconvenient.

Huh. It's kind of tempting though, considering how much I hate this experience.

Maybe if they played on a beach, where it's warm and sunny and people could bring me fruity cocktails with umbrellas in them while the athletes do their... sportsball thing it would be better.

The fight escalates. Other players are literally dragged in by their shirts. One guy has another one in a headlock, another has someone gripped so tightly by his shirt that any time the trapped player tries to move he wobbles on his skates.

The only player not involved is the goaltender... netminder? Goalie? Keeper of the gate?

Whoever he is, he's off to the side of the mob by himself, despite the fact that the melee has broken out right in his space. If that was me, I'd be yelling "Get off my lawn." But he just stands, face impassive, focused, leaning on the top part of his stick as he takes it all in. Is he bored, too?

The crowd is screaming around me, cheering the gladiators on in their battle. But the goalie just stares on.

I know I wouldn't be so calm if a fight broke out at my front door, but he just seems so chill. I wonder what that's like, to be calm in the face of chaos. Or, you know, at all.

Dad covers my hand with his, stopping me from twisting the hem of my shirt between my fingers. My stomach's churning. What if someone gets hurt?

For a second I think the goalie might feel the same way as I do. I don't want to call him a coward, I mean ultimately he's crazy enough to put himself in front of a really fast flying... something that people keep shooting at his face. But in this moment he's all the way off by himself.

My heart ticks up and races harder and faster as one player's helmet tumbles to the ground a split second before he lands on his ass. Instead of moving to help, the goalie shuffles a little further away.

I can't see his face through his mask-helmet-thing, but his fuck-off-vibes are pretty clear. He doesn't want to partake in anyone's bullshit. Though he kind of looks as though he might want to sweep them all the hell away from his goal with that broad stick of his.

I guess my attention is drawn to him because he seems to be a loner, just like me. Always on the edge of the action, but never brave enough to participate. The realization makes me shift in my seat, and Dad's hand covers mine again, pulling it from my face where I've been twisting the stud in my nose.

"This is just part of the game, Ellie-Rae." He pats my thigh in a bid to calm my anxiety. "They're all going to be fine."

When the game resumes, there's like five players sent to the time out box, and yet their benches don't look any emptier. The announcer starts listing off the reasons everyone's been sent to the naughty step as the referee drops the disc between two players.

Is it a ball? I can't really see from up here. It doesn't move like a ball, though, or bounce like one, so I could be wrong on what the black thing is that the players are now chasing around the ice like labradoodles scampering after a tennis ball.

My head's turned one way, watching as the athletes throw themselves over the barrier and glide over the ice. Why the hell don't they just use the door like a normal person?

Okay, so less labradoodle, more elegant, athletic, brick walls on skates, but in my periphery, the light over the goal lights up and everyone is on their feet screaming.

I missed another one. There have now been five goals scored in this game, and I've missed all of them. Every last one.

It's all just too fucking fast.

I have no idea why hats are landing on the ice, but everyone around me is throwing their ball caps and hats onto the ice. Why would they do that? Hats are freakin' expensive. I bought Dad a Hawkeye's baseball cap for his last birthday, and it cost me thirty bucks.

If he threw that thing onto the ice I'd be pretty pissed.

Where do all the hats go? Can you get them back? Are those people picking them up, hired specifically for that job? Hat picker upper?

"He scored a hat trick, Ellie. That means hats on the ice. You have like two weeks to claim them back." I'd say Dad's a mind reader, but he just knows me well enough to know how I tick.

There are fewer than five minutes left in the game. My eyes keep drifting to the goaltender. I'm pretty sure he just tripped that guy standing in front of him up with his stick. Can he do that? I mean, if someone was in my space and I had a big-ass stick like that, I'd wanna smack him with it too, but how come he wasn't sent to the glass box of shame?

I feel like the guy from the other team is kind of asking to get beaten with a stick. He's back in front of the UCR goal, and he's all up in the netminder's business. The goalie is very clearly unhappy about it, and when I take my eyes off the net for like a second to see if the referees are watching this guy pissing off the goalie, a blur of movement draws my attention back. The goalie has clearly taken things into his own hands. Quite literally. He's swinging his fists at the opposing player's face.

Man, they got undressed quickly. One minute they had helmets and gloves and the next, bam, fists in faces.

I'm not sure who's winning in this battle of the punches, but I can tell from the scowl on our goaltender's face that he's mad. Big fucking mad. I'm pretty sure those huge pad things covering his legs are getting in the way of him kicking that guy's ass, and he's mad about it.

But he's still standing, and that's pretty impressive. His hair is dark brown, or black, I can't tell because I think it might be wet, and he has a strong jawline covered with a smattering of stubble.

The visiting player lands a punch on the goalie, and despite the trickle of blood down the side of his face, the goalie grins. It's a dangerous grin, intense, full of assurance, and it sort of feels dazzling in all the wrong ways, like a lion grinning at an antelope right before he chows down on it for lunch.

The goalie bursts into action, and before I can blink the

other guy is on his ass on the ice. My muscles are so tense they're sore, and my stomach is clenched so hard it might squeeze dinner back up. This is... barbaric.

Holy crap.

I'm rubbing my chest, but no more oxygen gets into my lungs.

Dad's gripped, his attention firmly pinned on the action. The referees intervene, and one of the guys on the goalie's team hands him his weird looking gloves and stick.

Now the drama is over, the final few minutes tick down without incident. At the last buzzer, the crowd erupts. Final score six to zero in favor of UCR, and the team are loving on the goaltender pretty hard. I mean he did keep all the balls out of the net so I can see why they're so happy about it.

They all line up to either tap his pads, glove-bump him, hug him, or pat his helmet like they're trying to ruffle his hair through the plastic. When the other goalie from the Raccoon's bench gets to the guy at the net they jump into this chest-bump and hug combo that has my heart warming.

After all the seriousness of the game, the intensity, the bloodshed, this wholesome, bromance display of joy and open love is quite a shift. I'm totally here for it though. They're like one big family just hugging the shit out of each other right there on the ice for everyone to see.

Emotion wells in my chest. I find myself blinking back tears. As an only child to a widower, the yearning in my entire being for a squad like the one I'm witnessing on the ice is almost overwhelming.

Dad claps and whoops next to me. "What'd you think, kiddo?"

You'd think I was eight, and not eighteen from the nickname, but it's his way of showing affection. "I think some of those guys need to go away and think about what they've done."

His shoulders shake, but I can't hear his laughter over the still-roaring crowd. "Would you come again? There's another game next week and I think I'm in town for it." He's yelling, and I feel like my ears might explode from the noise ringing around the arena.

I'd rather pull my fingernails out one by one with a pair of pliers, then pour vinegar into my nail beds. But my long distance trucker Dad is around so little these days that I gotta take what I can get, because otherwise, it's just me, alone, and that's even worse than going to a hockey game.

To preorder Ares and Eloise's story, Pulling the Goalie, click here.

Also by Lasairiona McMaster

Two for Interference - Minnesota Snow Pirates book 1

Minnesota Snow Pirates books 1-3 Boxset

Freezing the Puck - Cedar Rapids Raccoons book 1

Two for Tacos - A Snow Pirates Novella

www.Lasairiona.com

Author Note

Over the last few years I've learned about The Enneagram of Personality, or simply the Enneagram. Wikipedia's description of it is better than what I could come up with: "it's a model of the human psyche which is principally understood and taught as a typology of nine interconnected personality types." My best friends Amber and Amy both knew I was a '4' before I even knew what an enneagram was or how to pronounce it.

I'll spare y'all the spiel and my nerding out over it, but if you're interested Google the Enneagram Institute and read up on it. But needless to say, 4s are emotional, we feel everything, we feel deep, and something I realized wasn't 'normal' for everyone is that our emotions tend to have very tangible, visceral, physical feelings in our bodies.

I wanted to write a hero that was a 4. I wanted him to feel everything, feel so deeply as though he could reach out and touch someone's emotions. I wanted to convey how exhausting it can be to be an empath. I was kind of terrified the more I got into this book. The more I dug deep into Justin, the more I shared of him; it felt incredibly exposing, because in so many ways, he is me. And that's an incredibly personal thing to share with the book world.

I know my other 4 friends will feel seen in this book too, and that's why I pushed through the icky and uncomfortable feelings of vulnerability and fear. My best friend is a 3 and she hates feelings, she pushes those suckers down and only talks to them every now and then—the idea of just existing in your feelings like I do is unfathomable to her bad self.

I also wanted to write a 'softer' hero. I know so many people love alphas, alphaholes, dominant guys who grunt and are standoffish and kinda cold for everyone but his girl. But I wanted to show another side.

Many of you know I have an 8 year old son, Lewis. And he's an empath, he feels big, and a few times already throughout his life people have told me he's soft.

People say *soft* like it's a negative thing. But I've never viewed my son's kindness, empathy, and love as something negative, or a weakness. Not once. And I know many men feel like they need to be tough, hard, and 'manly.'

I wanted to show that sometimes it's the feeling, the loving, the kindness that *is* tough, hard, and every bit as 'manly', that it's every bit as strong, sometimes stronger to feel, than it is to not.

This book was also a challenge because it's the first in a new series. I've read some series starters in new series by authors I love that just haven't set my soul on fire like their OG series, and I admit, I was freaking out a little.

As an author you want to grow, push yourself, and improve with each release, and I never want to feel like I stagnate or don't deliver on my reader's expectations. Even when my alpha readers gushed about Savannah and Justin and how much they loved their story, I couldn't let myself accept that it wasn't a steaming pile of crap.

Y'all, I know not every book is for every reader, and I know opinions vary, but I also know that every author I know has on some occasion or other, suffered from impostor syndrome.

It's a real asshole. It strikes at the worst times and can often do a number on us. It was only when someone close to me smacked me upside the head and shoved LOGIC in my face about this book that I was able to suck in a breath. It was a personal challenge to finish it, and I'm so proud of where it's ended up.

For those of you who don't know, my best friend lives in Iowa. When I met her online a million years ago (on Live-Journal for those of you old enough to remember,) she lived in Cedar Rapids. Over the past (almost) 20 years I've been there a lot, and I'm actually typing this author note from her dining room in Keystone, Iowa right now so it's kind of poetic.

When it came time to write a new series, Cedar Rapids was an obvious choice for my team. While a lot of the businesses and places are fictional, the city, the state, the people hold a very special place in my heart and I needed to write about that.

Also, for those of you who have received a ticket on I-380 like Athena, I feel your pain. I landed myself a speeding ticket on the same road, and when I told people I got a ticket, they knew where I'd been hit before I even said a word. Y'all know I love to write what I know ;)

Acknowledgments

Lewis—my son—knew I was struggling getting back into writing after traveling to author conferences and taking time out to master plot this series from the big picture view. I took an author course, Lewis and I both got sick, and there was a myriad of things that helped me procrastinate starting to write.

True to form, Lewis stepped up and kept me on track, hounding me daily for word counts when he got home from school and ticking sticky notes off with glee every day.

Tracie and Clare—my work wives. Thank you for stroking my hair and telling me everything would be alright during my writing process. I know my 4-ness can be overwhelming for your 5 and 1 selves, but I appreciate you holding space for me and my big 4 feels. My day isn't complete until I've laughed with you guys, and there isn't a day that passes when I'm not grateful to have your presence in my life.

The Jens—In 2020 I was supposed to go present at an author conference in Vegas, but the plague happened and you know how that went. In 2021, I couldn't go either, but I helped my dear friend and alpha reader Erika put together a group of trusted authors to help out with the author signing event at the conference—that group became affectionately known as The Jens.

The Jens are a fierce, strong powerhouse of amazingly talented authors from across various genres. When I helped set up the group I wasn't quite expecting the magic that came from putting together such a collection of (generally high strategic leading) people with the kindest souls, the biggest hearts, and the best senses of humor.

They've become a family to me. We talk daily—about anything from ad strategies, troubleshooting author things, encouragement, support, or just a safe space to exist when I need it even just for a second.

If it weren't for them I'd have stumbled and fallen way more than I have. They're the reason I've been able to get back up again so many times over the past year and I love them all more than they'll ever realize.

Micky—I miss you. Not just for your wicked sharp proofreading beta skills, but your presence. I don't think you had the slightest idea how much you meant to people, myself included, but when your light was extinguished all too soon this year (2022), we truly lost a good one. I love you.

My Alpha readers—Savannah, Amy R, Katie 'Violence' Wilks and Shani. **My Betas**—Robynne and Erika and my proofreader Corinne. Thank you for helping me become a better author and for helping me remember how commas work and how to spell really hard words like 'tacos' correctly. I appreciate y'all. A lot.

HUGE thanks to my editor Jessica Snyder for reminding me how to English proper... and my cover designer Kate Farlow over at Y'all That Graphic for bringing my boys to life on the covers.

And finally, to my ARC readers, my Facebook reader group *Margaritas, Men, and Mischief with Lasairiona*, and to each and every one of you who pick up this book: a bazillion thank yous. I truly hope you loved it enough to pick up the next one. Tell your friends! And if you're not in my group —come join us, we don't bite (unless you ask us to!)

About the Author

Lasairiona McMaster writes sassy, classy and badassy women and strong, yet vulnerable men. She challenges reader's expectations by openly dealing with mental health issues, often exploring tough-to-handle topics and 'taboos' and books with a whole lotta heart.

She can either be found enjoying a gin and lemonade by the Irish sea, or baking sweet treats in her kitchen while singing at the top of her lungs. When she's 'home' in Texas, and isn't eating fresh-popped popcorn while buying things she has absolutely no need for in Target, she can be found at Chuys eating her body weight in chips and queso and washing it down with a margarita swirl. She loves to make friends out of strangers.

facebook.com/QueenofFireLas

instagram.com/queenoffirelas